Select Praise for
Norman Lock's American Novels Series

On *The Boy in His Winter*

"Brilliant. . . . *The Boy in His Winter* is a glorious meditation on justice, truth, loyalty, story, and the alchemical effects of love, a reminder of our capacity to be changed by the continuously evolving world 'when it strikes fire against the mind's flint,' and by profoundly moving novels like this." —**NPR**

"[Lock] is one of the most interesting writers out there. This time, he re-imagines Huck Finn's journeys, transporting the iconic character deep into America's past—and future." —***Reader's Digest***

On *American Meteor*

"Sheds brilliant light along the meteoric path of American westward expansion. . . . [A] pithy, compact beautifully conducted version of the American Dream, from its portrait of the young wounded soldier in the beginning to its powerful rendering of Crazy Horse's prophecy for life on earth at the end." —**NPR**

"[Walt Whitman] hovers over [*American Meteor*], just as Mark Twain's spirit pervaded *The Boy in His Winter*. . . . Like all Mr. Lock's books, this is an ambitious work, where ideas crowd together on the page like desperate men on a battlefield." —***Wall Street Journal***

On *The Port-Wine Stain*

"Lock's novel engages not merely with [Edgar Allan Poe and Thomas Dent Mütter] but with decadent fin de siècle art and modernist literature that raised philosophical and moral questions about the metaphysical relations among art, science and human consciousness. The reader is just as spellbound by Lock's story as [his novel's narrator] is by Poe's. . . . Echoes of Wilde's *The Picture of Dorian Gray* and Freud's theory of the uncanny abound in this mesmerizingly twisted, richly layered homage to a pioneer of American Gothic fiction." —***New York Times Book Review***

"As polished as its predecessors, *The Boy in His Winter* and *American Meteor*. . . . An enthralling and believable picture of the descent into madness, told in chillingly beautiful prose that Poe might envy." —***Library Journal* (starred review)**

On *A Fugitive in Walden Woods*

"*A Fugitive in Walden Woods* manages that special magic of making Thoreau's time in Walden Woods seem fresh and surprising and necessary right now. . . . This is a patient and perceptive novel, a pleasure to read even as it grapples with issues that affect the United States to this day."
—**Victor LaValle**, author of *The Ballad of Black Tom* and *The Changeling*

"Bold and enlightening. . . . An important novel that creates a vivid social context for the masterpieces of such writers as Thoreau, Emerson, and Hawthorne and also offers valuable insights about our current conscious and unconscious racism." —**Sena Jeter Naslund**, author of *Ahab's Wife* and *The Fountain of St. James Court; or, Portrait of the Artist as an Old Woman*

On *The Wreckage of Eden*

"The lively passages of Emily's letters are so evocative of her poetry that it becomes easy to see why Robert finds her so captivating. The book also expands and deepens themes of moral hypocrisy around racism and slavery. . . . Lyrically written but unafraid of the ugliness of the time, Lock's thought-provoking series continues to impress."
—Publishers Weekly

"[A] consistently excellent series. . . . Lock has an impressive ear for the musicality of language, and his characteristic lush prose brings vitality and poetic authenticity to the dialogue."
—Booklist

On *Feast Day of the Cannibals*

"Lock does not merely imitate 19th-century prose; he makes it his own, with verbal flourishes worthy of Melville."
—Gay & Lesbian Review

"Transfixing. . . . This historically authentic novel raises potent questions about sexuality during an unsettling era in American history past and is another impressive entry in Lock's dissection of America's past." ***—Publishers Weekly***

On American Follies

"Provocative, funny and sobering." ***—Washington Post***

"*Ragtime* in a fever dream. . . . When you mix 19th-century racists, feminists, misogynists, freaks, and a flim-flam man, the spectacle that results might bear resemblance to the contemporary United States."
***—Library Journal* (starred review)**

Other Books in the American Novels Series

American Follies

Feast Day of the Cannibals

The Wreckage of Eden

A Fugitive in Walden Woods

The Port-Wine Stain

American Meteor

The Boy in His Winter

Also by Norman Lock

Love Among the Particles (stories)

Tooth
of the
Covenant

Tooth
of the
Covenant

Norman Lock

Bellevue Literary Press
New York

First published in the United States in 2021
by Bellevue Literary Press, New York

For information, contact:
Bellevue Literary Press
90 Broad Street
Suite 2100
New York, NY 10004
www.blpress.org

This is a work of fiction. Characters, organizations, events, and places (even those that are actual) are either products of the author's imagination or are used fictitiously.

Library of Congress Cataloging-in-Publication Data
Names: Lock, Norman, author.
Title: Tooth of the covenant / Norman Lock.
Description: First edition. | New York : Bellevue Literary Press, 2021. | Series: The American novels series
Identifiers: LCCN 2020027690 | ISBN 9781942658832 (paperback ; acid-free paper) | ISBN 9781942658849 (epub)
Subjects: LCSH: Hawthorne, Nathaniel, 1804-1864--Fiction. | Trials (Witchcraft)--Massachusetts--Salem--Fiction. | GSAFD: Biographical fiction. | Historical fiction.
Classification: LCC PS3562.O218 T66 2021 | DDC 813/.54--dc23
LC record available at https://lccn.loc.gov/2020027690

Bellevue Literary Press would like to thank all its generous donors—individuals and foundations—for their support.

This publication is made possible by the New York State Council on the Arts with the support of Governor Andrew M. Cuomo and the New York State Legislature.

Book design and composition by Mulberry Tree Press, Inc.

Bellevue Literary Press is committed to ecological stewardship in our book production practices, working to reduce our impact on the natural environment.

∞ This book is printed on acid-free paper.

Manufactured in the United States of America

First Edition

1 3 5 7 9 8 6 4 2

paperback ISBN: 978-1-942658-83-2
ebook ISBN: 978-1-942658-84-9

For Joyce Carol Oates

&

Charles Giraudet

How shall a man escape from his ancestors,
or draw off from his veins the black drop which
he drew from his father's or his mother's life?

—Ralph Waldo Emerson

. . . his doubts alone had substance.

—Nathaniel Hawthorne

Speak. I am bound to hear.

—Hamlet, to his father's ghost

Tooth *of the* Covenant

WINTER 1851

THE RED SHANTY

LENOX, MASSACHUSETTS

The snow keeps me indoors, and I've been fretful all week with boredom. I was saving this bottle of Barbados rum for Melville's next visit. He swears by it to sharpen the dulled wits that come from being shut up with one's self, like a spice to excite a vapid appetite or (to be modern) a galvanic battery to set a listless man twitching. I saw one resurrect a frog, or at least its hind legs, which remembered, in death, how to flee—too late to save itself, alas. Not that I have any great affection for rum, or frogs, either, though I sympathize with their racial fear of alien hands that would make a meal of them.

A story has been much on my mind of late, the telling of which may lay to rest the surly ghost of one of my ancestors, whose shame has long weighed on me. I wanted to tell it first to Sophia, but my poor wife is in bed with another of her headaches. She is a martyr to an overly sensitive disposition. Lidian Emerson is another whose nerves are finely spun. Waldo may be the nation's preeminent man of letters and philosophy, but he can be chilly. Remoteness is sometimes a penalty for thinking too much or too deeply, but one the thinker himself seldom pays. Biographies of illustrious men rarely mention long-suffering wives, except as they may have been an adornment to their husbands' reputations or, in cases of posthumous fame, vestals of their immortality. Although not of the first rank, I don't exempt myself from the egoism of the scribbling tribe.

Sometimes I wonder if it's worth all the fuss, but what are we if not our stories?

Although I don't much care for the taste of transubstantiated sugar beets, the fumes *are* delicious. Treats such as this dusky bottle of rum are a perquisite of employment in the U.S. Customs Service—not that I abused the high office of Inspector of the Revenue for the Port of Salem. The title is grander than the office itself. In our democracy, an appointment is often a bone of patronage thrown to dogsbodies in exchange for services rendered. I rendered unto Caesar sufficiently to hoist myself and family from the mire of debt without muddying my gaiters. Nevertheless, an article would sometimes vanish from a ship's hold and materialize inside the domestic establishment on Chestnut Street of Mr. and Mrs. Nathaniel Hawthorne. Sophia disapproved of my modest embezzlements, unless the contraband happened to be a fancy tin of Casparus van Houten's chocolates. Eve found common apples irresistible. Consider how much more tempting Dutch chocolate would have been than Eden's fruit, which once eaten must evermore be obedient to Newton's law of gravity, as well as nature's graver one called "death." I fear the rot that follows it more than the dire thing itself.

A little more rum, Nathaniel? Pour it to the brim, and if any should spill twixt the cup and the lip, so be it. Such an ardent draft may prime the rusted works of speech. My nature tends the other way from garrulousness. Emerson and Henry Thoreau tire of my silences, which are not eloquent but heavy, like a millstone, which can never know the nectar of a peach. But on paper—ah! I'm someone else. I am the prophet Jeremiah and also Solomon, who sang like a troubadour, even though his amorous serenades were meant for God's ears and not a mortal lover's. I would sing bawdily, but I'm a somber Puritan dogged by melancholy—"the Noble Prince of Melancholy," as that good man Evert Duyckinck dubbed me. My infamous ancestor settled his solemnity on me. Only on paper—like this sheet I rest my glass upon—can I speak heart and mind to you, reader, whose eyes and ears belong to me for as long as you are in thrall to my words. I say "reader" hopefully, since, for all I know, you may be falling asleep over these very pages or thinking of something by Dickens or Thackeray.

Fire in a bottle! I can see why a literary alchemist like Poe stoked the blazing furnace of his imagination with it. I prefer the lively Heidsieck. Sadly, I drank the last bottle at Christmas. In lieu of it, I will have a second glass of scalding rumbullion to fortify myself against the biting cold of a winter in the Berkshires under snow.

I am not one of those men of letters who write for posterity. I write to earn the price of a chop and something warming, to put a roof over our heads under which to settle our brains and ease Sophia's nervous strain, and to provide for the children. I write to be done, once and for all, with debt, which seems everlasting even now that publication of *The Scarlet Letter* has brought me fame. No, my brief is all with the past—in particular, with my great-great-grandfather John Hathorne, an examining magistrate during the arraignment of the Salem witches who handed down bills of indictment as if they had been sweets. Of the dreary and disdainful men who sat in judgment, he was the most zealous and unforgiving.

I'm preoccupied by his story, which is also mine. He is the grudge I bear and the thorn in my side, the speck in my eye and the needle in my heart. He's the reason for the altered spelling of the family name. He made me the man I am, one who walks in the shadow cast by Salem's gallows tree, whose heart is too heavy to be wholly glad and too chill to be completely warmed by any human joy. As Melville wrote of me, I am "shrouded in blackness, ten times black."

Snug inside the Red Shanty, in Lenox, Massachusetts, I ponder my guilty conscience, while its source, erstwhile Salem magistrate Hathorne, lies safely beyond reach of retribution, if not reproach. There may be enough left of him to make Brother Bones a clapper for a minstrel show or furnish a stage Hamlet with a prop to muse on in the graveyard scene, but the once proud adjudicator of others' guilt or innocence is unpoetical dust and no different from the mineral residue remaining to the victims of his stern intolerance.

I think some good would redound to me if Magistrate Hathorne could be brought at last to the bar and the rope. (I would spare him the agony of being pressed to death by stones laid, one by one, atop a condemned man's chest, undeserving though my ancestor be of mercy.) That I am saturnine and uncertain in society, I owe to his twisted root. It hobbles me with the gait and tongue of an awkward clod. I want to rip it from the stony ground, that root, where it took hold and became a blighted thing. Were it possible to dig up the man from where he waits to hear the last trump in Salem's old Burying Point cemetery, I'd do so, albeit I would find him chapfallen and deaf to my stammered curses. No, to be rid of him, I would need to cross a gulf of time wide and deep enough in which to drown. I needs must go to him, where, in his own age, he is raging, cruel and intemperate.

When I lived in Concord among the mystics, Thoreau gave me a pebble and said, in that sly way of his, which puts me in mind of an evangelist *and* a confidence man, that I could sense its longing to be reunited with its mountain, if I would yield to the magnetic currents everywhere present in the universe. "However base or obscure, all things desire to return to their origin."

To return to my origin, I require something far less antediluvian than Henry's pebble. I need a totem to excite in me a sympathetic resonance for the atoms of Magistrate Hathorne as he was when he walked the streets and breathed the air of Salem in 1692.

Fortunately, I have a pair of his spectacles, which descended through the generations that followed him, along with the odor of his misdeeds. For the Salem boy I was when I lived in my grandfather Richard's house in Herbert Street, they were more fabulous than Hans Lippershey's telescope. As I peered through their magnifying lenses, I fancied I saw what John Hathorne had seen in his day: the rutted village lanes, taverns, the parish house, blockhouse, pillory, and the meetinghouse where the younger Ann Putnam and her creatures eagerly manifested signs of a diabolical affliction—the cries, moans, gibbers, pains, and seizures visited on them by demons who had left the forest to destroy the city of the blessed. Fascinated and appalled, I would look through the twin panes of glass till I could bear it no more. The lenses had been ground for other eyes than mine. My vision was accustomed to the sights of a different Salem, the town where I was born in 1804 and spent my early years.

As a student at Bowdoin College, I read Latin and the classics. I'd have been graduated with distinction but for public speaking, which I could not do. Shyness has always dogged me. I envied the eloquence of my classmates Longfellow and Franklin Pierce, both of whom took the podium with the ease that a Baptist minister does the pulpit. The first became our national poet, the second a senator and a hero of the recent Mexican War. Lacking in oratorical skill, I became a customhouse hack and a scribbler. But a scribbler can create a world larger than the Mexican territories and more overflowing with raw life than what is bounded by stanzas. At Bowdoin, I became aware of my ancestor's infamy. Now eightscore years later, I intend to scribble a tale with which to bring him to book. I'll match his cruel sentences with my own and make his past a present Hell. If the Devil was at large in Massachusetts and his imps were eating into the Faith like worms into the pages of a book to set the Word at naught, my words will worm their way into my great-great-grandfather's guts.

My "envoy"—I'll call him Isaac Page—will travel to Salem as it was in the year of the witches and confront the man who bequeathed me a melancholy aspect and darkness of outlook. Perhaps he could have willed me no other, since the age in which he had his brief moment was benighted and the conditions harsh. Fear was ever present, and God less inclined to show His creatures mercy. But the fact remains that John Hathorne alone, of Salem's and Boston's civil authorities, did not repent of his terrible judgments, not even when Death or the Devil came to claim him at his end.

I say you *shall* repent, Grandsire, and release the innocents from their hard durance and bid the hangman put away his noose, or you'll die at the hands of Isaac Page, whom I intend to send to Salem to judge you and, if need be, execute you!

As I watch an ant cross the parlor floor, bearing a crumb of stale scone or a particle of eternity on its back (who knows to what purposes ants give themselves), I imagine myself in a room that even dust would hesitate to enter. I'm standing before a stiff-necked magistrate who is infuriated by the shouts of boys playing in the road outside his window—an affront to the gravity of a man who handles others' souls as washerwomen do soiled linen.

"What do you want?" he demands of me.

"To examine you," I reply.

"I am examiner here!"

"Then I would have you examine yourself."

"To what end?"

"To discover the absence of God in you."

"You are standing on the gallows, sir. It would take only a nod of my head to the executioner to have you taken off the Earth. Or perhaps you do not fear me?"

"I fear you well enough because I know the Devil has made himself at home in you."

With those words, I will begin the arraignment of my ancestor. If not those, then some others equally cogent. Ah, Nathaniel! You're never so eloquent as when you admit your love or vent your rage within the theater of your mind. But the words will *gush* from Isaac Page's mouth as they never could from mine. Isaac Page will voice my abhorrence for Magistrate Hathorne.

I'll see to it.

The Red Shanty's gate stands open. Isaac has only to step into the lane to begin his journey. The day is fine, the month April—I'll spare my surrogate a Massachusetts winter. And yet he hesitates, hobbled by uncertainty. But I am his author, and he is *my* creature—a thing of words, like the past itself and the people who walk there. I have only to write the first sentence of my tale to send Isaac on his way.

Tooth of the Covenant

A NOVEL BY NATHANIEL HAWTHORNE

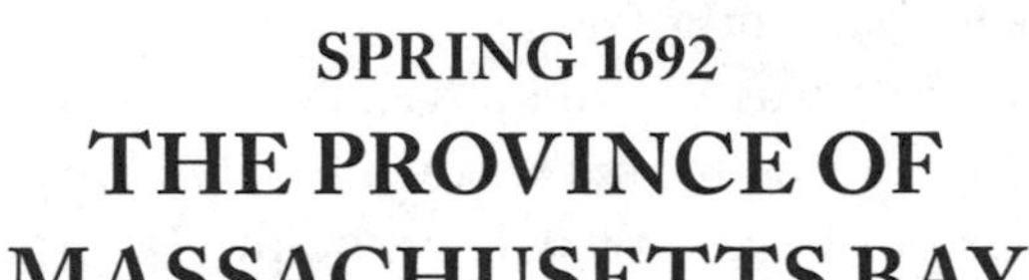

SPRING 1692
THE PROVINCE OF MASSACHUSETTS BAY

I

On an otherwise unremarkable April morning in 1851, Isaac Page, a writer of literary romances, prepared to set out from the town of Lenox, in western Massachusetts, to save Bridget Bishop from hanging. She would be the first of the witches put to death in Salem Town during the Year of Desolation, 1692, when John Winthrop's godly plantation in New England, which was to have been an example to all the world of a righteous commonwealth, withered, like an ear of corn in a field no longer green. Perhaps New England's shores were too stony a place on which to build a New Jerusalem or else God's chosen had become, in sixty years, mean-spirited, backbiting, tale-bearing Sabbath breakers no more worthy of His favor than the wicked of Sodom or Gomorrah. For whatever reason, He seemed to have turned His back on the Province of Massachusetts Bay. Or so His cold granite shoulder was interpreted in Isaac's own time by those of a religious bent who made a study of the nation's past, which will not cease to trouble its present till the course of empire shambles to an end and those who govern amid its ruins are forced to make amends or perish.

Isaac Page was not the pilgrim's real name, but a pseudonym taken to conceal the identity of his author from his great-great-grandfather John Hathorne, the Salem magistrate who did as much as the perjured girls of Salem Village to stoke the fever of unreason in the province. It was Hathorne who sentenced Bridget Bishop to death and set going the cruel engine that separated men, women, and children from their mortal husks.

The writer of romances who lived, together with his wife and children, in a farmhouse painted red, overlooking the Housatonic Valley, was not interested in Winthrop's "city on a hill," in God, or even—let him once be honest with himself—in forestalling a Terror that was inferior to Robespierre's only in the number of executions. (Seventeen thousand French persons were decapitated by order of the Revolutionary Tribunal.) Isaac Page wanted to save himself from the anguish of a guilty conscience. To do so, he would need to convince

John Hathorne that Bridget Bishop and the others whom he condemned were guiltless of sorcery. Should he prove deaf to persuasion, Isaac needs must knock sense into his head with a stick or, if worse comes to worst, cudgel the brains out of the man.

Naturally, Isaac knew that the past had been foreclosed on by time: the lights put out, the doors and windows boarded up, the drapes and carpets left to moths and rot. None can ever live there again, except in stories. But storytelling was Isaac's one and only skill. By it, he reasoned, he could travel to the Salem of his rawboned ancestor, whose shadow had eclipsed his own and darkened a nature that otherwise would have been genial.

Isaac buttoned a doublet over a linen shirt and put on leather breeches and stockings that red garters kept from becoming, as Ophelia said of mad Prince Hamlet's, "down-gyvèd to his ankle." These articles had served him as a costume for a recent patriotic tableau. For hat, he had a shapeless thing with a dented crown and a ruckled brim to shade his bristled face. Having let his hair grow long in the fashion of an earlier time, he tied it in a sailor's queue. In his doublet pocket, he carried a pair of spectacles that had belonged to the unrepentant magistrate who had taken in evidence the ranting of a pack of "afflicted" girls. Like the flagon of Hollands gin quaffed by Rip Van Winkle, the spectacles would convey Isaac backward in time, by the sympathetic attraction transmitted through the ether, which connected all things. Mostly, the so-called savage races were attuned to it, although some poets and writers among the "civilized" were aware of its presence, residing in a stone, in a talisman, or at the bottom of a glass of ardent spirits.

The spectacles had come to him by the law governing the transfer of a legacy. He had believed them to be of little value until one day he sensed an urgency rarely, if ever, expressed by objects—the wish (call it that) to return to their original owner. With them in his pocket, he had only to set out on the path that began not far from his farmhouse in the Berkshires, to know *in his bones* the way through space and time to the Province of Massachusetts Bay, where Bridget Bishop waited—along with eighteen others who would follow her to gallows and grave—for the great clock to tick forward to her end. Our bones belong not to us alone but also to our forebears, whose origin was Eden, if one happens to be religious, or a "center of creation," if one subscribes to Lyell's cosmography. (Isaac's friend Herman Melville would add that *his* bones belong to his creditors.)

After having said good-bye to his wife, Isaac walked along a country road into the forest and soon found himself amid towering spruce trees on a needle-sown path leading to Old Salem. Trodden centuries earlier by Indians of the Woodland tribes, the path had disappeared beneath Newbold cast-iron plows some years before, as a scar will fade and, in time, vanish. In the way of phantoms, however, the primordial forest had not passed entirely into history. It struggled on in the minds of Isaac and his countrymen, as real a place as Athens had been to the ancient Greeks, and still was to students of the classical age. Aided by the antique spectacles in his doublet, Isaac passed down the years toward one of time's stubborn tangles, purposing to unravel it or, if he must, to severe it as Alexander once did the Gordian knot.

One would expect the forest primeval to be a windless place outside history and beyond temporal disturbances. But isn't time said to be a wind at our back, pushing us into the future? As the poet Marvel wrote, ". . . at my back I always hear / Time's wingèd chariot hurrying near." Those vast wings—what a wind they would make, enough to sweep away all present things! In the case of a man who willed himself to walk toward a year whose leaves had long since been torn from tree and calendar, wouldn't he feel the wind of time on his face like a blast of musty air? Having risen in April 1692, one of time's ill winds buffeted Isaac, intending to drive him back to 1851 and to the red farmhouse where Constance, his wife, had gone to bed with a sick headache. In 1692, Isaac would often recall their parting kiss at the gate and the stirrup cup of rum she had given him for his courage's sake. Not that he needed courage at the outset of the journey. Isaac was brave in the way that people sometimes are who are overcome by passion—whether a desire to possess or an equally strengthening wish to destroy. He was in thrall to that desire and that wish, though he was conscious of neither. He thought only of his own small fate and of how he would alter it in Old Salem. To hold the thought in mind, however, was difficult because of the wind. The serpentine path seemed to writhe. His face burned, and his lips were chapped. His eyes were made to water by flying particles of grit. Creeping vines tripped him; nettles stung him; burrs fastened onto his bootlaces and woolen hose; the trees pummeled him with gall- and hickory nuts. He felt time slipping through his fingers like nubs in raw silk.

He had not expected a wind, and he fretted over it. In the red farmhouse, Isaac had often dreamed of the forest where he now walked, painfully. Like a vast timbered cathedral dressed for the risen Christ in sweet fern and Spanish moss, purple flags and hyacinth, it had stretched from Baffin Bay to the Florida Straits, from the Atlantic Ocean to the Pacific. Silence had reigned over the sylvan colonnades—a silence in which a leaf might turn, a movement so slight and fitful that it was mistaken for stillness.

He told himself that he was being foolish and that no malign agency harried him—this man from Lenox of no special importance, whose mind was prey to fancies. The wind is in your head, he said, which is opposed to your proceeding against your own interests, which lie behind you in the farmhouse, in Constance's arms, and in modern Boston, which publishes your books and whose nighttime streets are illumined by gaslight. There is nothing for you, Isaac, in a city on a hill that shines only in a figure of speech—nothing anymore in Salem Village, which is, at the middle of the nineteenth century, a place to visit and smirk at the simplemindedness of men and women who believed in the Devil's mark and witches' teats hidden beneath their skirts.

As he made his way through the crowding trees, he asked himself the everlastingly futile question: Who can understand the ways of God? In reply, he adjured himself to ". . . lean not unto thy own understanding." Or was it the trees who admonished him?

Isaac leaned into the wind and held on to his hat. "The strongest wind cannot stagger a Spirit," Thoreau had written.

But I'm not a spirit; I am a material man!

Through this improbable wilderness, Isaac ventured onward, that is to say backward—one hand on his slouch hat, the other on a satchel of carpenter's tools. He did not hunger, nor did he thirst. The peevishness that he had felt at the start left him. He had walked beyond weariness and had been granted the elation experienced by a climber who ascends to a great height.

"Where else may the forest path lead?" he asked of no one.

A voice that may have come from the forest or from Isaac himself replied, "To the origin of life, the first green leaf and flower. To the sowing of Earth with stones and the upraising of its mountains. To the shore of the ancient ocean and the first night. To the day before creation."

Suddenly appalled at the arrogance of his undertaking, Isaac shivered. Or was it only the wind that made him do so?

"How far is it from Lenox to Salem?" he asked aloud of whatever spirit—virtuous or foul—might be inhabiting the place on which he had trespassed.

"One hundred and fifty miles, more or less. Between *more* and *less*, a chasm opens, large enough to engulf an elephant. Between *more* and *less,* kindness can sour, smooth become rough, forgiveness vengeance, and goodwill enmity. A fit man can walk the distance in four or five days—seven in snow. To tread one hundred and fifty-nine years, however, takes no longer than it did for you to open and close your front gate. What seems to you a far pace of time is nothing but the crumbs of time you carry in your pockets."

"Is the forest dark?" Isaac asked anxiously, because his sensations were confused.

"Dark as night and, at the same time, not. The forest is touched by paradox. *Twilight*, then—perpetual and shadowless—like the setting of a dream or an allegory," said the voice, which could have been Isaac's or his Creator's. (Or the Devil's.)

In that remote age, New Englanders feared what lay beyond the reach of common day and the ambit of their candlelight. Wampanoag and Narragansett trod in stealth, and ravaging sickness was visited upon the people by an angry God. Hunger and sharp winters, blight and drought, cholera and smallpox smote them for backsliding. In the Book of Isaiah, the people's tribulation had been foretold.

> And they shall look unto the earth; and behold trouble and darkness, dimness of anguish; and they shall be driven to darkness.

An impenetrable, even inexplicable, forest must come to an end. Coming out from the trees, Isaac noticed a pall hanging above a village, as if gloom had transpired from the Puritan temperament, like dirty water from a rag. His eyes were unaccustomed to the dim view taken by benighted minds fearful of the unholy wonders of the invisible world. The Age of Enlightenment had not yet dawned in New England, where pillory, whip, prison, and noose extorted obedience to ironbound dogma. Faith—the genuine article—does not fear for its life, does not answer for itself, does not bring fire and the sword to heretics and infidels. The Province of Massachusetts Bay, however, was a faithless place, whose people did not trust in God's mercy, but in His wrath, and would not believe in their neighbors' goodness, but only in their malice.

Isaac would not soon be rid of the "dusk" of self-doubt. Now and then, he would repent of having flouted the universal law of time—a blasphemy that had brought him to a place hostile to reason and goodwill. He would become frightened that his arrogance had lost him his rightful time and he would never see his wife and children again. Then he would recall the silver dollar stamped with the year of its minting, 1851, buttoned in his doublet pocket. Like the spectacles, the coin could overcome time itself by the operation of nostalgia, or by the "contagion of objects," as the affinity was known by the Puritans and the East Anglians before them. Isaac had only to clench the coin to return to the middle of the nineteenth century, when witchery was a game for children and magistrates did not examine them for the seal of the Devil's covenant.

Sixteen hundred and ninety-two was a frightful year in Massachusetts. The brutal winter promised a meager spring, sickness went abroad, and New England's failed assault on Quebec had crowded the streets of Salem Town with refugees from Maine, fleeing the Abenaki and the French. Men who coveted their neighbors' land or livestock, together with their spiteful wives, whose tongues could curdle milk, were crying "witch" against one another. Few there were in the village and the town who were not afraid.

II

saac arrived in Salem Village on April 19, 1692. On that day, Bridget Bishop was examined at the meetinghouse, where inquisitors probed for cankered souls. Though he stood miles from the village crossroads, he heard voices. One voice, a man's, was cold and imperious; the other, a woman's, defiant.

"I am no witch."

"If you have not wrote in the book, then tell me how far you have gone. Have you not to do with familiar spirits?"

"I have no familiarity with the Devil."

"How is it then that your appearance doth hurt these girls?"

"I am innocent."

"Why you seem to act witchcraft before us, by the motion of your body, which seems to have influence upon the afflicted!"

"I know nothing of it. I am innocent to a witch. I know not what a witch is."

"How do you know then that you are not a witch?"

"I do not know what you say."

In 1630, when the Winthrop Fleet made safe harbor on the Charles at the start of the Great Migration, the Puritans brought the idea of the Devil with them from East Anglia, together with his Powers, Principalities, Thrones, and Dominions. They hopped like fleas from the gaunt bodies of the starved, seaworn passengers into the endless, lightless forest, where they would henceforth "worry and annoy" the new colonists, whose infants' blood witches drank in unholy communion and whose names they sought to write in Satan's book.

"How can you know, you are no witch, and yet not know what a witch is?"

"I am clear: if I were any such person you should know it."

Silence flooded the meadow where Isaac stood like someone not entirely in the world or outside of it. And then he heard several cries and shrieks of pain, so that he needs must take his head in his hands to keep it from breaking. Having read Cotton Mather's account of the trials, Isaac knew that Tituba, the Reverend Parris's Indian slave brought from Barbados, and his daughter, Betty Parris, as well as the young Putnam girl, Mary Walcott, Abigail Williams, Mary Warren, Elizabeth Hubbard, Mercy Lewis, and Susannah Sheldon, were playacting for the village gawkers. Although unseen by Isaac, those girls—vipers whose poison had been turning every man against his neighbor—were twitching and writhing in a simulacrum of possession.

The counterfeiting girls had begun their notorious careers with "little sorceries," such as "turning the sieve" or gazing in a Venus glass to see the shapes of future husbands. Soon they were miming agonies caused by an imp or a poppet pierced by a sewing needle, at Ingersoll's ordinary. By curse, charm, and effigy, witches were believed to be at large in Salem, making cruel sport of the innocent children who were now crying out against them. Salem people knew that the girls had only to point to send one or the other of them to Arnold's jail. They may have been irked by the discipline imposed on their young lives or terrified of being whipped to within an inch of them for having been caught frisking naked in the forest by the Reverend Parris. They may have craved attention, which their histrionics brought them in abundance. Had the saints in the New World not outlawed playhouses, the girls would have had a proper stage on which to "saw the air" and "tear a passion to tatters"—the melodramatic playacting style despised by Hamlet. As it was, the frustrated thespians tore their neighbors to pieces by pretense and lies.

Later in the universal frenzy, others would cry "witch" in envy, spite, or dread of being hanged for sending out *their* specters to sicken or murder their neighbors. Spectral evidence was sufficient to condemn them: Accusers need only descry a witch's familiar—a mastiff, such as Black Shuck, which had ravaged Yarmouth's Long Sands, a black hog, or a yellow bird with the tiny head of a woman—for the magistrates to convict the accused of keeping company with the Devil. Such infernal entities were invisible to all but the bewitched. In Salem, there were few brave hearts to call them liars.

Another exchange of voices was audible to Isaac. They were as clear to him as if he had been standing at the meetinghouse window. John Hathorne was interrogating four-year-old Dorcas Good at her mother's arraignment. The child was terrified, the magistrate cunning.

"And did you never play with a familiar?"

"I had a little snake."

"Did it leave its mark on you?"

"A deep red spot, about the bigness of a flea bite."

Dorcas showed the magistrates the tip of her forefinger, where the snake would suck.

"Who gave you the snake? Was it the Devil? Think carefully, child, else you keep your mother company in Arnold's jail."

"It was my mother gave it me—not the great Black Man."

Gulled into betraying her mother, the child would spend that night and many another in terror, hunger, and chains.

Having heard his ancestor flay Dorcas with sharp arguments, Isaac could have cut the man's throat as readily as the Hebrews did their sacrificial lambs' or a New England farmer of his own time does a stout's. Isaac would have gone at once to the meetinghouse and dispatched John Hathorne, but like a shackled prisoner or a man in a trance, he was unable to move an inch from the spot where he stood at the outskirts of the village. The magisterial voice, which mixed blandishment and coercion, arriving from underneath a century and a half of grass, snow, and mud, in their seasonal round, unnerved Isaac. He could not reconcile the fact that the man was dead with the fact that he had just spoken. Momentarily bewitched, Isaac could as well believe that fiends lurked in the thatched darkness beneath the soaring trees surrounding Old Salem as that invisible agencies were the cause of cholera or smallpox. And then his Yankee skepticism declared itself. Evil originates in the mind, he told himself. It does not creep into a man's soul, like a tick into his clothing.

"Say you have conjured! Say who else has supped with the Devil, and you will go free."

"I am innocent."

Isaac's purpose now grew larger: He had not only to lift the family curse, which blighted his nature, but forestall the hanging of nineteen innocents, the pressing to death of Giles Corey, and the imprisonment of 150 men, women, children, and milk-toothed babes in Boston jail for "the horrible crime of witchcraft practiced by them and committed on several persons." He must do so for their sakes, as well as his own. God had decamped in that grievous time and taken His mercy with Him. His representatives in Salem and Boston were unpitying. Could there be a more outward display of broken charity than to charge the husbands or the wives of the condemned for their bed and board during their imprisonment and, if need be, for their coffins and burials? Their envious neighbors got their grasping hands on a number of farms confiscated from those whose grief was ample but earthly treasures small, in payment of the debt.

Once again, John Hathorne's voice sounded in Isaac's mind, together with that of another of the accused "witches."

"Have you signed the Devil's book?"

"No."

"Have you not toucht it?"

"No."

Borrowed from the Whirlwind, a lesser wind arose, and the words scattered like leaves. You must be as ruthless as the pest that sent a host of New Englanders and a horde of savages writhing to their separate afterlives! Isaac exhorted himself. Mercy is dead in Massachusetts.

III

n a lane skirting Wilkins Pond, Isaac hallooed to a young woman wringing a wet rag into a bucket. The firmament appeared to have drowned in the pond. An elegant pair of swans paddled through the sky's reflection until a cloud

eclipsed the sun and the monogamous birds returned to their native element.

"Whose house is this?" asked Isaac, admiring a plain, though substantial, plank-framed two-story residence with a slate roof, two brick chimneys, and diamond-paned windows, which the woman had been washing, her sleeves pushed up above dimpled elbows.

"John Buxton's, sir, son of Master Anthony and his goodwife, Elizabeth."

Isaac had encountered John Buxton's name in court records of the time. He and Thomas Putnam had denounced Sarah Wildes, Sarah and Edward Bishop, Nehemiah Abbott, Jr., William and Deliverance Hobbs, Mary Easty, Mary English, and the slave Mary Black for "sundry acts of witchcraft . . . whereby great hurt and damage hath been done."

Those persons would shortly be in Salem jail. Whether they would ride in an oxcart to Proctor's Ledge was in men's hands and not, as the magistrates and ministers declared, in God Almighty's. Before the year was out, Buxton himself would take the ferry from Noddle's Island to Boston to think upon his sins in Arnold's jail for having compacted with the Evil One. None was immune from the spite and envy of his neighbors.

"Who might you be?" Her shape and comeliness would have kindled a spark in a younger Isaac, needing only a little fanning to blaze.

"Isaac Page, of Lenox, Massachusetts."

She tilted her head to one side, a quizzical gesture he

found charmingly comical. Isaac had forgotten that, in 1692, the town of Lenox, Massachusetts, had yet to be founded and would not be until 1767 by pettifogging and deceit. The student of history might well conclude that empires—be they as large as Alexander's or as small as a neighbor's dooryard—cannot be established by any other means.

"You may not have heard of the place," he said offhandedly. "It's no more than a gristmill and a handful of habitations too mean to be called houses."

Isaac was relieved that the girl did not question his manner of speaking, which he had laboriously acquired before leaving his own century. He had read John Winthrop's journals, Election Day sermons, tracts, jeremiads, and ancient pamphlets preserved among the rarities of our nation's past at Harvard College. He had gotten by heart verses of Anne Bradstreet's and strophes from the *Bay Psalm Book.* To complete the subterfuge, he befriended Henry Shaw, a philologist and scholar of Colonial American writings, who taught him to shape the East Anglian vowels of our most native speech—save those belonging to the continent's aboriginals.

"What brings you to Salem Village?"

"I'm an itinerant carpenter," he replied. "I travel the country in the hope that my skills will be useful to someone and profitable to myself. I seldom make a profit that cannot be eaten cold or by which I can take shelter for a night or two in someone's barn. New England's flinty soil raises flinty men."

She lifted her face to the sun, which had come out from behind the cloud and turned the pond again to sky. Isaac saw her features clearly; they bore evidence of smallpox, and he was glad the malady had not laid a heavy hand on her. He knew that even virtue, when seen up close, may appear less than perfect. Isaac did not doubt the young woman's virtue. Her countenance was too frank and unclouded for her to be secretly troubled by vice, nor did he find her face less appealing for the pox. Her beauty, though flawed, enchanted him, as did her dimpled arms.

"What's your name?"

"Smyth."

"May I know your Christian one?" asked Isaac, aping the urbanity of a Virginia cavalier.

"Hannah."

"Hannah," he repeated softly, as though he had never heard the name pronounced.

"But you must not call me that!" she scolded. "They will say we are too familiar—you, for using my Christian name, and I for allowing it."

"Who are 'they,' Hannah?" He knew the answer. "They" are those who sit in judgment of the tribe.

"The people of Salem Village."

"Do they speak as one?"

"There be few who would not take pleasure in rebuking us. You're a stranger here and do not know their ways."

"And are they not yours, Mistress Smyth?"

For answer, she nudged the bucket with her shoe.

The gray water rose up one side of it but did not overflow. Was the nudge a minor act of rebellion?

"What do you know of Bridget Bishop?" he asked.

"They say she curtsied to the Devil."

"Do you believe it?"

Hannah frowned, smoothed her skirts, and replied, "I believe in charity."

"I'm grateful for yours, Hannah Smyth."

"I've given you no charity that I'm aware of, goodman!" she replied tartly, as the sun dimmed again.

"Your willingness to answer plainly this pilgrim's questions is charitable."

"You said you're an itinerant workman. Now you call yourself a 'pilgrim.'"

"Since I'm a carpenter traveling from pillar to post in search of work, I am the former; because I've come to Salem to pay my respects, I am the latter. In other words, mistress, I am both." He smiled and doffed his hat.

"Have you come to pay them to Master Buxton?" she asked warily.

"I'd sooner pay them to you." He smiled a second time and put his hat back on.

"You're very forward!" she chided him playfully.

"I mean to see John Hathorne, whose righteous work against the Devil's spawn I've heard praised everywhere by God-fearing souls."

A shadow fell over Hannah's face, although a lofting wind had uncovered the sun. The decorous swans moved across the face of Wilkins Pond, where reflected clouds sailed, sedate as icebergs. Hastily, she picked up the wooden pail. Gray water slopped onto the flagstone steps.

"What is the matter, Mistress Smyth?"

"My work obliges me to bid you good day."

Standing in the doorway, she gazed pensively at the trees round about and bit her lower lip. Perhaps like John Winthrop, the father of the colony—now a province—she saw that New Englanders "were compassed with dangers on every side, and were daily under the sentence of death, that they might learn to trust in the living God." She tossed her head in annoyance, as if to rid it of a pest.

"And, goodman, if you truly are one, I'm not mistress of this or any other house!"

She turned and shut the door behind her.

IV

saac had last eaten on an April morning in 1851. He was hungry, though less than one would expect after so long a fast. He fancied that he had been traveling through some outer borough of eternity, where rare spirits, who neither ate nor drank, went about their Father's business. In Lenox, he had jeered at the notion of seraphim and cherubim. On his first day in the province, he did, as well. But the longer he would stay in the New World, which was really an old one, the more willing he would be to accept the prevailing opinion concerning

the invisible world, which, in the seventeenth century, was as teeming with evil and well-meaning spirits as a drop of water is with animalcules.

In 1851, Isaac was open to ideas as long as they were sensible. In exile, however, his intellectual toleration would lead him to an uneasy recognition of Satan and his cohort. That was no more astonishing than clear water's turning dark by the process of infusion—a minor marvel witnessed in a pot of tea. Isaac did not shut his mind to modern science on the first day among his remote countrymen, nor on the second, or the tenth. It had to steep awhile in the superstitious age in which he found himself. Superstitions are derided in retrospect, but while they reign, they are meat and drink for the most scholarly of men. (Women were believed to make poor scholars in Isaac Page's day as well as in John Winthrop's.) As the juice of the grape can, after achieving perfection in the wine, turn gradually into vinegar, a mind can sour and its thoughts grow caustic. Thus would Isaac Page's nature warp away from reason until some recollection of his former life (one could as easily say his "future life") woke him to himself. A dog ought not to be punished for doing what dogs do.

Leaving the Buxton house, sumptuous for its time, Isaac followed the windings of Pout Brook to Rowley Village, also known as Boxford. Not far from an ironworks stood Croft's ordinary. *Slumped* was more apposite to its ramshackle condition. The alehouse's sagging door was open to let in fresh air and let out an atmosphere rank with the sweat of laborers from the foundry and nearby fields, indentured servants from the farms thereabout, sour barrels, bitter hops, and the heavy smoke of tobacco imported from plantations in Virginia and the Indies. In Boxford, uncovenanted souls may have felt safe from the jaundiced eyes and spiteful tongues of Salem villagers and the carnivorous appetite of steeple-hatted ministers for the wastrels in their midst. They may have been careless of damnation. They reminded Isaac of the revelers in Edgar Poe's tale who had retreated from the pestilence to Prince Prospero's castle.

Not everyone who gathered at Thom Croft's was a rogue or a reprobate, although by Salem law and God's ordinances, which were the same, they sinned for exceeding the limit of Puritan jollity. Coming from an impure age, Isaac knew that anyone might yield to temptation when temptation comprehended the smallest vanity or stumble along the way. He was prepared to forgive all but the most grievous sinners. To the black-suited men of sober countenance, their eyes alight with God and fanaticism, the residents of Salem Town and Salem Village—having been sown in corruption—required constant surveillance and chastisement. God's own men, it was understood, were beyond reproach. Theirs was the religion of "Thou shalt not," even unto absurdity: Thou shalt not pull hair, neither a man's nor a woman's, howsoever thou art tempted by rage or lust. Thou shalt not drink unto drunkenness, sell strong water to the Indians, dance profanely, or indulge in the "creature called tobacco," which is the Devil's weed.

The pipe that is so foul within,
It shows man's soul is stained with sin;
It doth require
To be purred with fire;
Think of this when you smoke tobacco!

Isaac was about to order a jar from the innkeeper, when he recalled that he had come from the nineteenth century with neither a note printed nor specie minted in the seventeenth. He had only the silver dollar in his doublet to pay for his passage home. Had his pockets been stuffed with banknotes backed by God and gold, they would have been useless here. He was a person without means. Although the earnings of an author of romances had inured him to indebtedness, he felt like a man washed up on an alien shore, with none to vouch for him or lend him the most trifling sum. Charity, Isaac understood, was not meant for him; it was given only to brothers and sisters in the faith and even then with stinginess.

"What will you drink?" asked landlord Croft, a large man whose erect carriage, strong voice, and mane of steely hair belied his threescore-and-ten years.

Croft gave the appearance of someone who did not entertain fools or beggars gladly, so Isaac adopted the pridefulness of a man who'd rather die of thirst than beg for water or listen to his belly grumble than crawl on it.

"I've not the means to a gill's worth of foam, but what I lack in coins, I have in talents."

Croft's frank look unsettled Isaac, who nonetheless held the other man's gaze.

"What manner of man are you?" asked Croft coolly. His cheek, Isaac noted, was faintly scarred by a brand that might have been, when new, the letter *P*.

"A carpenter who would barter his skill for victuals and, if it pleases you, a place to stay."

Having suffered martyrdom to the communal ideal at Brook Farm, Isaac was familiar with hammer and saw and bore their calloused warrants on his palms. To further his imposture, he had borrowed tools from an old millwright in Pittsfield, who had them from his father, who had had them from his. They were identical to those Isaac had seen among artifacts displayed at the Boston Museum.

"What say you, Master Croft?"

Croft considered Isaac's proposition and replied, "So long as your talents are worth your keep, you can sleep in the shed and take your supper in the taproom. I would rather be fair than generous."

The man went to the hearth and, spooning a stew of venison and turnips onto a tin plate, invited Isaac, with a grunt of sufferance, to eat. His hunger had caught up to him, and he set to its appeasement with the relish of a famished man, while the other put a mug and a hunk of bread at his patched elbow. Having left not an ort of stew to prove the plate had ever been otherwise than clean, Isaac sucked a lacy remnant of ale through his teeth, wiped his lips on a sleeve, as uncouth persons do, thanked his new master, and went outside to earn his keep.

They could have been reared on different planets—so very much at variance were their characters. Nonetheless, Isaac took a liking to Croft, and Croft to him. In the weeks that Isaac spent mending the spavined roof, leaky casements, and sagging door, the two were often in each other's company, when the taproom was closed to trade in observance of the laws hammered out on the obdurate Calvinist anvil, which the Puritans had lugged with them from England. It was a wonder John Winthrop's fleet of Nonconformists had not sunk to the bottom of the ocean under the terrible weight of solemnity it carried.

The twenty thousand Puritans who arrived in the Massachusetts Bay Colony during the Great Migration of 1629 to 1642 believed that the Church of England—to their mind, idolatrous and lax in its admission of unfit priests and irredeemable congregants—could be purified by the covenanted saints of His Invisible Church, who had been saved before the world of time began. Nothing could be done for the rest of Adam and Eve's numberless progeny—children of His wrath, born into sin and damnation—regardless of how strenuously they professed their faith or how godly they behaved. None could will or wish his way into Heaven. The matter had been decided before the first day of creation. But the saints must work to be worthy of their election, uncertain of it though they may be.

For the boisterous patrons of Thom Croft's ordinary, matters of greater consequence centered on the miraculous fermentation of barley and the distillation of grain. The roisters were blithely unconcerned by controversies surrounding the Geneva gown, the placement of the altar rail, man's depravity, election, redemption, the kissing of one's wife in public, or playing shovelboard on the Sabbath. They cared not a whit whether babes were sprinkled or dipped in baptism, nor did they obey the Puritan dictum concerning strong drink—"one and done." The thirsty souls in Master Croft's keeping were pricked immoderately by appetites sharpened after the Fall, when grain could be turned into something other than bread, and grapes into the means of an ecstatic communion having nothing to do with the Supper in Emmaus. Wine consoles us for the loss of Eden and reminds us that things ripen *toward* perfection and not away from it. Beauty is achieved in time and, because of its transience, is the more moving to behold.

Rough-hewn, coarse, sometimes sottish and bawdy, Croft's patrons were nearer Isaac's sort than the disputatious Puritans of the Bay. He took pleasure in the spicy fumes of Thomas Croft's tavern. He would have been nauseated by the stale opinions aired at the meetinghouse, which he avoided, or the odor of sanctimony at Deacon Ingersoll's ordinary, where the afflicted village girls performed in the chief spectacle of the age—the examining and arraignment of the witches. The pious and the indecently curious alike would gather there to enjoy the amateur theatricals.

"This afternoon I've some business in Salem," said Croft, joining Isaac in the shade of an elm tree, where the latter was digesting his supper. "Why don't you come?"

"Not today, Thom. I want to get started on the roof."

"Your industry does you credit, Isaac, though I take to heart the proverb 'All work and no play makes Jack a dull boy.'"

"Aye, but my name's not Jack."

Like a man who steps into the shallows to accustom his body to the chill of the ocean, Isaac stayed away from Salem, where hearts were likely to be cold. He was safer amid the dregs. A man can enjoy being shunned by the majority, as long as a jolly minority keeps him company. The virtuous of Salem kept their distance from the scruff, as they would from a plague house or leper colony. With a partial knowledge of men, which he had cultivated as a storyteller (none can claim a perfect one), Isaac suspected that many of the "Sticklers" envied the freedom of the little congregation of the damned, whose hearts were gay. A few of the saints, overcome by curiosity, would peek through the tavern window. Their smirking would turn to gawping as they watched some "perishing sinner" bouncing a lusty girl on his knee. Sitting on stools drawn up to the fire, the hellions were heating mulling pokers and roasting partridges while they sang a bawdy song.

Sometimes I am a Taylor,
And work with Thread that's strong Sir;
I have a fine great Needle,
About two handfulls long Sir;
The finest Sempster in this Town,
That works by line or leisure;
May use my Needle at a pinch,
And do themselves great Pleasure.

The dissolute were sometimes fined or whipped for flouting heavenly ordinances, which were also the laws of the province. A few of the reprobates had seats in the stocks, as well as in the tavern. But the government had need of them, since their number included men who carted away filth, bore the stink of the tannery, dug lime pits, cellars, and graves. When sober, they could be depended upon to hunt savages, when a hue and cry was raised against an uprising. Among their caste were trappers, sawyers, indentured servants, and wharf rats from Salem Harbor. Piety was not the sole business of the Province of Massachusetts Bay. As in every other place on God's round Earth, His kingdom in New England rested on a midden heap.

ONE EVENING, ISAAC AND THOM CROFT spoke with an openness encouraged by aqua vitae, the fellowship of outlaws, and the impending darkness, which falls kindly on those who may be spurned in the light of day. As men who are brought together by circumstances sometimes will, the two talked about themselves—each wanting the other to know the life that had been given him, the strains that may have warped it from his youthful imagining, and the moment, which might have been brief or long, when he exerted himself—perhaps for the first time—to shape his own end, regardless of how destiny had roughly hewed it. Most of our bedeviled kind may be incapable of exertion and granted only a crumb of courage or selflessness before Death closes our eyes in the rounding sleep and snatches the crust from our nerveless hands. The nut of ourselves, which we have saved against the endless winter famine, is hulled and eaten by a hungry squirrel.

"You've done many things in your life," said Croft after Isaac had told his story, which, of course, was mostly invention. He manufactured a great variety of plots and skeletons of tales, and kept them ready for use, leaving the filling up to the inspiration of the moment. "Now I'll tell mine."

Croft had been a musketeer in the Andover militia during the native uprising of 1675, known as King Philip's War, waged against New England by the Wampanoag, Nipmuc, and Narragansett. Chief of the Wampanoag, Metacomet had taken the Christian name Philip to show his goodwill toward the English, who showed theirs by taking still more of the Indians' land, as well as their muskets, and, for good measure, stretching a few red necks on an English gallows. In reprisal, Metacomet, a son of the sachem Massasoit, who had fed the famished separatists at Plymouth in the lethal winter of 1621, led a confederacy of aggrieved tribal nations against the English. Among the militiamen were descendants of *Mayflower* planters, who gave thanks to their Indian deliverer by drawing and quartering his "doleful, great, naked, dirty beast" of a son, in Rhode Island's Miery Swamp, at Mount Hope, near Bristol. They hung his parts in the trees and set his head on a pike at the entrance to Plymouth. For twenty years, he scowled at the white trespassers and thieves, who gloated as they passed the black and shriveled remnant, until nothing remained.

Not content to have dismembered Metacomet, the militia, aided by Pequot and Mohawk warriors, harried the surviving Narragansett into the Great Swamp and burned their wigwams, along with their shrieking occupants, mostly women and children, whose spirits flew by the hundreds to their creator, a lesser deity than the Christian's God. Those escaping the pyre fell to English carbines, halberds, and axes or, like Metacomet's two sons, were sold as slaves to sugarcane plantations in Bermuda. (Just prior to the rising, the savages had considered it a good omen when Earth's shadow, in the shape of a scalp, fell across the moon. But the heavens, like the American continent, belong to the white man.)

Thom Croft's story was not uncommon for the age, save in its particulars, which are the hinges on which a story can be hung. The door is the same for all; we open it and, after a time, close it—or hear it close—behind us. Between the opening and closing of the door is the subject of tales, which writers put to paper in the hope that they will profit by them, as do the makers of coffins, graves, and funeral goods from the actuality of death. Isaac already knew that Croft had lost his wife and children to fever and his farm to an avaricious neighbor who connived with the assessor to have him put off his land.

The two had been walking beside the Great River, which goes to Ipswich. They halted at the confluence of Beachy Brook. Where trees had gathered in a shade, they made themselves comfortable. Croft took off his hat, rubbed his nose, and kicked a stone loose with his boot heel. By those tokens, Isaac understood that his friend had not yet finished his story, whose thread stitched up the fabric of his life. He had first to tell of his youth in the Old World.

"I was a young man when I left the Dorset coast, where I was raised in the Church of England. My father's faith was lukewarm. I've always thought his trade made him irreligious. He was a barber-surgeon, and as many times as men's innards were open to his inspection, he'd never seen anything like a soul. He was a skeptic and would have likely been hanged had he not been a discreet man, as behooves a barber. He kept his mouth shut and his thoughts to himself."

Croft worked a cottonwood twig down his back and scratched it.

"When I was twelve or thirteen, my father began to instruct me in the mysteries of his trade, but I had no stomach for it. The smell of blood and putrid matter overcame me each time I stood beside him and watched him cut."

Croft examined his hands, first the backs, with their raised veins, and then the calloused palms, as if he might see his past inscribed on them. He had not much future left.

"I apprenticed at a forge. Being a muscular fellow, I soon earned my master's approval. I wasn't dissatisfied with the life. I took pleasure in my skill and strength. I'd have a forge of my own in Dorset instead of a rundown tavern in Massachusetts Bay if not for an argument over a horse."

"A horse?" repeated Isaac stupidly. He was distracted by Beachy Brook, which had its own tale to relate. He could not decide whether it was a cheerful or a tragic one—or something else, which, to fathom, would disclose the meaning of everything. Brooks have more uses for storytellers than as settings for drowned lovers. "A horse," said Isaac again, as if trying out the word in his mouth for the very first time.

"A mare. She belonged to the justice of the peace for Shaftsbury, a swaggering midge whose powdered wig reminded me of a hedgehog squirming at the bottom of a sack. He burst into the forge one morning, calling me a whoreson this, that, and the other thing and shouting that I'd lamed his horse. He demanded five pounds' compensation, or I would see the inside of Shaftsbury jail before the noon meal."

"You struck him, I suppose." Croft's confession demanded a serious response from Isaac, which he found difficult because of the picture in his head of the justice's wriggling periwig.

"My blood was up," said Croft, shrugging his broad shoulders. "I hit him with the first thing that came to hand—a hammer, which I brought down on his head and turned his brains to mush. He looked even smaller sprawled on the blood-soaked floor. I felt wonder—only that—at what can happen to the human head when sufficient violence is brought to bear against it. I knew I'd be hanged as a murderer. With no way to conceal my crime, I ran from it. At the time, New England and the Indies were much talked about, and the idea of starting anew where land could be had at the cost of four, or six, or seven years' service or apprenticeship was enticing." He scratched his cheek with a ragged nail. "I decided to take passage on one of the westbound ships as a deckhand—or a smith, if I was lucky."

Isaac's thoughts had wandered once again to the brook, where a momentary shadow on the water betrayed the presence of a grass pickerel.

"You'd show some interest if I'd killed him because of a woman!" growled Croft.

"Let me hear the rest," said Isaac, breaking the snare that had caught his attention.

"I forged a brand and burned the letter *P*—here." He touched the scar, as though he felt its heat. "I'd seen the like on other men's faces, put there by the Anglican royalists after Charles the First dissolved Parliament to quash Puritan opposition and began to fill the Tower with luckless saints. I dressed it to hide my 'stigmata' till I could make use of it, and with my father's blessing, I walked to Yarmouth, where Winthrop's fleet waited to set sail for Massachusetts. The Puritans took my branded cheek as prima facie evidence of righteousness."

"You talk like a lawyer."

"Most everyone hereabout knows the law, since few have not stood before a magistrate to complain about a neighbor's pig trespassing on their vegetable patch or to sue a man who sold them a cow that died soon afterward. Giles Corey"—in our time his name has come to signify a man who will not recant—"has been thirty-three times in court. He's a fractious fellow. I doubt there's a more backbiting and contentious race of human beings than God's chosen people in New England, and the worst of them live in Salem Village."

Their descendants will be equally malicious and covetous, thought Isaac, who excepted himself from the forecast.

"I was taken onboard the *Talbot* for my experience at the forge as much as my avowed faith. Lacking the five pounds needed to pay for the crossing, I couldn't have emigrated otherwise."

Catching sight of the pickerel threading the brook's weeds, Isaac shied a hickory nut at it.

"I applied myself to my trade, which was much in demand. The following year, I married a Lincolnshire woman, who'd arrived on the *Ambrose* in 1630, when Winthrop was made governor. We had a house and garden and a child and could be said to have thrived wonderfully in Salem, and would be thriving still had God shown us mercy. But He's not obliged to be kind or gentle, and the Puritans of Massachusetts Bay prefer a dark and inscrutable Deity."

"Do you know John Hathorne?" asked Isaac after a silence in which the brook raised its voice again.

"I would sooner know a snake!"

"Is he so very wicked, then?"

"Not by his lights or by those of the congregation of saints hereabout. He glories in the reverence they show him. He's a wall against the Devil for the fearful and a champion for the spiteful, who look to him to punish neighbors who happen to be better off than themselves."

In the palm of his hand, Croft had been weighing a stone pried up by his boot, as if to judge it.

"Massachusetts came down with witch fever before this," said Croft. "The colony was not yet thirty years old when Margaret Jones, a midwife, was hanged at Boston Neck for having a 'malicious touch,' which caused deafness, vomiting, agonies, and suchlike evidence of Satan's favor in her victims. Goody Jessup claimed that Jones had dried up her cows. She was arrested, tried by the General Court, and 'watched' in her cell, as prescribed by Matthew Hopkins in *The Discovery of Witches,* which is a merry thing to read, Isaac. One of her teats withered before the eyes of witnesses. Governor Winthrop himself swore he saw an imp feeding at her breast 'in the clear daylight.'"

"It may be she was a witch for all that," said Isaac, and was instantly amazed at himself.

Croft's eyes pierced Isaac's like wimbles, making him squirm. "It had more to do with some natural misfortune that befell her neighbor's milch cows than witchcraft. They dried up by themselves!" Croft threw the stone into the brook, saying, "When stones don't sink, I'll believe women ride on brooms and cuddle with the Devil." His hands muddied by the stone, which could have lain in the damp earth since the days of Genesis, he wiped them on the grass and stood as if to set the carpenter at defiance.

Isaac's mind was on graver things than brooms and milch cows. The idea of killing John Hathorne had stolen into his thoughts, insinuated by the brook's muttering, which had been gay five minutes earlier but now spoke of sinister matters, as the Three Witches had to Macbeth.

"And you say John Hathorne is a wicked man?" asked Isaac.

"What is he to you?" asked Croft, suspicion and anger proportionate in his tone.

Isaac shrugged and would say no more. He would sometimes act contrary to his best interests and, in doing so, put himself at risk. His reckless words and acts would call to mind Edgar Poe's observation in "The Imp of the Perverse," which Isaac had read (how long ago it seemed!) in *Graham's Magazine*: "We perpetrate them merely because we feel that we should *not*."

The two men left the hickory trees and the flowery pink ribbons on their branches. They were like a pair of sullen children, each nursing a grievance as he walked back to the tavern. As the light died out of the sky, the witch hazel bushes beside the brook were transmogrified into sarsens and the brook turned zinc.

At one point, Croft stopped and took Isaac by the arm. "Did I misjudge you?"

"I won't be judged by you, old man!" he replied, roughly shaking off the other's hand. Much later, Isaac would regret his anger, realizing that he had mistaken Croft's disappointment for resentment. His thoughts had been on his great-great-grandfather, whom he had come from so far away to judge. And what if he should turn the table and judge *me*? Isaac had been asking himself when Croft brought him up short.

A conciliatory gesture, a kind word spoken, either would have been sufficient to make amends, but Isaac couldn't bring himself to make the gesture or say the word. So has it always been for our prideful, stiff-necked race. When a man has the Devil gnawing at his heart, there is nothing that will defang it.

At the end of the week, Isaac took his satchel of tools and the rucksack in which he kept the few things that he had brought from the red farmhouse and left Thom Croft's ordinary. The two men, who had liked each other and then fallen out, parted ways without so much as a nod to each other.

Isaac had broken the bowl that fed him.

V

At Log Bridge, on the road to the village, two laborers were dressing logs. A rude bridge had been hastily thrown across the Great River by a previous generation and was in need of repair. One was barking a branch with a drawknife. Isaac could see that he had not much skill with it. Isaac sat on a rail fence in the hot noon sun and watched them sweat at their work. He offered them water from his bottle. They put down their tools and thanked him for his charity.

"My name's Geoffrey Hance. This fellow," he said, cocking his head at the man who had been ill-using the knife, "we call 'Dilly.' He was born William Dill and is accounted a simpleton, though he speaks sense sometimes."

Dill grinned. He looked like the sort of man whose life was measured in plowed fields and the copses where he hunted birds and rabbits. His view of the world was what he could see of it from the top of a hill. In this, he was no different from most.

"Isn't that so, Master Dilly?"

Dill nodded and scratched his ear, which was hidden underneath a quantity of unruly hair.

"And who might you be?"

"Isaac Page."

"Dilly and I've been dancing on the Devil's own skillet all morning, Isaac Page." Hance wiped his stubble on a dirty linen sleeve, laid a patched waistcoat across the rail, and sat beside Isaac. Dill followed suit. "We could do without shirts, but the elders would frown," said Hance.

"What quality of men might they be?" asked Isaac cautiously.

"The elders? Oh, the usual sort." Hance spat into some jimsonweed. "There be not much variety in men, or women, either, hereabout—except for the Indians and the unregenerate."

Dill snickered. Hance silenced him with a sharp look.

"These days Salem streets are crowded with English refugees from Maine scared off by the French and the Wabanaki. The saints don't like them, and they don't much like the saints."

"Aye," said Dill as he chewed on a blade of timothy.

"And there's a few Jersey families who follow the king's religion out on Salem Neck. They'd be shunned if well-off folks didn't need their ships to bring them window glass, fancy spoons, Spanish pots, and suchlike foreign goods."

Isaac watched in fascination as a green thread of drool swung from Dill's lower lip.

"You're not from here, I think," said Hance shrewdly.

"Nay," replied Isaac, "I arrived three weeks ago."

"Maybe he's an unregenerate," said Dill, biting the thread with his teeth.

"Were you among the Germans and Dutchmen in New York? I've a cousin living with the English colonists who does not much care for them. They smell of sauerkraut, and their beer is vile."

Isaac shook his head, signifying that he had not been in New York.

"You don't look like a man who's been picked clean. God's truth, a Dutchman will steal buttons off a dead man's coat and the pennies on his eyes! They are this greedy." Hance rubbed a finger against a thumb, as if to conjure a banknote. Then with the delicacy of a monkey nosing a tempting piece of filth, he sniffed Isaac's doublet. "You don't smell like a German, either."

Hance took a worn briar from his waistcoat and plugged it with a twist of fig tobacco. He sparked a nest of lint into flame and, drawing breath through the stem, set the twist to crackling. His face showed that contentment seen in men with a pipe of "good creature tobacco" clamped between their teeth. Isaac, also, had savored it till Constance scolded him for the "wormholes" in his vests, bored by tiny embers, and he'd had to give it up. Now and then he would smoke a cigar rolled in some fetid New York tenement by a hollow-eyed Jew or a half-starved Chinaman.

"I guess there are no Chinamen in Salem," said Isaac, whose thoughts were often at the mercy of his mouth.

"I haven't seen one since I left Weymouth docks, where they were swarming over the East India ships."

"The goodies of Salem do stitch their mottoes with Chinese silk thread," remarked Dill, who clicked his tongue against the roof of his mouth, as one does when "speaking" to ducks and chickens.

"They do, right enough, and on New England linen,"

said Hance, tamping down the live coal of tobacco that had risen in his bowl.

Isaac took a sip of tepid water, then handed Hance the bottle. "I'm a carpenter by trade," he said while the other two drank turn and turn about. "I was in Rhode Island and have come to Salem to fill my purse and belly."

He told them that he'd done work in Boxford for Thom Croft, neglecting to mention their unfriendly parting. Hance knew the man, and after having pronounced him "an honest landlord" and praised his venison stew, he argued the merits of the village's drinking holes and those of Salem Town, on the seaward side of the North River. A man need not go thirsty in seventeenth-century Massachusetts.

"Samuel Beadle waters his beer. . . . The tars at the Ship Tavern tend to be pugnacious when they've drained a hogshead dry. . . . Matthew Howes is a busybody. . . . A man can't enjoy a jar at the Blue Anchor for the bottle flies staggering across the sticky tables. . . . These days, Deacon Ingersoll's is crowded with folk come to gawp."

"What cause have they to be at Ingersoll's?" Isaac knew the answer, but as a stranger to the place, he thought it prudent to pretend to be ignorant of Salem matters.

"They have their sport there."

"What sport is that?"

"One better than a cockfight," said Dill.

"Aye, for them who like to see old women run to ground by a pack of shrieking girls!"

"It may be Master Page has heard naught of our village girls," said Dill, glancing slyly at Isaac.

"Who has not heard of them?" replied Isaac vehemently. Dill turned his gaze on Isaac, which, at that moment, betrayed some little intelligence—or so Isaac thought.

"Are they that famous, then?" asked Hance, tamping down the dottle in his pipe.

Like so much dust, Isaac swept away the question with his hand. "Have you any cause to doubt their honesty?"

"If foaming mouth and bucking hips can make them so, then they be honest girls." Hance spat. "Or rare playactors." He put his pipe between his teeth and fumed visibly, then took it out again. "Annie Putnam's the ringleader; she pipes the spiteful tune and makes the others dance." His anger turned hot. He shouted his resentment that a girl of twelve should have set a province on its ear: "Goddamn her for a bitch!"

"And John Hathorne?" asked Isaac casually, as a man might ask after his neighbor's sick dog.

"What about him?" His blood on the boil, Hance had spoken sharply.

"Is *he* honest?" Isaac waited with a childish expectation to hear his ancestor decried.

"I don't see plainly how he profits by the business—though it's certain that he does."

"He has a covenant with God!" said Isaac, and

wondered if he had mocked the magistrate or, for some reason, had defended him.

"They all do!" cried Hance. "It's what makes them appear lofty, that and their tall hats."

"Then you are not one of them?" asked Isaac.

"My hat is as you see it. But I don't cheat my neighbor or play shovelboard or stoolball on the Sabbath. I give the Lord His due."

"And the Devil?"

"There is no Devil here, though there be many covetous souls among us. What say you, Master Dilly? Have you trafficked with the Black Man? Does he sneak up and kick you on the arse?"

"He do kiss my backside with his boot!" Dill rubbed his muscular arm and whined, "And he sticks pins and needles in my arm."

"That's what comes of arm wrestling with Old Nick, my sweet dafty."

"I arm-wrestled John Proctor and beat him!"

"Now they're saying that he's the Devil's man! God help him!" Hance gave himself up to his pipe, which he smoked thoughtfully for a time. "Well, we had best get to our work. We thank you for the water, friend."

"I'm handy with a drawknife, if you've another to spare."

"You can take Dilly's. He can't shave his own neck without nicking his Adam's apple."

Dill laughed happily, his eyes fixed on a cow munching grass at the river's edge. Sitting on the split rail, he aped the way the animal rolled its tongue around a tuft, took it into its mouth, and, with a jerk of the heavy head, pulled it from the ground. Isaac was near enough to the beast to see a glassy string of green saliva hanging from its chin.

"You don't mind if I borrow your drawing knife?"

"I don't mind," replied Dill, who had discovered a pippin in his apron pocket. He chewed it with the same deliberateness and satisfaction as the cow did its grass. "Tuppence is tuppence," said Dill, his mouth full of fruit.

The three men went to work on the pile of felled trees. Isaac barked and shaved, while Hance and Dill pegged the rough-hewn timbers into place. By six o'clock, they had finished. Seven miles to the east of them, a sea wind rose and brought the rich odor of the salt marsh at Noodle's Island. Dill's nose snuffled like a horse's, relishing the smell of brine and marsh mud spiced with sulfur, rotting fish, and clams.

"Good smell, eh, Dilly, my lad?" Hance gave his friend an affectionate clap on his broad back. "Dilly has a fancy for smells you and I might turn up our noses at. Ah, but feel the breeze, man!"

"A breeze is a wondrous thing!" declared Dill.

As the sweat dried from his clothes, Isaac luxuriated in the cool air. "Aye, 'tis wondrous indeed, Master Dilly!"

"You'll be wanting your wages, I suppose," said Hance, drawing a tentative figure in the dust with the toe of his boot.

"They stand between me and the poorhouse."

"I thought as much," said Hance. "To be round with you, I'll have none of 'mistress' money till Saturday, when Thomas Putnam pays for the work." He held up a hand to silence Isaac's protest. "I don't intend to tell you to go scratch for it. Go home with me and share our fish pie and peas. You can sleep in the buttery, which is cool, and on Saturday, you shall have your two shillings."

Isaac agreed, and the three men walked eastward to Fairmaid's Hill, where the Hances—Geoffrey, Zipporah, their daughter, Alice, and Geoffrey's senile father—lived in a four-room house on Andover Road. Dill continued to Thorndike Hill and the disused cowshed where he put up.

VI

Isaac was amazed by Zipporah's sky blue gown.

"My brother is a hand at Shattuck's dye house, and I get a bolt of cloth, now and then, for me and little Alice."

In Salem Town, Isaac would see cloaks and kirtles cut from bolts of yellow, orange, blue, green, purple, even cloth of gold. Yet Bridget Bishop's attire was considered extravagant. She wore a black cap and a red paragon bodice worked in various colors. To dress in a color that would incite a bull to charge was a reason to condemn her, in the eyes of many enough to send her to Proctor's Ledge.

"The Devil wears black," said Alice, a girl of seven or eight, whose eyes sparked with mischief.

"That he does, child," said Zipporah.

"Reverend Parris wears black, too," said Alice. A more costly dye and given to fading, black was worn by solemn deputies, counselors, magistrates, and haranguing ministers, who pulled long faces on the Sabbath. "Mother, is Reverend Parris the Devil's man?"

"It does not follow!" she replied harshly.

"Reverend Parris said Satan has come to Salem to smite us for our wicked ways."

"Eat your peas, Alice!" scolded Zipporah, vexed by her daughter's interrogation.

"Father, is it so, what Reverend Parris said in church? We're going to be smote for our faith's improvement."

"*Smitten*, you little imp! And the Reverend Parris is an ass."

"I won't stand for such talk at table!" chided Zipporah, who bore the name of Moses' wife and strove always to deserve it.

Hance ignored her and addressed the child sternly: "There is no Devil in Salem, Alice, and those who say so are—"

"Geoffrey!" Zipporah gave him a look that matched her voice's flint. Had *she* been wife to Moses, not merely her namesake, he'd have lived considerably fewer years than his six score. "Tell the girl the truth, or you'll sleep in the buttery along with your friend!"

Hance turned to Isaac for help or pity. Isaac stared at his plate and a constellation of peas that he had arranged there in his distraction.

"The Devil lives in the forest, which is why you must

never go there alone," said Hance, subdued. "Or with them who mean to dance in the woods."

"More fish pie, Goodman Page?" Zipporah would be cordial now that Geoffrey had been silenced.

Alice pushed her peas around her plate with a tin spoon.

"Tituba could read your future in those peas," said her father slyly.

Glaring at him for having broken the peace, Zipporah scolded Alice. "You'd be grateful for those peas, mistress, if you had nothing to eat except boiled acorns, like them that came with John Winthrop!"

"Who's Tituba?" asked Alice ingenuously, to bedevil her mother.

Zipporah noisily cleared the table of the supper's remains. From the lean-to built against the house, her anger was audible in the clatter of dirty plates and cutlery, which she emptied into a tub of boiling water set on brick and iron braziers.

All Salem Village knew of Tituba. Annie Putnam and other of the bewitched girls used to visit her in secret for a glimpse of their future husbands' faces reflected in a cup of water or some other forecast in a drop of egg white floating there. Tituba had excited their childish interest in white magic's naughty arts, which she had learned as a slave on a sugar plantation in the Carib. Little Betty Parris's father, the Salem Village minister, had once owned both the plantation and the slave. His congregation despised him for insisting on silver candlesticks for the altar, when plain pewter was good enough for the unassuming Lord. Who was this upstart divine to grouse that he had yet to see a penny of his wages? Was he ignorant of Christ's admonition to the disciples: "The life is more than meat, and the body is more than raiment"?

Hance led his guest into the hall, which, in Isaac's time, was called the parlor, and filled two cups of cider from a Spanish jug, which Isaac thought he'd seen in pieces under glass at the Boston Museum—or one very like it.

"I've heard things said about Salem's magistrates that would trouble a reasonable man," said Isaac.

"If you can find a reasonable man in Salem, no doubt he would find them troubling."

"You are such a one, I think," said Isaac cautiously. "A reasonable man."

"Aye, I hope to be! But the reason for all things only God knows."

With a jolt, Isaac realized that Hance, though he might seem cynical and irreligious, was rooted in his own age and country, which lay snug against the Atlantic between the Narragansett and Connecticut Rivers. Only with difficulty, if at all, could Hance's thoughts escape the pillory of his origins. Just so was Isaac Page a man of 1851. Breathe, as he must, the air of the seventeenth century, neither his lungs nor the brain pickled in his skull had altered by so much as an atom. He felt the bumps on his head and, by the science of phrenology, declared himself unchanged.

Alice was playing with a cloth doll. Zipporah came

in from the lean-to, wiping her wet hands on her apron. Seeing the doll, she flew into a rage.

"I'll have no poppets in my house!" With one hand, she tore it from the girl's grasp and with the other slapped her face hard enough to mark her cheek. Alice yelped. "Where did you get this wicked thing?"

"Annie Oaks give it me."

Zipporah threw the doll into the fire.

Alice was too terrified to whimper, much less to object.

"Annie Oaks is a wicked girl!"

"Wife!" said Hance, rebuking her. "You're frightening the child!"

"Don't you know it's witchcraft?"

"But there be no pins in it, Mama!"

Hance's old father came downstairs in his nightshirt, his bare feet creaking on the worn oak treads. "What are you on about now?" he asked his daughter-in-law querulously.

"Go back to bed, Father, while I have a word with Goody Hance."

The old man shuffled over to a sideboard and, from a lacquered box, took a biscuit, which he gummed. He had already forgotten the squabbling that had awakened him from his nap.

"Geoffrey, I will speak no more on it! Mark you! Look how it burns!"

The poppet had ignited in a crackling blaze, such as a dead pine tree will do when struck by summer lightning. Entranced, Isaac could not tear his glazed eyes from it.

"Stuffed with straw, how else *would* it burn?" jeered Hance.

Dolls intended for wicked purposes were packed with hog bristles. This rare fact Isaac knew from reading Cotton Mather's tedious, often delirious, tome *The Wonders of the Invisible World: Observations as Well Historical as Theological, upon the Nature, the Number, and the Operations of the Devils*, published in Boston in 1693, the year the witch fever burned itself out, as plagues and fires do.

Zipporah spluttered.

Hance winked. Whether the cause of his eyelid's flutter was the smoke twisting from the hearth or the wish to nettle his goodwife, whose face had turned the color of stewed beets, Isaac could not tell.

"Alice, get me the bone-handled knife," said Hance as he searched the iron rack beside the fender for a stick of wood to carve. "What would you like to keep you company tonight?"

"A papoose!" replied Alice happily. "Like the one you made me the other day."

"I would never whittle a heathen image!" he said, glancing sidelong at his wife. "Not in a Christian household! It was baby Moses in his papyrus boat I whittled you."

"But Indians are Christians, Father. Goody Proctor told me so."

"She meant those that gave up their heathen ways

and live in the prayer towns. Savages belong to Satan." Hance glanced at Zipporah, the barest of smiles on his lips. "Think of some animal instead."

"I can't decide," said the girl after rubbing an earlobe with her thumb in deliberation, a gesture Isaac had seen her father make.

"A cow, then. Master Page and I saw a fine cow by the river this afternoon."

"I should like a cow," she said seriously. "What color were it?"

"It was a red cow."

"Make mine red, too!"

"We'll stain it tomorrow with pokeberries." Hance gave the child an affectionate pinch.

"Witches send their specters out to pinch little children. The minister told us."

"He spoke truly!" said Zipporah, giving her husband a scalding look.

He returned it sweetly.

Afterward, Isaac and Hance sat on a rough bench beneath a dogwood tree. Its blossoms, radiant the week before, had begun to rust. Hance kept mostly silent, puffing his pipe. His mind seemed elsewhere. Isaac wanted to speak of the witches but could not think of a way that would not raise the other man's suspicions.

"Be the women of Rhode Island as sharp-tongued as ours?" asked Hance. "They say that Anne Hutchinson was a great scold and a brazen heretic who whelped thirty unfinished creatures in a single monstrous birth."

When she had dared to argue theology with

Governor Winthrop and John Cotton, they plucked her out of the company of saints and sent her to Rhode Island to live among the Narragansett. Sitting in Hance's dooryard, Isaac wished that his ancestors had been other than Puritans. In the New York of 1692, the mercantile Dutch grew fat on beer and oysters, while the Quakers in Philadelphia lived in a peaceable kingdom—partly real, partly a delusion. In Massachusetts, all was a delusion, save for the gin and the rules regarding shovelboard, which were real. The peace of Salem and Boston, where the Council of Assistants and the General Court dealt with matters appertaining to the province, was disturbed by bickering over piety and property. The law courts were sized to narrow minds, as was the dogma of the day.

"They're a quarrelsome lot," replied Isaac, who knew nothing of Rhode Island women or shrews. Constance was inclined to patience and gentleness. He recalled some harsh words he had spoken to her and keenly regretted them.

"Our goodwives would do well to think on the covenant of marriage and gentle their dispositions." Hance studied the lofty pile of a cloud, as if he could see gentlewomen dressed in cloth of gold on its airy porches. "They do order their poor husbands about like servants. In my father's day, such wives as we have now would have been dunked in Wilkins Pond or shut up in the root cellar."

"Your goodwife seems a pious woman," observed Isaac, hoping to turn the conversation to graver matters.

From his research into Salem's history, he knew that he had only until June 10 to act. On that day, Bridget Bishop was—would be—hanged. As Isaac watched Hance whittle a stick into the shape of a cow, the tumult that would whip New England into a frenzy had not yet drawn blood. When it did, the universe would shrink to Arnold's jail, Thomas Beadle's tavern, where the accused were examined and arraigned, Salem Town House, where their death warrants were signed, and Proctor's Ledge, where they were hanged.

"Our women think God whispers in their ears," complained Hance, knocking the spent tobacco from his pipe against his boot heel. "They scold us, as Moses did the Hebrews when he came down from Mount Sinai and, in a fit of temper, smashed the Tablets of the Law. They preen themselves in their pews while we sit sulking like boys who've gotten their ears pulled."

"Are Salem husbands less virtuous and industrious than their wives?" Bridget Bishop's tryst with the hangman is a month away, Isaac told himself, his mind drifting like the smoke unraveling from the Hance's chimney pot, to his eyes a miniature of Geoffrey's briar.

"We apply ourselves in obedience to the Lord; we toil like the biblical ox or ass," replied Hance as he picked a red pokeberry flower to pieces. "I heard John Arnold is getting Boston's jail spruced up for all the witches and wizards who'll be staying there." Hance made a sour face, and as if to rid his mouth of a bitter taste, he spat. "He ordered two hundred board feet of lumber from Dodge's sawmill, as well as chains to keep Sarah Good and Sarah Osborne from turning their specters loose upon the town. Lord knows how iron can bridle apparitions! I nearly forgot to mention that Goody Arnold bought two blankets for Sarah Good's infant, who does poorly in prison. I suspect, by this, she hopes to prove herself a charitable Christian woman." Once again, Hance spat into the dust and ground the damp spot underfoot. "Is this drought the Devil's work or God's punishment on the poor in spirit?"

"I've heard that there be much 'gripping, and squeezing, and grinding the faces of the poor,'" said Isaac, who, as a student at Bowdoin, had read Urian Oakes's exhortation against usury in the Bay Colony.

"They will be given fine clothes to wear in the hereafter." After a silence, Hance said, "John Arnold might have work for a carpenter, if you've a mind to see the sights of Boston."

"I wouldn't care for such work."

Hance grunted and brushed a leggy spider from his knee. Isaac saw that his refusal had pleased his host. "We're raising a barn at the Buckley place. If you care to work for your supper, there'll be better fare than fish pie and peas."

"A man cannot rest in Salem," said Isaac, sighing extravagantly.

"We are God's children in the New Jerusalem. He intends for us to enjoy the fruits He has set within our grasp, if we are willing to sweat our arses for them."

Isaac concluded that Hance's argument was not with God, but with His human creatures, especially those who were likely to dance on their neighbors' graves. There would soon be many new graves in Salem.

VII

Early next morning, the two men broke their fast with pease porridge and coffee, "that grave and wholesome liquor," and walked to the Buckley place, their shadows dogging at their heels. The parched fields ought to have been green with spring wheat. Indifferent to drought, clouds sailed across the azure bowl of sky, dragging their bluish shadows over the brown hills. "We have no rain for you!" the clouds taunted in a voice disguised as wind. "And what of September?" asked the fields. "Will the stalks of corn incline their tasseled ears toward the earth, as if to hear Aristotle's *primum movens*, commonly known as God?"

The framing for the new barn lay in pieces on the ground. The odors of raw wood and recently turned soil would—150 years hence—intoxicate the mechanic, hoer of bean fields, and natural philosopher Henry Thoreau, a New Englander whose nonconformity cost him only a night in jail. At the Buckley farm, a score of men—some burly, others thin as rakes—were rolling up their sleeves, while a muster of women, dressed in bright colors befitting a May morning, set trenchers of bread, cold beef, and ham on planks thrown across sawhorses. The men picked the platters clean. By the time their shadows had dwindled to no more than midgets of themselves, they'd been swarming over the beams and rafters of the rising barn for hours, each man armed with a saw, mallet, or chisel, according to his proficiency. They chewed on wooden pegs, as if they were stalks of sweetgrass, which common folk called "holy."

Isaac had been present at raisings in his own century. The frame that slowly grew by the work of many men had always reminded him of the sketch of a barn, which they would finish and sunset embellish with the golden brushwork of falling light. He liked the sweetness of a good join and took pleasure in the words of the craft, which he would repeat to himself, as if they held a secret known only to carpenters: *beam, spar, batten, lath, joist, spline, girt, tendon, mortise, post, purlin, scarf, sill, plank.* He remembered the joy with which he had beheld the Phalanstery at Brook Farm, which he helped to build, and how he had grieved when the great assembly hall of the communalists burned to the ground.

Having read much of the history of Salem, Isaac knew that the barn, along with the house and furnishings, would pass into grasping hands when, later that spring, Goodman Buckley's wife and widowed daughter were clapped up for witchcraft—unless Isaac could prevent their imprisonment. He had begun to question whether or not he had the courage to intervene. It was one thing to hatch bold schemes in Lenox while lending half an ear to a distant locomotive chuffing in the Housatonic Valley and quite another to stand on a rafter in Salem Village and hear the wind moaning in the forest, where, for all he knew, the Devil did preside over a dance of degenerate souls.

More and more, Isaac would come to see through a glass darkly as he doubted himself and wondered at his skepticism. He had not seen tooth marks left by witches and wizards on maiden flesh, nor had he been in the watch house at the inquest of Daniel Wilkins, the "greatest part of whose back seemed to be pricked with an instrument about the bigness of a small awl." Isaac had not been present at the examination of the boy's murderer, John Willard, who had only to chew his lip nervously before magistrates Hathorne and Corwin to cause Annie Putnam and Mary Warren to cry, "Oh, he bites me!" Isaac had read accounts of these things just as he had read, in the Acts of the Apostles, the words with which the disciple Paul had rebuked King Agrippa, also called Herod: "Why should it be thought a thing incredible with you, that God should raise the dead?" You were not in the forest or at the village watch house any more than you had been in Judea when Christ returned from His harrowing, he told himself. You were not so much as a speck of dust. Truth is easy to accept when all the world proclaims it. When doubt assailed him, Isaac would examine himself, as if he were the accused and the magistrate in the same person. Who am I to meddle in time—God's curse on the race of Adam? My forebear's bones have lain these thirteen decades in the grave. Who am I to dig them up and interrogate their former owner in absentia?

As a boy, Isaac had willingly joined the others in

schoolyard hectoring. Years later, he regretted having let an opportunity to show moral courage pass him by, one that had come and gone unrecognized. Next time, I'll do right by the harried and abused, he promised himself. But would he? If he had been at the Sacramento River in 1846 when Captain Frémont and his men slaughtered two hundred Wintun Indian men, women, and children, would Isaac have lifted a finger or raised his voice to stop them?

—∿∿∿∿∿—

WILLIAM DILL HAD ALSO GONE to the barn raising. Isaac marveled at his strength. He could take the weight of a dragon beam on his broad back while six other men drove the dowels home. He had the brawn of an ox and, now and then, would shake his shaggy head to rid it of a pest, a bead of sweat, or, perhaps, an unwelcome thought. Isaac could not have said why he'd been shy of Dill all day. Happening to look down from the truss beam on which he was cutting a mortar, he saw that Dill was regarding him with an uncommon intensity.

"Good day to you, Master Page."

"Good day, Dill. You look broiled."

"They say it be hotter by a hundredfold in Hell." He wiped his damp face and chest on an old sack.

"Who says?" Isaac climbed down from the beam, took off his sweat-stained doublet, and laid it on a stump to dry.

"Them that have been there do say it." Dill laughed with an almost imbecilic glee.

"Do you mean those that send their spirits abroad to cause others mischief?"

"Nay, Isaac Page. If those have been in Hell, they do not say it. I mean them that describe 'its exquisite agonies, and anguishes.' You never heard Cotton Mather scare the people out of their wits with Hell's pains. 'And another that was broiling in the fire of such troubles, roared in this manner, O might I have this mitigation of my torments, to lie as a backlog in the fire on the hearth, for a thousand ages!' Now there be the true meaning of broiling!"

"Aren't you frightened by such a picture of Hell?" asked Isaac, amazed at Dill's sudden articulateness.

"Dilly has no wits to be frightened out of." He laughed again, as if at some fabulous joke.

"I wonder if that is true," said Isaac, as much to himself as to the other man.

Dill shrugged his sunburned shoulders, cinched his mallet in his belt, and climbed up to the ridgepole as agilely as a monkey.

Isaac took up the chisel with which all morning he'd been cutting mortises. He delighted in a snug piece of joinery, as once he had in a well-wrought sentence. Increasingly, there were days when Isaac could not have said if Lenox was a memory of a previous life or a premonition of one that awaited him. Salem Village is no figment, he told himself. Thus does time lay traps and snares for those who travel recklessly in it.

That evening, the weary men ate supper at the makeshift tables. The women had brought chickens, and while the men had worked toward sundown, they slaughtered, plucked, and boiled them, which they then served, together with corn and parsnips from the Buckleys' cellar. Matthew Howes, the landlord, contributed a hogshead of beer, in exchange for a dozen bushels of potatoes payable at the fall harvest. (Given the drought and the tardiness of the growing season, his barrel of beer was an act of munificence.) After the meal, a scraggly fiddler plied his bow with the fervor of an Indian straining to light a fire with a bow and drill. Reminiscent of a lewd Morris dance, the tune would have made the blood of Thomas Morton and his licentious crew run hot at Merry Mount. An affront to the pious of New Plymouth Colony, the idolatrous maypole was cut down in 1627 by sobersided John Endicott. Later in the gloomy history of Massachusetts Bay, Miles Standish, whom Morton had belittled, calling him "Captain Shrimpe," put an end to pagan revels at Merry Mount, scattered the wastrels, and exiled the profligate Pilgrim to the rocky Isles of Shoals.

Having finished her chores at John Buxton's house, Hannah Smyth was helping at the tubs. With a look of disapproval contending with a blush of pleasure, she consented to partner with Isaac in the Haymakers' Dance, judged to be a naughty figure by the Sticklers, if not quite an indecent one.

"Your gaze is oppressive, sir!" she chided when they met together and commenced the promenade, whose measure the by-now-tipsy fiddler accelerated.

"And how, Mistress Smyth, might a gaze oppress, its being nothing more substantial than the ether?"

"I do not know what ether may be, but a gaze can fall heavily enough to leave a red mark on a lady's cheek."

"My gaze, like any other gentleman's, approaches your cheek but stops short of touching it, howsoever my lips may wish to come nigh."

"You're uncommonly forward, Goodman Page!"

"You are uncommonly pretty, and my gaze has the weight of admiration, which cannot shift a balance beam so much as a hairsbreadth."

"Mind your feet! You're not a pretty dancer, sir, though I admit the tune does gallop."

"It's the fault of my boots. Roger de Coverley himself would trip over them."

"They were made for clodhopping and not for dancing."

"Then won't you walk with me a little, Hannah?"

"Where would you have me walk?" she replied suspiciously, but she did not resist when he took her arm and led her away from the rest.

"To yon clump of trees."

"Not so far as that! I'll accompany you only as far as the light of the bonfire falls."

"One step farther, please!"

Having read chivalric romances, Isaac was amused to find himself in a coy exchange with a young woman whose menial situation could not have prepared her for a conversation found in the pages of a novel by Jane Austen. Later, he wondered whether he had imagined it—no, not imagined, but translated it in his mind, as he did the vernacular into artifice in his own tales. Isaac believed in words more than in actions, since a man will often do nothing, but it is seldom he won't speak, if only to himself.

"Not one step more, or we'll be talked about in church on Sunday," replied Hannah to Isaac's courtly pleading.

"Gossip is another thing that has no weight."

"It has a sting notwithstanding."

The deadweight of a hanged man or woman will often begin in gossip.

"You reduce me to beggary," said Isaac.

"There are no beggars in God's kingdom."

"Is that where we are?"

"Some say so."

"What do you say, Hannah Smyth?"

"That in such a time and place as we do find ourselves, we should keep our thoughts to ourselves." She had spoken apprehensively.

The couple stood at the light's deckled edge and watched it gild the giddy phantasms in their dance.

"I think it be too like the old maypole not to annoy the Reverend Parris," said Hannah, referring to the night's frolic around the fire.

Salem Village was not Merry Mount, where greenmen and glee-men, bears and wolves, mummers, rope dancers, mountebanks, horned gentlemen, and Morris dancers—all the merry crew of Comus—used to disport themselves around a festooned pine tree to the music of pipes, cittern, and viol.

> Drink and be merry, merry, merry boys;
> Let all your delight be in Hymen's joys.
> Io to Hymen now the day is come,
> About the merry May-pole take a room.

Merry Mount meant wine; Salem meant water—and tepid at that.

"The dancers take an innocent pleasure in one another," said Isaac.

"Increase Mather would not consider it so. I've heard the minister read from *An Arrow Against Profane and Promiscuous Dancing Drawn Out of the Quiver of Scriptures* so often, I know the words by heart."

"What does *your* heart tell you?"

"'That we have tarried enough in the dark."

They walked back toward the barn. To Isaac's dismay, Hannah curtsied saucily and bid him a good night.

"Shall I see you again?" he asked.

"Salem is not London, Master Page. Nor even Boston."

Isaac joined a knot of revelers and swallowed a fiery draft to ease his disappointment. A sentence he'd composed for a sketch fifteen years before (or would do nearly a century and a half hence) came to mind: ". . . it was high treason to be sad at Merry Mount." Would that the same could be said of Old Salem, which seemed a fount of sorrow.

What *could* be said of Salem was particularized in the words of two women, who were gossiping nearby.

"I was at Beadle's tavern when Constable Osgood brought Abigail Soames before the magistrates to answer for having sent out her specter against Mary Warren. Of course, the witch denied it. But no sooner did Soames lay eyes on Mary than she cried she were being stabbed in her belly. They searched the witch and found a great botching needle hid in her skirts."

"Matthew Hopkins said that specters are 'venomous and malignant particles ejected from the eyes.'"

"Better not look a witch in the eye."

"It's enough for a witch to look at you with hers. Though you be blind, you shall be possessed."

"Best not look anyone in the eye."

VIII

Mistress Smyth is a pretty thing," said Dill, coming up behind Isaac as he stood and stoked his ardor with brandy. Passions, be they grand or mean, are not easily put away. "She be a reason to stay, I think."

"Stay?" asked Isaac, fuddled by drink and disappointment, which self-pity embittered.

"In Salem Village. I say the pretty wench is good reason to keep you here with us . . . unless you have another put by," said Dill slyly.

Isaac regarded him with mistrust and, after a moment's pause, asked, "What kind of man are you?"

"A clever one, I hope," replied Dill, laying a finger aside of his nose.

Isaac put down his cup. "I would hear more of what a clever man has to tell."

The two men eyed each other like a pair of bantams searching for vitals where blood could be drawn. Isaac sensed that Dill wasn't the daft fellow others supposed. The imposture made the erstwhile writer of romances both curious and apprehensive. He was himself a dissembler.

"You're welcome to visit me," said Dill offhandedly.

"Now?" Isaac would not sleep that night, he knew, without hearing what Dill had to say.

"If you're not too weary from dancing." His reply struck Isaac like a challenge or a taunt.

They walked east on Meeting House Road and then struck across the fields to Thorndike Hill. They were silent—Dill like a man nursing a grievance or a hope, Isaac like one waiting to hear something of consequence. The night, which had begun happily when he walked Hannah to the gold light's flickering edge, had turned dark and sullen. Beloved by readers of romantic tales, a mist had risen. The gibbous moon had been erased, and the fires of numberless stars quenched. The night had an unpleasant odor—"sulfurous" Isaac would have said if he had not belonged, in principle, to an enlightened age. For many, the Inferno existed only as an image given shape and substance by Dante's book.

Dill unlocked the cowshed where he lived by the sufferance of an ancient widow named Matilda Stowe, who, forty years earlier, had been his wet nurse. He lighted a grease-filled lamp and waved Isaac to the only chair.

"My house is not commodious like Hance's, but then his was given to him—or rather, to his father, a hero of the Pequot War. He set fire to two villages at Mystic River. In the words of Captain Mason, Hance had 'laughed his enemies and the enemies of his people to scorn making the Pequot fort as a fiery oven.' Three hundred aboriginals were burned to death, as surely and completely as the Canterbury martyrs had been set ablaze during Bloody Mary's reign. 'It must have been a fearful sight to see the savages fry!'"

Isaac could hear them in the greasy sputtering of the lamp.

"The General Court deeded Hance a parcel of land, and John Winthrop paid for a house to be built on it for his use and enjoyment and that of his heirs. Famous by the age of twenty, he rested thereafter and, for more than fifty years, bored anyone within earshot with that single tale of cruelty. We thanked the Lord when senility took his mind away."

Being a man of letters, Isaac was more interested in the books stacked on a plank table than in the elder Hance's glorious pyromania. He was amazed to see Milton's *Paradise Lost*, several plays by Shakespeare, Marlowe, and Ford, Thomas Hobbes's *Leviathan*, as well as *The Bloudy Tenent of Persecution, for Cause of Conscience, Discussed in a Conference between Truth and Peace* and *A Plea for Religious Liberty*. The two latter works had been penned by Roger Williams, whom Winthrop and the General Court had banished to Rhode Island in 1635 for apostasy. Williams did not believe "Tis Satan's policy, to plead for an indefinite and boundless toleration," but that God was a broadminded Deity, who would hardly recognize Himself in His mean-spirited creatures settled in the Massachusetts Bay.

"Do you approve of my library, Master Page?"

"I'm surprised."

"The widow's husband was a worldly man. The New World killed him. Or is it that a simpleton can read that startles you?"

"Aye. In truth, Master Dill, it does."

"I was raised in Rhode Island and educated in the home of Roger Williams, a person with too large a mind for Massachusetts Bay and too ardent a faith not to have enflamed the elders."

"His views were heretical," said Isaac, parroting the prevailing opinion of seventeenth-century Massachusetts as though it were his own.

"Heretical? Because he believed that our settlements rightfully belong to the aboriginals or that the magistrates ought not put to death women taken in adultery?"

Adulterers (men were never accounted such) might be pardoned if they exhibited tokens of irresistible grace and were not sluts, to whom mercy must be withheld. Such tokens were not easily discerned, however, and the women were almost always charged as whores and hanged.

"Do you believe in the Devil?" Isaac asked with too much eagerness.

"I believe there be many in Salem with an appetite to do the Devil's work." Dill perched on the edge of the table and, with a finger, reverently traced the tooled leather binding of a book, as though its contents, if only they could be fathomed, would untie the knots by which our kind has been pinioned since the riddles posed by the first philosopher. But the book was only Ford's *'Tis Pity She's a Whore.*

"And Hell?"

"What of it?" asked Dill, whose face appeared to glower in the tawny light cast by the Betty lamp.

"In your opinion is there one?"

Like many another educated man of his time, Isaac scoffed at the notion of Hell. His own moral tales were ambiguous on the subject, which, in their epics, Dante and Milton had made palpable. Isaac was a modern man who rode in steam trains and elevated cars, cooked on a Rathbone stove, and hobnobbed with the literati of his age. To the Europeans of seventeenth-century Salem, Hell was gaudily real and its gate nearby. Why, one could swear that the damned were just beneath the hearthstone, when the fire in the grate was hot and roaring!

"If the Pequots' burning villages weren't Hell, I don't know of another," replied Dill.

"There was something you wanted to tell me." Isaac had assumed a jaded tone to let the other man know that whatever he might say could be of no consequence.

"You asked what kind of man I am."

Isaac studied his fingernails.

"I would ask the same of you, Isaac Page."

"You know what I am."

"I know what you say you are."

"Then you know all that's worth my saying and your knowing."

"Is there nothing else?" asked Dill, fixing Isaac with the needle of his gaze.

"Nay, fellow, there is not."

"Why do you look away, if there be nothing else?"

Isaac longed to lie down on the chaff bed in Hance's buttery, at peace amid the fragrant oaken casks. The air was bad in Dill's shed, and Isaac's head hurt.

"Your face looks ghastly in this light," said Isaac.

"You're nervous, I think."

Isaac glowered at him to show that he was not.

"I think you're a liar," said Dill.

The words stung, as though envenomed. Isaac would have struck him had Dill not taken a coin from his pocket and, giving it a fillip, made it ring against the tabletop.

Isaac was startled. In an instant, his weariness had turned to wariness. The coin, he saw, was the silver dollar he had brought from Lenox. "That belongs to me!" He made to snatch it from the table, but the other man was too quick for him.

"I've been wondering all evening if you would dare to claim it."

Isaac ought to have disavowed ownership of the

silver piece, but to do so would estrange him from what he knew best of Earth and all he cared to know. Salem would be for him a Hell, inescapable and desolate as Milton's is for the fallen angel Lucifer: "As far remov'd from God and light of Heav'n / As from the Centre thrice to th' utmost Pole." Constance and his children were Isaac's Heaven, and he would not lose them to save a multitude from hanging—especially those who had been already hanged by the neck until they were dead.

Dill gave no sign that he sensed the turmoil into which Isaac's mind had been thrown. Did he mean him harm, or had he another reason for turning on his guest?

"What do you want?" asked Isaac when he could once more harness words to thought.

"I'm not Dilly the oaf and simpleton—a beast fit only to live in a cowhouse and bear burdens on its back!"

Why had he chosen to reveal himself to Isaac? Dill may not have been able to answer, except that happenstance had given him a confidant or, if Isaac spurned him, a victim.

"What do you want?" repeated Isaac, whose terror was turning into rage. They share a pivot—fear and anger, as do love and hatred; one can be made to swing round to its opposite by a mere touch or breath of wind. Isaac was no match for Dill, who, at that moment, looked very like a beast. But a weaker man, his good judgment in abeyance, will sometimes fly at the throat of a stronger one. Isaac would have done had Dill's voice not modulated into awe.

"It is wondrous!" Dill held the silver piece and described it front and back: The phrase *United States of America* arched over an eagle clutching three arrows. Below it were the words *One Dollar.* On the obverse appeared a flag, a canopy of thirteen stars, and *Liberty* spelled out on a shield held by a seated woman draped in Attic fashion. Most puzzling of all, however, was the year engraved beneath her—for surely the four numbers must be that!—1851.

"What does it mean?" he asked.

Isaac could not explain it without telling a story the other man would not believe. Yet there was evidence: Dill held it in his hand. Even Thomas the doubter, who'd needed to touch the hole in Christ's palm, would have had to believe in the miracle of Isaac's arrival in Salem. But what would Dill do with this piece of intelligence? That was the question whose answer terrified Isaac.

Should I deliver myself into the hands of this man, who seems my enemy? Or should I make light of the coin or invent a plausible reason to have it? Can't a man have a coin made to mystify his friends? To produce an object from the future—what an excellent jest it would be! Those thoughts passed through Isaac's mind while Dill waited for an answer. Isaac wished he could read the other's mind and was not encouraged by his growing anger, visible on his face and in the clenching of his fists.

"Well, Master Page, what am I to make of this necromancy?"

Isaac flinched. It was neither the time nor the place in the history of his countrymen to bandy such a dark word.

"It's not necromancy!"

Dill sniffed the coin and said, like a bad actor in a miracle play, "Methinks I smell the stink of burning pitch and roasted human flesh. I do believe the Black Man paid this piece of silver into a sinner's hand for signing away his soul."

"Now that I've taken a closer look, I think the coin belongs to someone else," said Isaac, having decided to renounce it. Better to spend the rest of his life in the past than to cut short his present and forestall any possible future. Thorndike Hill was only seven miles from Proctor's Ledge.

"Nay, Master Page, I took it from your own doublet, which you'd set on a stump beside Buckley's new barn."

Isaac squirmed in the chair, as if his bowels were roasting.

"How came you by such a rarity?"

Isaac felt his neck itch, as though the hangman's hempen rope were already chafing it.

"Tell me, or I will say the Devil has come to Salem Village in the shape of Isaac Page!"

"I will not say!"

"Then I think there will be another wizard in Arnold's jail tonight."

Isaac repeated his refusal. Won't Dill's fantastic story

prove that he has lost his few remaining wits? he reasoned. But there is the coin. . . . Let Dill show it to the magistrates; I'll deny ownership! But might they hold me while they send a marshal to Rhode Island to verify that I had worked there as a carpenter or send a man to Lenox, which will not exist for another seventy-five years? Very likely! And I may find myself in the same oxcart as Bridget Bishop when it rumbles across Town Bridge toward the ladder, whose rungs lead to Heaven, Hell, or neither. Isaac could not escape the horns of his dilemma, save by telling Dill a plausible truth. Then a greater horror dawned: If Dill should squeeze the dollar in his fist, would he fly back to Lenox and the red farmhouse, to Constance and Isaac's bed?

"One last chance before I drag you to the watch house!" He took Isaac's arm in his powerful grip. "I could break your neck and bury you in the pigsty, and none would be the wiser."

"I'll tell you what you want to know, but first you must set the coin aside."

"Wherefore set it aside?"

"So that it may breathe!"

"Breathe, is it?" Dill pressed his thumbs into Isaac's windpipe.

Isaac croaked, "Let me speak!"

"Very well." He set the coin next to the Betty lamp, where Isaac could not get at it.

Isaac told him that he had come to Salem Village from a Massachusetts town called Lenox. He told him that the year stamped on the silver dollar was that of his departure.

"How was the trick accomplished?" asked Dill, beside himself with excitement.

"It's not a trick!" Even at that dangerous moment, Isaac bristled to hear his feat derided as a conjuror's swindle. There were many capital crimes in the Province of Massachusetts Bay, and one would do for Isaac as well as another. He might swing at Proctor's Ledge for vanity as readily as witchcraft. His neck would stretch not a whit longer.

"Call it what you like, but tell me!" Dill had brought his face near enough to Isaac's that the latter could smell roasted capon from supper on his breath—that and something else: the odor produced by a body in the heat of an overwhelming emotion. Isaac couldn't help but smile at the other man's gullibility. Naturally, a greedy man will believe anything that promises to gratify his appetite. Dill once again put his hands around Isaac's throat; it would need but a little tightening to send time's pilgrim to eternity or extinction. The pink tip of Dill's tongue was visible between his teeth. It was obscene, Isaac thought afterward, a thing to shudder at. "Do you mean to make a mockery of me?"

"No!" gasped Isaac, trying to pull away the other's hands. Dill watched him struggle for breath and then let go. Later, Isaac would wonder if fireflies shut up in jars by his son, Jack, felt as he had in Dill's beast house. What would Waldo Emerson say, or Thoreau? Is there a scale of pain and sorrow? Does a whale suffer more anguish than an ant? A man more than a bug?"

"Let me get my breath; then I'll tell you how I came to be here."

"Say first whether the coin be the Devil's work."

"Aye, inasmuch as men are devils."

Sweeping his books onto the floor with an arm, Dill sat on the table, his legs drawn up in Indian fashion. "Go on, then, and be quick! I'm at the end of my patience."

To save himself, Isaac did as a storyteller would: He let loose his imagination, which was inclined to be fantastic, in the "infinite space" of Dill's cowshed.

"In Lenox," he began, "I was an alchemist."

"I could have you hanged for an alchemist as readily as for a witch!" cried Dill.

"I was an alchemist in 1851; now I'm a carpenter!" retorted Isaac.

"For the sake of argument, let's say I believe you." Dill waved a hand at Isaac, as if signaling his readiness to hear an incredible story, like a schoolmaster humoring a boy who claims his dog ate his primer. "Why would a man of 1851 wish to be in Salem in 1692?"

"I came here by accident. I was searching for an elixir that would grant eternal life."

"'The life of man' in Salem is 'solitary, poor, nasty, brutish, and short.'"

Ignoring Dill's gibe, Isaac went on with his tale: "At a bookseller's in Paris, I happened on an extraordinary copy of *Mutus Liber,* or *Silent Book*. Twenty-four copies, each containing fifteen woodcuts without annotations, were known to have been printed at La Rochelle in 1677. Not even a rumor of a twenty-fifth copy containing an additional woodcut had ever been heard. Most surprising of all, it was annotated! After an hour's scrutiny, I realized that the twenty-fifth book contained the Grand Elixir of Immortality, which alchemists had been toiling to discover since Zosimos of Panopolis and Mary the Jewess."

"Plainly, they were witches."

"There are no witches!" cried Isaac, pretending to be vexed.

"In the Valley of Ben Hinnom, there were. King Manasseh 'used enchantments, and used witchcraft, and dealt with a familiar spirit, and with wizards: he wrought much evil in the sight of the Lord.' Second Chronicles."

"Only the simpleminded believe in witchcraft, and you, Dilly, claim to be otherwise." Isaac fretted, notwithstanding. His skepticism in matters of the black arts had been diminishing. It would be the same for a bird caged for so long a time that it could barely remember the sky.

"I profess what my neighbors do," said Dill airily. "It's foolish to show the hangman your neck before you're asked." Of a sudden, he shook a fist at Isaac. "And I warn you, Isaac, not to call me Dilly!"

Isaac waved it away as he would a fly, having found his courage and also his conviction that he was, indeed, a reasonable man regardless of the madness surrounding him. "Witches exist only in the overheated fancies of their malicious neighbors. The condemned of Salem Village are innocent."

"Though they be as innocent as the Gadarene swine, Salem's witches will hang. I pity the poor beasts that Jesus filled with the evil spirits of a madman." Dill's glance took in the limits of his small domain. "As you see, I live in an old beast house."

You smell of beast, said Isaac to himself.

Dill studied the other man's face. "You're too long in the tooth, Isaac, to have tasted the liqueur of eternal youthfulness."

"I got it wrong! I misconstrued the sixteenth diagram. Or perhaps it had been drawn to gull any poor soul who might find it. The compound I prepared and swallowed opened a path between your time and mine. I'll grow old and die like any other man—but at least I'll be rich. The people of my day will pay handsomely for the merest thimble from yours. I've only to fill my pack and satchel and return to 1851."

"And peddle our old pots?"

"Aye, and make a handsome profit by them!"

"Isaac Page, you're a rogue, as surely as if you've lived all your days in Salem Village!"

Isaac was not surprised at how readily Dill accepted the lie. Although he was educated well beyond the common, Dill had been born in an age of unreason, when pins stuck into a cloth poppet could prick Mary Walcott's arm, Abigail Williams's stomach, and Mercy Lewis's foot while an imp unseen to all but them danced upon a rafter. Dill knew that a witch's familiar in the shape of a cat could lick the breath from a babe, and he had seen an Irish washerwoman named Ann Glover hanged for speaking in the Devil's own tongue, which, later, proved to be Gaelic.

"And you say the people of your time will pay money for . . ." With a quick glance, Dill assessed the contents of his hovel. "For that stone jug?"

"Aye, and more were it glazed Delft."

"Widow Stowe has Delftware and German brown platters from Frechen." He had spoken to himself as much as to Isaac.

"You've no idea of the value of the most commonplace things around you. Antiquarians of my time would go mad were they to dig up your jug, even if it were in pieces!"

Dill wet his upper lip with the tip of his tongue. "I wonder that anyone should give a fig for Salem and its folly."

"People of the nineteenth century are fascinated by Salem's witches."

"As are we, Isaac Page."

Secretive, avaricious, and spiteful, Dill was, nevertheless, a bondman to belief, which is little more than a consensus of opinion. In its name, men do tear other men limb from limb, burn their wives, and skewer their children. Doubt—its antithesis—is the tooth of the covenant we inherit; it can bite and gnaw where conscience has its quick. But what doubt could possess a mind like Dill's, or Hance's, for that matter? Both had been steeped since birth in the vinegar of communal ignorance—a sourness that tasted sweet to them.

"To modern minds, witches are as fantastic as Saint George and the Dragon. One author in particular, a Massachusetts man—I know him well—has written tales about the Bay Colony that are much admired. 'Young Goodman Brown' is particularly fine."

"An old stoneware jug . . ."

"The wealthy of my day will pay dearly for a tin spoon or a caudal cup."

"And where be this Lenox of yours?" asked Dill after a moment's pensive rubbing of the jug, as though he might summon a jinn to satisfy his wishes in a less roundabout way than Isaac proposed.

"A town in the Berkshire Hills, some hundred and fifty English miles west of here. But the town won't be founded until 1767."

Dill fingered his stubbled chin thoughtfully. A silence ensued, in which Isaac heard the jarring cry of a night bird, a faint crackling made by an animal scuttling through underbrush, a creaking floorboard, and a moth desperately beating its wings against the lamp's glass chimney for a purpose as hidden as Isaac's own. That his might also prove futile, even fatal to himself, was a possibility he would not allow himself to entertain.

"Then you know the future!" said Dill, as though his wits were slow, indeed, and an idea slow to dawn on him.

"Not as Tituba claims to know it. I cannot see it in a dish of water, a spill of grain, or a cloud of gnats.

I can't read the sky or the guts of a dead animal for portents. I know the future of the Province of Massachusetts Bay as it's written in books." He opened one of Dill's, *The Bloudy Tenent of Persecution*, and noticed that Roger Williams had inscribed it: "With Affection for his Pupil William Dill." "I'm no soothsayer; I can't foresee the remnant of your years or days, your portion of fame or shame, any more than I can what you'll eat in the morning. I know the future of Massachusetts, as any schoolboy of my time does."

"There must be a way to squeeze a shilling from it," said Dill. His eyes had a faraway look, as if he saw himself as rich as merchant Philip English of Salem Town. In time's dark slurry, what magic might not be performed in the future to Dill's advantage?

"Now if you'll give me back the coin . . ." said Isaac slyly.

Dill became wary. His gaze narrowed, and his eyes seemed to grow smaller, as if he had donned a mask signifying Avarice. His hand closed around the coin in a fist whose meaning was covetousness and wrath.

Isaac trembled, as a man does who fearfully lays a finger on a galvanic generator to make his hair stand on end. He waited to see whether or not Dill would disappear into the future—Isaac's own present, where, at that moment, he desperately wished to be. But Dill did not vanish, and Isaac relaxed. This coin, which was carried here by me, will take none but me home, he assured himself.

"What means this coin to you?" asked Dill.

Having begun his tale, a nimble storyteller will ride it—however wildly it careens—until he finishes it or breaks his neck in the attempt.

"My daughter, Alma, gave it to me to buy a bag of sweets for the train. The coin is all I have of her, and I keep it close."

Dill put aside his mistrust. Tugging at Isaac's sleeve, like a child greedy for candy, he would not be satisfied until Isaac had explained what he meant by train. The pilgrim compared it to a great iron ox snorting black plumes of smoke as it dragged a line of wagons behind it on a pair of silver tracks. The picture he drew on the slate of Dill's mind increased the latter's awe of the future and his resolve to profit by it.

"What price would the Reverend Parris's Bible fetch in 1851?"

"An exorbitant one."

"Or, say, some of Winthrop's papers or a manuscript of Cotton Mather's?"

"Any price you cared to name."

Dill's eyes blazed.

"Of course, you couldn't spend it here," said Isaac, liming the branch to catch the bird that would prey upon him.

The blaze was dampened.

"In the Massachusetts of 1692, you'd be like Dives of the parable, whose riches could not buy him an icicle in Hell with which to slake his thirst."

Dill cosseted the buff-colored jug as a mother would her babe.

"What would this get you in the village marketplace?" asked Isaac.

"A kick in the arse."

"Better to be a rich man in 1851," said Isaac.

"You mean me to go there with you?"

"You can, or I'll be the agent for the two of us."

"I don't trust you to go without me."

"Then you can go alone."

"To your time?"

"Why not?"

"What's to keep me from staying there?"

"Your cupidity. You won't be satisfied with what you can sell in one trip. And even should you be and stay, I'll have Mistress Smyth to console me."

Dill folded his hands as if in prayer, which is only another word for hope—an attitude toward life as familiar to covetous men as to religious ones.

"God gave men hands to take from the abundance He provides," said Isaac, happy to be leading the man by the nose in his own beast house, which still bore a faint odor of animal sweat and dung.

"It is His covenant with the visible saints," responded Dill, his mouth split open in a grin.

"And shall you and I make a covenant between us?"

"Aye, partner Page. When can I leave for Lenox?"

"I must gather the ingredients and prepare the elixir. Then you have only to drink it and be away."

Dill's eyes glazed; perhaps he saw himself as a gentleman dressed in fine clothes, riding behind a giant fire-breathing ox.

"I'm curious, Dill, why you pretend to be simple-minded and choose to live meanly."

"No one envies a poor man, and none fears a simple one." As if he had remembered an urgent duty, he got into his doublet and put on his hat.

"Where might you be going at this hour?"

"To Samuel Parris's house to steal his Bible. He's gone to Boston. If not his Bible, there are certain to be papers of value to the future."

"What of John Winthrop's?"

"I can't wait to pluck them! The present chokes me, and I must fly from it or die!" He paused on the threshold, if a cowshed can be said to have one. "I'll tell *you* a secret, Master Page. My mother's father's father was Philip Ratcliffe, whom John Winthrop ordered whipped and his ears cut off for 'most foul, scandalous invectives against our churches and government.' Were that hypocritical cunt alive and sleeping in his bed, I'd cut off something more precious than ears and sell it for a fortune to the curious of your day!"

The venom behind Dill's words frightened Isaac. "Will you give me back my coin for Alma's sake?"

"I think not, Goodman Page. I'll keep it in my pocket in case I need it for the toll keeper on the road to Lenox."

"And if I refuse to send you there?"

"Then Magistrate Hathorne shall have the coin and you to make of what he will."

Again Isaac wondered who had invited Death to set up shop on Proctor's Ledge, where the gallows waited to turn men and women into corpses; what had extinguished the light of John Winthrop's city upon a hill, which was to have been "a brand plucked out of the burning"? A light to light the world.

IX

Early the next morning, Isaac searched the woods for hazelwort, described by Nicholas Culpeper in *The English Physitian* as "a plant under the dominion of Mars, and therefore inimical to nature." The whitish roots have a sharp, though not unpleasant, taste. In measure, they have beneficial properties. Culpeper commended them to the cautious use of the herbalist, leecher, and surgeon. "This herb, being drunk, not only provokes vomiting, but urges downward, and by urine also, purges both choler and phlegm."

Isaac's first thought had been to administer *Artemisia absinthium* in a potion that would have racked Dill with convulsions similar to those mimicked by Salem's afflicted. He could as easily have dispatched him with a mallet, but Isaac feared that, like the murderer in Poe's "Tell-Tale Heart," he would become conscience-pricked and give himself away. "I admit the deed!—tear up the planks! here, here!—it is the beating of his hideous heart!"

He had become familiar with plants, medicinal as well as poisonous, at Brook Farm, a utopian community near West Roxbury, Massachusetts, organized on the principles of Charles Fourier, the socialist philosopher. At the farm, Isaac read *The English Physitian* and concocted curatives for the well-being of the tiny commonwealth. Though Brook Farm had come to naught, Isaac had begun to write a romance shaped by his two years there, which he felt would add luster to his fame and money to his purse once he returned to Lenox and finished it.

Having filled his pouch with hazelwort, Isaac walked back to the cowhouse, where he ground the roots into a milky curd.

Isaac had sent Dill after a jar of honey. He returned with it, radiant with greed. He rubbed his hands together, like a fly contemplating a turd.

"Wealth is our reward for doing His bidding and a symbol of our redemption," he said, eagerly subscribing to the commonly held fallacy of God's affection for the Israelites of the Bay. That Dill had broken His eighth commandment by stealing Parris's Bible, a draft taken down in his fussy, ministerial hand of the testimony of several witches, and Tituba's Venus glass was of little matter to the impostor of Thorndike Hill.

Isaac stirred the macerated roots into a jar of honeyed water, which clouded. "Now close your eyes and imagine the world of eighteen hundred and fifty-one, as I described it to you."

Dill put the cup to his lips and was about to drink but stopped, and, in doing so, nearly caused Isaac's heart to do likewise. "Have you a message for Constance and little Alma?"

Afraid his voice would betray him, Isaac shook his head and urged the other man with his eyes to drink. Dill sniffed the liquid, wet his lips with it, and smiled at its sweetness. And still he seemed to hesitate.

For the love of Christ, drink!

He drank half the potion, and as he made to put down the cup, Isaac stayed his hand and encouraged him to drain it to the lees. "You must drink it all."

"To Constance and Alma!" said Dill, winking unpleasantly. "I promise to return the silver piece to her and give your wife news of you and Hannah Smyth."

Dill finished the cup. Almost at once, his complexion turned a deathly pallor. He dropped the cup and sat heavily on his cot. He lay down and commenced to groan. "I feel as though I've swallowed brimstone!" He held his stomach and writhed. Soon enough, the potent draft had the desired effect, to the dismay of the one and the disgust of the other. Relief came to Dill, and with it an appalling smell, as Isaac picked his pocket.

"Put away any thought of revenge!" he warned, holding the silver dollar. He tucked Dill's copy of *The Bloudy Tenent of Persecution* under his arm. "What would the magistrates say were they to read Roger Williams's fond inscription? You might as well have signed your name in the Devil's book as to have that renegade's name in yours. I'll take this, as well." He slipped *'Tis Pity She's a Whore*, which bore the name William Dill on the frontispiece, into his pocket. "The elders would hang her, and you, also, for reading depraved literature. And now, 'Master' Dill, I leave you to your privy."

X

n Northfields, four miles south of Thorndike Hill, Isaac stopped to bathe in Humphrey's Pond. He did so with the deliberateness of a Hindu in the Ganges or Thoreau in Walden Pond. Isaac had first met Thoreau at the Lyceum in Concord, when Emerson read aloud his new essay entitled "Nature." Isaac had twice visited the secluded spot with Thom Croft, who took him there for the pike and pickerel. Wishing to purify himself after his defeat of the minor devil William Dill, he chose the pond as the likeliest place for his own ritual bath. His spirit, he imagined, was as rank as his clothes, which stank from the Betty lamp, and something worse besides.

He undressed behind a screen of balsams, whose resin offered up an incense apt to Isaac's devotional purpose. Like a savage or a pioneer, he beat his clothes against a rock and wrung them, if not dry, then damp, and then he washed, beat, and wrung them once again, until he was satisfied they were clean. Slowly, he washed himself, pumicing his skin with a flat stone, as though to mortify his flesh. He let the late morning sun fall full upon him and felt with pleasure the gentle warming of his skin. The thought of home revolved briefly in his mind, and he beheld the image of Constance's face framed by glossy rings of chestnut-colored hair. He was not inclined to dwell in fond recollection on her—strange for a man who had loved his wife above all else. He did not ponder the meaning of his growing disinterest, dismissing it as an effect of his dislocation. A journey such as his must wrench the mind from its habitual orbit. In time, Isaac would come to remember his past as one does a dream—pale, fragmentary, and absurd. Many desperate souls have yearned for the blessing of forgetfulness, but memory is as stubborn as a stain and not easily pumiced from the mind.

Waiting for his clothes to dry, Isaac read, for a second time that day, a broadside printed by Richard Pierce, of Boston. Two years previously, Pierce had published *Publick Occurrences Both Forreign and Domestick*, intending to inaugurate the first newspaper in the colonies. The governor and council of Massachusetts had declared their "high resentment and disallowance of said pamphlet" and suppressed it. The broadside named those cried out as witches since the end of February.

PERSONS SUSPECTED OF COMPACTING WITH THE DEVIL;

Cried Out In Salem Village & Salem Town By Elizabeth Parris, Abigail Williams, Ann Putnam Jr., Elizabeth Hubbard, &c.

{Published at Boston, on the 11th day of May, in the Year of Our Lord 1692}

29 February. Tituba, Sarah Good, & Sarah Osborne are arrested.

12 **March.** Martha Corey, age 71, a "Gospel Woman" and fully covenanted member of Salem Village Church, is arrested.

23 **March.** Dorcas Good, age 4, is arrested.

24 **March.** Rebecca Nurse, midwife, age 71, is arrested.

28 **March.** Elizabeth Proctor, wife of John Proctor, is arrested.

3 **April.** Sarah Cloyce, sister of Rebecca Nurse, is accused.

11 **April.** John Proctor, husband of Elizabeth Proctor, is arrested.

13 **April.** Giles Corey, age 80, husband of Martha Corey, is accused.

19 **April.** Abigail Hobbs, Bridget Bishop, Giles Corey, & Mary Warren are examined by magistrates Hathorne & Corwin at Salem Meetinghouse.

22 **April.** Nehemiah Abbott Jr., William & Deliverance Hobbs, Edward & Sarah Bishop, Mary Easty, Mary Black, Sarah Wildes, & Mary English are examined by magistrates Hathorne & Corwin at Deacon Ingersoll's ordinary.

2 **May.** Sarah Morey, Lydia Dustin, Susannah Martin, & Dorcas Hoar are examined by magistrates Hathorne & Corwin at Nathaniel Ingersoll's ordinary.

4 May. Sarah Churchill & the Rev. George Burroughs, former minister of Salem Church, are examined by magistrates Hathorne & Corwin at Ingersoll's.

10 May. George Jacobs Sr. & granddaughter Margaret Jacobs are arrested; Margaret confesses to "sundry acts of witchcraft" & denounces Jacobs & Rev. George Burroughs, "a wizard & conjurer." On this date, Sarah Osborne (age 49) dies in Boston jail of sickness after 9 weeks & 2 days' imprisonment, leaving an unpaid bill of £1:3:0.

Pierce's broadside gave no hint of his opinion in the matter of witches and wizards, and Isaac could not decide whether he meant to uphold the proceedings or to show—by the number of arrests, Goody Osborne's death, and the extremes in age of the accused—the folly abroad in Salem Village.

Before the year was out, 162 persons would be denounced by the dissembling village girls or by some of those cried out by them as witches in order to escape the gallows ladder. Fifty-two would be imprisoned, including eight children. Threatened with earthly and infernal punishment, four-year-old Dorcas Good would affirm that her mother "had three birds one black, one yellow, and that these birds hurt the children and afflicted persons." Sarah Good would be hanged in July, and Dorcas's infant sister, Mercy, would die in prison shortly afterward. Nineteen innocents would be hanged at Proctor's Ledge, and an old man, Giles Corey, pressed underneath a weight of stones until his ribs cracked. He died in agony and arrears, owing his jailer £11:6:0 for his upkeep. May God forgive us our debts, for none else will.

Witchcraft aside, not all of the imprisoned were of spotless character. Quick to anger, Giles Corey had beaten the half-wit Jacob Goodall to death sixteen years before the former refused to stand trial for having signed the Black Man's book. Venerated in Isaac's time as an upright man, Corey braved *peine forte et dure* not for his principles, but to save his goods and property from seizure. Bridget Bishop was a notorious scold, who wore a red bodice and played shovelboard on the Sabbath to spite the town. The town was all too eager to believe that her apparition went by night to George Herrick's bed, capered on a rafter in Ingersoll's cowhouse, and bewitched John Bly's sow, which became "stark mad." William Stacy swore before the magistrates that Bridget's specter had picked him up and flung him at a wall and, more grievous, had murdered his infant daughter by means of devilry.

Bridget Bishop won't be carted off to Proctor's Ledge for weeks yet, Isaac told himself. Before rushing in, I must think further on the matter. More hangs in the balance than one cantankerous woman. I needs must be circumspect in how I go about the business, which is more complicated than I had imagined in Lenox. I must act, but not rashly. I would not dare to disturb the universe.

Isaac's mind teetered, like a top spun on a table—none

knowing which way it will fall. The argument went thus:

All men and women are equal in guilt and besmirched by sin. This is a New Englander's bleak view, and in that I am one, I take John Hathorne's point: The men and women who stand in the pillory and the dock and who will stand on a rung of the hangman's ladder are guilty, if not of witchcraft, then of some other venal act. Must I destroy my ancestor for being a product—even an exemplar—of his age? A judge wears the opinions of his day as snugly as his judicial robe. I might as well condemn the blue jay for stealing a sparrow's egg to satisfy its hunger. Or the house sparrow for pecking to death the purple martin chick in order to annex its nest. We are obedient to urges and, also, obligations that are imposed upon us by natural laws.

And yet the accused suffer greatly in prison as they await their doom. If able, am I not obliged to end their misery?

So Isaac picked at his conscience, which would not entirely crust over its wound. To allay the tooth of doubt, which gnawed at him, he would claim to be an instrument of justice—God's or man's. Then he would chastise himself for presuming to be an agent of either. He rode a balance beam, which would raise his self-esteem, only to send it plummeting to self-loathing. He would rejoice in his purpose, which was a righteous one, and then suspect that his motives were impure and his heart was morbid. He was a New Englander; his blood was infused with Puritanism. Its stain had darkened his mind's complexion throughout his maturity. His somberness went largely unnoticed in Salem, where all was overcast in gloom and sanctimonious men and covenanted women spoke a language of pious mottoes worthy of being stitched in Chinese threads on fine New England linen.

He recalled having seen one hanging in the Hances' main hall, beside an old-fashioned harquebus belonging to the senile elder.

Vincit qui patitur

HE WHO SUFFERS CONQUERS

Such words do sorrow bring, thought Isaac, who came very near to clenching the silver dollar in his fist and going home. Then he saw a pickerel dart; its powerful body was a glance of gold in water tinctured brown by the roots of cedar trees bending over the murky pond like divining rods. Truth, he admitted, is as elusive as this fish, and divination only a guess.

His clothes having dried in the blaring sun, Isaac dressed, but not before sewing the silver coin into his breech's pocket. He walked up Norris's Brook and on to the Great River, which he followed as far as Log Bridge. Thence he cut across a corner of Reading Village until he reached Wilkins Pond and the nearby house of John Buxton.

XI

ood morrow, Isaac Page," said Hannah as she scattered dried corn for the chickens strutting in the yard. "What brings you to the far edge of naught?"

The afternoon sun fell aslant her face, causing her to squint—an expression, Isaac noted, that brought out the mischief in her hazel eyes.

"I've been drumming up trade."

"Have you managed to drum up much?" Her tone of voice was impudent, like her gaze.

"None to speak of. I hope to change my luck at your mistress's house."

She turned her back on him to tend the chickens.

"Do you think something can be found for me to do?"

"I wouldn't know," she replied without turning around. Had he mistaken the meaning of her parting words spoken the night before?

Temporizing, he sat down in the dust, careless of his clean clothes, and untied his bootlaces and then tied them again. His heart beat loudly above the gritty noise of dry feed spilling into a tin trough. He was about to take himself off sheepishly, when she turned and, eyes bright with teasing, said she'd ask the mistress of the house. As he waited for an answer, he turned his gaze on the pond to see if the monogamous swans were still gliding amid islands of cloud. In August, it would be choked with water lilies, leaving scarcely enough room for a Jesus bug to skitter. In August, Martha Carrier, George Jacobs, Sr., George Burroughs, John Proctor, and John Willard would be hanged unless Isaac screwed his courage to the sticking place and wrecked the machinery of the law, like a Luddite, to stop its heartless progress. In August, Isaac hoped to be far away from Salem.

"I'm to show you the stile at the bottom of the field," said Hannah, untying the apron in which she tended the geese and chickens and forked up the midden heap. She pushed an untidy lock of hair beneath her cap. Hannah's hair was the color of a cello, Isaac thought, and as bright as a long-held note played on the D string of that most poignant of instruments.

They walked across a pasture, surprisingly green after the dry spring and a harsh winter that, scholars of the Salem madness would later speculate, had disposed the colonists to morbid fancies. Hunger and misery can undermine reason's government, especially in those given to argument or grudges.

To say that Isaac and Hannah walked side by side is not to suggest immodesty. Heaven forbid they should hold hands, lock arms, or let their shoulders touch! Having become used to the Puritan way, Isaac was careful to observe its proprieties. Of the two, in fact, he was the more decorous. Between yard and stile, she smiled warmly at him—even boldly, he'd have thought had he been thinking at all. That afternoon, however, he was inclined to let things go. Perhaps the cause of his sangfroid was his defeat of William

Dill or the fine weather and the feeling of well-being after his bath. He was experiencing the pleasurable sensation that comes to children—even Puritan children—taken unaware by a warm sun, a tonic breeze, the odors of grass, clover, and, barely perceptible on the wind, the rich scents of woodland and loam.

As they walked the hundred rods or so from the chicken run to the stile, Hannah chattered gaily. Near the end of their walk, she sang a ditty, such as might be heard on a gust of raucous insobriety from the window of an alehouse where "one and done" was not the rule. It began with "Room for a lusty lively lad, / dery, dery down" and ended in a pinch—one that she gave Isaac on his thigh.

He chided her with a line from *The Two Gentlemen of Verona*: "'You, minion, are too saucy!'" He had meant to be amusing, but she had felt him flinch.

"Are you the same man who walked with me in the dark?"

Isaac had the naïveté of many of his sex who will chase a woman and, amazed at having caught her, are frightened by her "impudence."

"Well?" she asked, having stepped into his path, her hands on her hips. "What do you have to say for yourself, Master Page?" Like William Dill, she was in the habit of seasoning the word *master* with a pinch of sarcasm. At that moment, scorn seemed predominate to Isaac's ears.

She'll think me a dull Jack and turn her attention to some lusty country boy.

"Forgive me, Hannah; I couldn't sleep last night," he said slyly, knowing that he must play the part of a lovesick swain.

"Oh? And why not, sir?"

"For thinking of you."

The compliment pleased her. Her eyes searched the four corners of the field. Satisfied to be alone and unobserved, she kissed him on the mouth. Her lips had not lingered, but his blood grew warm. Her lips had tasted salty—no, not salty. Peppery.

"Do you have a sweetheart?" she asked. Lacking experience of amorous young women, he was unable to tell whether she had spoken curiously or coyly.

"Nay," he replied. "I do not have a sweetheart." In that he had a *wife,* the statement was true. But it was equally true that he had forgotten her as she waited for him in Lenox, their son and daughter fretful in his absence. Husbands are capable of forgetfulness. Yet how could he be said to have forgotten what would not come to be for a century and a half? Time had been reorganizing Isaac's mind; his previous connections were being broken; more and more his memories seemed figments of a dream.

They reached the stile; much of it had rotted.

"There's wood in the barn," she said, "if you do not scorn a niggling project."

"Did your mistress mention what it's worth to have her husband escape a broken neck?"

"Good church folk disdain talk of money!" replied Hannah airily. "Especially with the Reverend Parris, who has the gall to ask for it, as if to preach God's Word to imbeciles is not reward enough."

"Aye, they do natter on about sanctity. But shouldn't they honor the Covenant of Works, and am I not a worker for hire?"

"It is one they make with God and not with itinerant carpenters, whose rough cheeks can stand a razor." She laughed and would have happily played Phyllis to Isaac's bearded Strephon if she had read Edmund Spenser. She was a natural for an Arcadian pastoral, although theirs was unfolding not far from Wilkins Pond, in a resolutely prosaic age. (Fifty years before, Cromwell and the Puritans had pulled down the Globe Theatre, a place of "lascivious Mirth and Levity.")

"I ought to have known better than to come among flinty Puritans!" he said, pretending to be sullen and hoping for a second kiss, no matter that her lips were chapped.

"Well, you will not starve, and there's a place for you tonight among the cows. I'll show you where the lumber's stored."

Isaac wondered if it was to be his lot in Salem to sleep where cows dreamed the sweet dreams of kine—fresh grass, cool brook water, and an end to the scourge of flies.

Beyond the fence and broken stile, an old white horse galloped away in the meadow.

XII

ore bird, Goodman Page?" asked the stout Master Buxton as he sawed a leg from a goose sitting, solemn and headless, on a silver platter. Evidently, the Buxtons stood too high in Salem society for plain pewter.

Isaac chewed on a thigh and anticipated—his mind growing torpid—a good night's sleep on a mattress stuffed with feathers having once belonged to the goose's kith or kin.

John Buxton was not one of those stringy Christians whose scowling faces could spoil meat and sour milk. Though he had a seat in the meetinghouse proportionate to his girth (his rotund goodwife had another) and knew the *Bay Psalm Book* front to back, he believed in a Jovian religion of the flesh and would gladly have made one with the jolly crew at Merry Mount had it not long ago been dispersed by killjoys. An admirable fellow, he bore, without complaint, the gout and other maladies common to those who would not show ingratitude to the Almighty by ignoring the plenty He set before them by refusing the smallest crumb. "God would not have given me an appetite if He had not intended for me to satisfy it" was a thing Master Buxton often said in the company of his corpulent brethren.

To say that Mistress Buxton was plump was not to do her justice. Her figure, which, in her youth, had verged on voluptuousness, had achieved the perfection that fruit does just before it falls and rots.

Neither husband nor wife appeared any the worse for a famishing winter or the recent aggression of the Indians. The pair of them was as well padded as the goose whose juices were beginning to thicken around the carrots.

"Did you suffer much in Rhode Island, Goodman Page?" asked Goody Buxton. "They say the winters be perishing cold there."

"No colder than Massachusetts's," rumbled the provider of the feast, who was zealous in matters pertaining to his province's reputation.

"I can never remember if Providence is north or south of Boston."

"Providence is everywhere for God's elect. All others be damned," said Hannah.

"Hannah, do be quiet!" admonished the mistress of the house, shaking her finger at the flippant servant. Though lacking in volition, her three chins also shook, as if they had a mind of their own. "Get into the kitchen, where you belong, girl!"

"Massachusetts winters are intended to mortify us and make us worthy of Divine favor," said Buxton, who wore a dimity waistcoat and a fleck of mashed potato on his cheek. "Is it not so, Elizabeth?"

Her eyes riveted on a buttered biscuit, Elizabeth made no reply.

Isaac's attention was caught by a shaft of evening light burnishing silver cups and platters and by the oak wainscoting made glorious by coats of beeswax applied, doubtless, by Hannah, whose indentured status was somewhat higher than a slave's. As in the case of a slave, a servant could be beaten at and for the master's pleasure; unlike the slave, the servant's back could not be flayed with impunity—in theory at least. "You've many fine things," said Isaac, a hint of disapproval in his voice.

Buxton received the remark as a compliment and reflected on the exquisite nature of his conscience. "The poor are luckier to have nothing that will give them pangs of guilt for breaking sumptuary laws. I assure you, I have qualms, Goodman Page, and they trouble me constantly."

"Poverty is its own reward," said Isaac with an irony that went unnoticed.

"Jesus said the same in the Sermon on the Mount," assented the mistress, who delivered herself of a polite belch, which caused her wattle to wobble.

"'They that will be rich fall into many temptations and snares,'" intoned Buxton gravely. Immediately, he shouted, "More goose!" as he wiped sweat from a bald head that reminded Isaac of the dome of Saint Peter's Basilica, which he had once seen on a rainy day in Rome.

Hannah returned from the kitchen, where she had been worrying over the jam tarts. Slyly smiling at Isaac, she carved more bird and heaped the master's plate with meat. His mouth full of peas and potato, he pointed toward Isaac's with his knife, and before his guest could swallow his claret, Hannah had served him likewise.

"Excellent goose, my dear!" Buxton mumbled to his wife, who had not fed it, beheaded it, cooked it, or put it on the table, though she would suck the bones of marrow before Hannah took them to the midden heap.

"My goose always turns out well," she replied complacently, spilling her ruby-colored tipple down the purple front of her brocaded gown.

Isaac Page, he said to himself, you've stepped into an engraving by Hogarth, who, in five years, will be born in Bartholomew Close and will be laid to rest at Chiswick in St. Nicholas's Churchyard forty years before you yourself have drawn your first breath, in a red clapboarded house, at 27 Hardy Street, in Salem. It is a thing to think upon and marvel at!

"Tell us, Goodman Page, if Rhode Island be the godless colony it was when Roger Williams and that obnoxious Hutchinson woman were banished there," said Buxton. Without waiting for a reply, he continued: "The Siwanoy murdered her at Pelham Bay, along with her children, after the villain Kieft stirred up the tribe against the English in New Netherland. She ought to have remained in Providence, near her friends the Narragansett." Buxton wiped his perspiring face on his sleeve, leaving behind a glister of goose grease. "Have no truck with Dutchmen; it is a wise saying, and true." He picked a morsel from between his teeth with the point of his knife. "When he was dead and buried, Williams's house fell down into its own cellar. We took it as a judgment of the Lord on his deluded soul."

"Praise Him!" mumbled Goody Buxton, wetting her finger in the claret and then sucking on it delicately. "Hannah, where are the tarts?"

"The tarts are a disaster," she announced, wiping floury hands on her apron. "The meal was weevily."

"Bring them forthwith!" shouted the master in high resentment and disallowance. "I will eat the jam out of them."

"I threw the lot out the back door for the squirrels."

"Damn! It be a terrible sin to waste God's bounty on squirrels!"

"It was done according to His will," said Hannah, putting on a solemn face.

"What? Are my raspberry preserves lost?" asked the mistress in great distress, although she had not picked the berries, washed, mashed, boiled, or jarred them.

"There be some still in the jar."

"Bring it, you careless wench!"

Hannah brought the stone jar to the table, and the couple stoically made do.

"God provides!" intoned Master Buxton, licking his apostle spoon.

"And to those of His elect, He giveth jam," recited his goodwife.

"And to the damned, He giveth their just deserts!" said Hannah, wearing a smile for Isaac.

"It matters not at all to them if they be weeviled!" complained her mistress, thinking of the lost tarts.

"Sinners are not fussy," replied Hannah with a toss of her pretty head.

"They are like the savages, who are content to gnaw on roots," agreed her master. Having swallowed another draft of claret, Buxton showed his magnanimity toward his nearest fellow man by saying, "I inspected your workmanship, Goodman Page, and it were well done!"

"I'm glad to hear it," said Isaac. "And I thank you for supper and a bed in the cowshed."

The mistress of the house clapped her dimpled hands delightedly. "Why, Isaac Page, you made a rhyme! It must be a lovely thing to be a poet."

"I hope you be not choosy, sir!" admonished the master of the house, trying to get a leg up on his high horse. But he was too wheezy. "It would be churlish to turn your nose up at a cowshed!"

"God provides for the dung beetle and the louse," said Hannah. "Our guest would not ask for more."

"Well said, Hannah! Goodman Page, the Lord loves you as much as He does the meanest of His creatures."

"The cross would have been a pretty piece of joinery," said Isaac, "seeing as how the Lord made it."

Buxton gasped not by reason of Isaac's impiety but from the weight of his lordly gut sitting on his lungs.

"My husband, who knows about stiles, said ours is

one to admire," said the mistress, her eyes glazed like the skin of the goose, which she was daintily nibbling.

Buxton pulled a thread from the Gospel of Matthew: "'His lord said unto him, Well done, thou good and faithful servant: thou hast been faithful over a few things, I will make thee ruler over many things: enter thou into the joy of thy lord.'"

"It will give the carpenter joy if you'll put a few talents in his pocket," said the naughty Hannah.

Buxton turned to her and snarled a thread from the Book of Malice: "And as for you, Mistress Sloth, I say unto the Lord, '. . . cast ye the unprofitable servant into outer darkness: there shall be weeping and gnashing of teeth' over the ruined tarts!"

Hannah filled the portly pair's flagons to the brim. "I ought to have baked a witch cake," she said, winking at Isaac. "For surely it was a witch who weeviled the flour."

"It be very like a witch to bedevil a tart," said the mistress of the house, suppressing yet another belch.

"Satan is the patron saint of tarts, drabs, and trollops!" said the plainly besotted master, pleased with himself.

"It be blasphemous to say Satan is a saint!" cried Hannah, looking to Heaven in mock consternation.

The mistress guffawed into her claret cup.

"Pray you, straighten the Delft," said Master Buxton, pointing to a cockeyed ceramic plate hanging on the wall, by which token the little world of Salem knew him for a man who laid up treasures for the love of God.

Having done as bidden, Hannah furtively knocked awry a portrait of her mistress, whose youthful complexion resembled a dish of curds.

"I cannot draw breath!" gasped Goody Buxton. "Lord, save me, for I feel I am like to die of it!"

"You're being strangled by your corset, Elizabeth! It's too tightly cinched."

"Hannah does it to spite me!" carped his goodwife, fanning her red face with a pudgy hand.

Hannah smiled serenely.

"Girl, fetch your mistress a cup of water!"

Hannah had not taken two steps when the master gave a second order: "And more wine!"

"Tomorrow you'll be on your way again," said Buxton in a tone that left Isaac uncertain whether he had spoken in the interrogative or the imperative. He was inclined to think the latter. Isaac was eager to be away from the fatuousness of the wife, the buffoonery of the husband, and the greediness of the pair of them. They were like rats in a pharaoh's granary, eating themselves to death. If God be an indwelling spirit, as the Antinomians maintain, Isaac could not imagine Him sitting, serene and majestic, within the Buxtons' lard-caked hearts.

Master "Rowley Powley" became fabulously sick. His great face, with its massive jowls, inclined dangerously toward his plate, where the goose's remnant bones were embedded in the sauce. Hannah saved the plate in time, but the man's profusely perspiring head fell hard against the table. Elizabeth Buxton stared, perplexed.

"Goodman, will you help me lug Lord Gut to bed?" asked Hannah.

"Aye," said Isaac, and between them, they raised the beef-faced sot, dragged him over the doorsill of his chamber, and put him into bed, boots and all.

"Will he live?" asked Isaac, mopping his own face after having struggled with a grampus, which was presently snoring with the might and dignity befitting a landowner, slaveholder, and a covenanted member of Salem Village Church.

"I live in the hope he will not." Then she sang a lilting air over the inert lump of flesh and sated appetite, as the Devil himself would have sung over the bloated corpse of a hypocrite:

Let such a hog
Lap whey like a dog,
While we drinke good Canary.

"Hannah, will you walk with me tonight?"

"I will."

She led Isaac out the door. Goody Buxton, her extravagant headdress askew, had managed to get herself into a wing chair and was snoring in concert with her husband.

—~~~~~—

Isaac helped Hannah over the stile. His hand trembled when he freed the hem of her dress, which had caught on a splinter.

Teasing him, she sang:

O Hangman, stay thy hand,
And stay it for a while
For I fancy I see my true love
A coming across the yonder stile.

He took her arm, and they crossed the meadow. The sun was low in the sky, and to the east, on the other side of the Great River, black night draped over blacker Hathorne's Hill. Near Thorndike Hill, William Dill lay like a dead man on his cot, having not the strength to light the Betty lamp. At the far side of the meadow, where the Buxton place bordered the Putnam family burying ground, Isaac once again saw the white horse.

"It's a beautiful animal."

"What is?"

"Buxton's mare."

"Molly's in her box. I put her there myself before I made the supper." She turned in the direction of his gaze. "There's no horse there. It may be an apparition that you see."

"I don't believe in a spectral world, where wicked girls watch invisible spirits flit from the Devil's consorts into the minds and bodies of their victims!" He had spoken emphatically, as one would have done whose resolve was loosening. Certainty is a two-stranded skein: thought and action. The former unravels first. (Many a time there is a third strand, called "doubt.")

"You believe, then, that they are wicked?" she asked seriously.

"I do!"

"I, too, have thought that they be wicked girls, who want only to do mischief."

In Hannah, he saw the immature strain of a skepticism that, a century hence, would ripen into the Yankee temperament. He could not see so far as a barleycorn into her heart, however, to be certain of her motives.

"Then you don't believe in the spectral evidence being used to condemn those they cry out?" Isaac could have been a magistrate examining a suspected witch instead of a man out for a country walk with a girl.

Hannah shook her head, signifying . . . What? he wondered. That she did not believe in an invisible world of malicious agents? She scoffed at the notion that they were apparent only to Annie Putnam and her claque? Or might it be that Hannah could go no further into the matter than to shake her head in uncertainty? Always, for as long as Young Goodman Brown lived, he would doubt the virtue of his once-dear wife, Faith. And so, too, would their author, Isaac Page, for his sins—no, for his great-great-grandfather's sins.

"And yet the magistrates be godly men," said Isaac.

In just such a tone, Mark Antony had incited the Roman mob against the noble Brutus.

She gave no reply, and they walked on together in silence.

“My eyes ache,” said Isaac to change the subject. They did, in fact, pain him.

“Shall I send out my specter and heal them with a kiss?” asked Hannah, having recovered her good humor.

“When I first saw you, I took you for a witch,” he replied, only half in jest, because of a disconcerting sensation that he felt first on one eyelid, then on the other. “You turned my wits.”

“It’s a power the Devil gives to women to ensnare a man,” she said, smiling.

Turning his head sharply, Isaac saw the white horse and, where the last light of day was dying into night, a woman in the shape of Goody Buxton making haste toward a towering pine that could have been the very tree set blazing by Captain Standish when he subdued Comus and his crew at Merry Mount. Isaac could almost hear the pine shriek.

Frightened, he turned to Hannah. Her eyes were cold; her mouth seemed full of teeth.

He rubbed his eyes with the heels of his hands and saw again the gaily smiling girl, her auburn hair peeking from her cap.

“Isaac, you look as though you’ve been bled! I thought the greedy fool had stuffed and swilled himself nearly to death, to have been made so sick, but perhaps the goose was spoiled. You'd better sit before you fall flat."

So shaken was he, he let her help him sit.

"Rest your head in my lap." She was all tenderness and solicitude.

As Isaac fought his rising gorge, he could not believe that, moments before, her pretty face had appeared bestial. Doubtless, his distempered fancy had betrayed him. Might he not have been mistaken in the white horse, in podgy Mistress Buxton's phantom, and in the infernal tree? Surely, they'd been figments of an imagination inclined to morbidity, intensified by a rich dinner and the impression left with him by the master and the mistress that the world was turning helter-skelter! He shivered in momentary fear.

"You're cold!" Hannah took off her shawl and covered him.

Yes, he told himself. Something I ate disagreed with me, or else the noxious air wafting from the kitchen midden has made me sick. The smell had been appalling.

"Shall I get Dr. Griggs to come?" she asked.

While preparing for the journey, Isaac had encountered Griggs in John Hale's *A Modest Enquiry.* In Salem Town, on the afternoon that Isaac mended the stile, Roger Toothaker, one of the "cunning folk," was being watched by William Griggs, the court's physician, for evidence of diabolical operations and mischief. Griggs had previously declared that the accusing girls, who sniffed out witches like pigs do truffles, "were bitten and pinched by invisible agents; their arms, necks, and backs turned this way and that way . . . so as it was impossible for them to do of themselves, and beyond the power of any epileptic fits, or natural disease to effect." In the doctor's opinion, Abigail Williams and her sorority of spites were "sadly afflicted of they knew not what distempers" and likely "under an evil hand." Griggs's testimony was as good as a writ, and a writ a death warrant. Roger Toothaker would die in Boston jail on June 16—six days after Bridget Bishop flew.

"Dr. Griggs has often attended my mistress and master with physic and leeches."

"Nay, I'm feeling better now."

"You scared me, Isaac Page!"

And you, me, Hannah.

"Will you rest awhile longer?"

"Help me up. The grass is wet with the evening dew." After she had done as he asked, he said, "Let's walk on."

"If you're able."

"Aye, a walk will do me good."

She laid a palm on his brow. "You are too warm, I think."

"The cool night air will soon fix that."

"What way shall we take?" she asked.

"There where the tall pine tree stands like a finger pointing heavenward."

"It does seem a finger, now you say it."

"Does it enjoin us to look to God, or does it accuse Him?"

"You mustn't say so, Isaac!" she whispered. "There be people abroad in the woods at night. You need take care not to be misconstrued."

"What sort of people go abroad in the forest after dark?"

"They are not all like us."

"And do they dance?" he asked slyly.

"Aye, there be some girls who like to dance among themselves."

"Do you like to go dancing in the woods, Hannah?"

"Sometimes." She had hesitated in answering him. Had she seen the tall pine burst into golden flame? Had she seen the birds fall like torches from their burning nests? Did she hear, as he did now, the fire roaring? Did she smell its acrid smoke?

"Aren't you afraid of meeting the Devil when you dance?" he asked, helpless not to cast a look over his shoulder.

"He's shy of dancing girls—afraid that we'll step on his tail in our merry reels." She had made light of the Devil, but Isaac sensed that her bold words were shadowed by apprehension. Suddenly, she took his hand and cried, "Oh, Isaac, I saw the awful fear on Mary Warren's face when the imps stopped her mouth as she tried to tell the truth! She swore to the magistrates that they threatened to burn her with 'hot tongs . . . to drown her and make her run naked through the hedges!'"

"Mary Warren," said Isaac, as though she had stepped out of the forest and curtsied to him. "Mary

Warren," he repeated like a man who had become stupefied or entranced.

He knew the story of the Proctors' hired girl from his past—that is, his future—research into the trials of the witches. Racked by the magistrates' relentless examining, Mary had come to believe, as they declared, that having confessed to shamming and then recanted, she'd given the Devil license to assume her form and torment the afflicted who cried out on her in court. Mary must make one with the girls again, she knew, or be destroyed.

And was she herself not mocked and hurt by the apparition of Alice Parker, who had killed Mary's mother and stricken her sister deaf and dumb? Mary was caught in a tightening noose, whose braided strands were fear and vengeance, so that she must cry out more witches. Among those Mary had condemned were John and Elizabeth Proctor, who had tried to compel her silence to save themselves from hanging—or so Mary Warren claimed and, in time, came to believe. Who can know the truth where liars reign?

"It was the Devil's book, my master Proctor brought me," Mary had sworn to John Hathorne and Jonathan Corwin, who beamed on her, leaned back smugly in their chairs, and flounced their neck cloths complacently.

That great pine tree, Hannah; say it does not burn!

She did not reply. Had he spoken aloud or only in his mind?

Isaac and Hannah walked into the woods. Now and then, he would turn his head sharply, wanting—and at the same time dreading—to see a phantasm beyond the periphery of his vision. As a child, he had believed that another world existed just out of sight; whether it meant him good or ill, he could not have guessed. He would gaze into a mirror in the hope of glimpsing in a corner of the reflected room a face not his own. God's face. He'd search the looking glass until his eyes pained him. More and more, his eyes hurt him now, as if he were keeping watch.

WINTER 1851
LENOX, MASSACHUSETTS

his rum is a fiery concoction! Nature intended its raw essence to sweeten our coffee or reward a restive horse and not, in its distillation, as a means to rout reason, corrupt the Indians, or barter for slaves. Thus are innocent purposes often bent. The world is ceaseless alchemy, and only a few poor scribes, like destitute and defamed Edgar Poe, can sometimes transmute reality's base metal by plying the aqua regia in their inkwells. I have not the skill to produce the noble metal gold (or a morsel of chocolate for Sophia). My genius, if I can call it that, is to turn a shameful doubt into stories, guilt into tales. In any case, it scarcely matters whether one is a giant of his age and trade or Barnum's Lilliputian; time's maw swallows them both with equal relish.

And so to you, the lately wretched Mr. Poe, and to my friend Melville (though he does tend to force himself on one), I drink—and to all else who spin straw into nothing but baskets, and empty ones at that. Certainty, like liquor, is a corrosive that eats away at truth, which is said to be sober. How easy it is to rebuke this woman or exculpate that man when one is convinced of his own rightness! Because they dwell in uncertainty, philosophers would make poor judges and worse theologians—or authors of romantic tales, whose readers want a pretty ending.

Nathaniel, you would do better to pour libations than drink them! Ah, writing is a mean occupation. I've heard it said that the portion of rum that evaporates during its manufacture is called the "angel's share." It's a lovely conceit, and so from this bottle, I offer up the *spiritus* to the fallen angels of my tribe.

"Nathaniel, you've drunk enough for one afternoon!"

"Sophia, my dear! You startled me. Are you feeling refreshed?"

"Not in the least. Nathaniel, you're never so talkative as when I want to take a nap!"

"I ask your pardon. My voice and I do get on well together. Excepting you, I can think of no one else I'd rather talk to, although I tend to speak foolishly when there's no one by to hear. Come and sit. Have you heard enough of my new tale to offer an opinion?"

"'All things desire to return to their origin' is far-fetched even for you."

"It was Henry Thoreau's conceit, you know, and he must take the blame for it."

"Husband, I hope you're not so small-minded as to sulk at a criticism."

"I'm not sulking! But you've got the little end of the

horn. The interest of my tale lies in the Salem of 1692 and not in time travel."

"Then I'd leave your great-great-grandfather's spectacles out of it."

"Ah, but they have another part to play. I entreat you, Sophia, to withhold judgment!"

"Very well."

"But what of the story itself?"

"I think you should give the Devil his due. He makes no appearance. Readers ought to feel the horror of creation's bogey, or they'll believe that Salem folk were fools, or worse."

"I cannot write the Devil! He is beyond my skill. Readers can get their fill of horrors in Dante's and Milton's books!"

"Don't be peevish, Nathaniel! It's unbecoming in a man of your eminence."

"I'm a parvenu in the business of letters. I envy those artful Salem girls the cunning of their embroidery. Their stories were so rich in uncanny detail that I ask myself if they weren't indeed tormented by specters—or with the writer's itch at least."

"Nonsense! Sit down and finish your tale. If you like, I'll play the part of scribe."

"Won't you take the barkeep's part first and pour me a glass of rum?"

"Dypsomania is an unattractive quality and unworthy of your—"

"Noble name?"

"Nathaniel, I'm sick of your unending argument with a dead man!"

"I can no more separate his story from my own than I can skin water!"

"Then for Heaven's sake, finish it."

As soon as she came near all fell into fits.

"Bridget Byshop, You are now brought before Authority to give acc'o of what witchcrafts you are conversant in."

"I take all this people [turning her head & eyes about] to witness that I am clear."

—The Examination of Bridget Byshop
at Salem village
19. Apr. 1692, by John Hauthorn &
Jonath: Corwin Esq'rs

SUMMER 1692
THE PROVINCE OF MASSACHUSETTS BAY

I

saac no longer felt a stranger in Salem Village. With every breath, he tasted the animated atoms of what particularized it in time. They were as stimulating to his tongue as if he had drunk cold water from a limestone spring. Each thing's novelty, the character of each person, so unlike that of people five generations hence, stung like an astringent on a wound. Now and then, he thought of Constance, but the very idea of a wife was shrinking like ice on a hot skillet.

It was already the fifth of June when Isaac realized with a start that he had yet to walk the mile separating Thorndike Hill, where William Dill had his cowshed, and the heart of the village, where the meetinghouse, watch house, pump, and pillory marked the crossroads. On nearby Andover Road stood the parsonage, where Betty Parris had first nursed the viper at her childish breast that had set neighbor against neighbor like teeth on edge, and Ingersoll's ordinary, where Hathorne and Corwin interrogated the accused witches brought before them by Deputy Sheriff Herrick. Five days were left till Bridget Bishop's soul would be unhoused, and her body rudely planted in the ground, to come again as bane.

Bridget was being irresistibly drawn toward the gallows while Isaac dallied with Hannah Smyth. Now like a vexing tooth beyond salving, his conscience pricked. He knew he must act or be no better than the man he'd gone to such lengths to confront—worse, in fact, since Isaac had the benefit of a retrospective view. And yet his rancor toward John Hathorne was less sharp than it had been the week before. Isaac, who, in Lenox, had pictured himself as Joshua, was, in Salem Village, more and more a Judas.

His day's work done, Isaac put away his tools and went to meet Hannah at the stile. Taking an eastern route, they crossed the Great River at Indian Bridge and went on to Mile Brook, which skirted the Birch Plain at the border of Wenham, where the old plantation farms were already shrouded in darkness. The pleasure they took in each other was not an uncommon one in Salem, not even under the stern, beetling authority of the New Jerusalem. Next to the willows aslant the brook, they lay together in the grass.

Except for a faction whose narrowness made them sullen, Puritans were not the ascetics Isaac had supposed, although in that dangerous year, they made a greater show of pious living than heretofore. A woman's skirts might not have billowed, but neither were they drab. Dressed in a brocaded waistcoat, a wealthy man would serve his guests Madeira in chased silver goblets rather than cider or ale in tin cups and take pride in his jade chess pieces. He might have stood before a magistrate and confessed to having fornicated with another sort of jade, but he'd be forgiven because his wealth and standing were a proof of his heavenly election. Though the saved might stumble and fall on the way to their foreordained reward, they would find their footing and pass, in God's time, through the eye of the needle. Those predestined for glory will achieve it—struggle against it however they may; this is Calvinist doctrine, and on it rested the Puritan state.

"What troubles you, Isaac?" asked Hannah, putting her dress to rights. "Is the work at the sawmill not to your liking?"

"I've been neglecting a duty."

"What is it?"

"I cannot say."

"You are unfriendly!" she chided.

"It was an oath taken long ago and in another place. It doesn't concern you, Hannah."

"You speak harshly, and I wonder if I've not been reckless in confiding what *I* kept most secret. Are we not now very like a husband and wife, Isaac Page?"

"It pleases me to think it, but not everything a husband knows can be told to his wife."

"Does the opposite hold true?" Her pretty mouth was screwed into a pout.

"Aye."

"Henceforth, I'll keep my secret safe from you!" She'd spoken with a vexation that Isaac had not heard before in a voice that had been either flippant or beguiling.

"Hannah, don't be cross! I must do this one thing first."

"And you won't tell me what *thing* you must do?"

"I've business with the magistrates."

"I shudder for any who has business with them."

"Will you be patient with me?"

"I'll bear it awhile. But hear me, Isaac; I'm not Hagar, and I won't be cast out into the wilderness!"

He wanted to ask what she had meant by "wilderness," but he let the matter drop.

The next morning, Isaac crossed the Great River at Log Bridge and walked east on Meeting House Road toward the village's seat of government, spiritual and civil. Although he was not yet ready to speak to him, Isaac wanted at least a glimpse of his great-great-grandfather, who was a frequent visitor to the meetinghouse and Ingersoll's now that he had souls to weigh. As Isaac drew near to the crossroads, he was overcome by the fear and nausea that had stricken him in Andover Woods. His skin prickled, his legs buckled, and he bent forward toward the dusty lane, as if his spine were a rod conducting an electric current between the heart of Salem Village and his own, which beat so fast, he feared his ribs would crack. The antique spectacles in his pocket had reached their magnetic source, he supposed. They yearned to rejoin their owner, Magistrate Hathorne. The intensity of the moment terrified Isaac. He felt, he would later say, as one pegged out on the ground, waiting for the fire ants to devour him.

He turned and fled like a man with the Furies at his heels. He hurried south on Ipswich Road and, between Governor's Plain and Orchard Farm, entered the town of Northfields. He crossed the North River on a ferry pulled by a team of straining mules. He hardly stopped for breath until he reached the wharves of Salem Town. Like any other port, Salem's was a basin in which the dirty linen of many foreign nations steeped. There men and women compacted with their own devilish appetites and wore their sins like finery, indifferent to constables, ministers, and magistrates. They were stains on the hem of the town, frustrating the resolve of the most beefy-armed of washerwomen to scrub them clean.

II

saac stopped fifteen miles short of the place where John Winthrop and his bedraggled flock of saints had made landfall at Boston, on the Charles, in 1630, at the start of the Great Migration. By the time Hathorne, Jonathan Corwin, Bartholomew Gedney, and other of Salem's magistrates had taken in hand the righteous winnowing of "the precious from the vile," towns and villages surrounding the city upon a hill had become a home to informers,

their meetinghouses courts of no appeal, their ministers autocrats, and the moral high ground where their covenants had taken root a wasteland of stony hearts. In the "redeemer nation," of Massachusetts, moral and civil law were identical and administered by pious men, who would trample, in big black boots, over the rights of man, which had yet to be proclaimed by Thomas Paine. The high ground in Salem Town was occupied by the place of execution. (Is it not often so?) Zeal is a pivot by which love can turn to hate, sanguine hearts become sanguinary, and the hangman's rope grow taut.

Spellbound, Isaac watched Massachusetts Bay tremble, a dazzle of gold coins minted by the evening sun. In time to come, the wharves would multiply from a handful of wooden fingers resting on the water till, in 1846, when Isaac was appointed Inspector of the Revenue for the Port of Salem, fifty piers fretted the harbor, crowded with stevedores, ropewalkers, sailors, merchants, carters, draymen, and drabs—all clamoring in the tongues of several nations, amid warehouses, custom sheds, chandleries, counting-houses, rum holes, and brothels.

The bay that sprawled before him in 1692 was the same Isaac had studied through his glass from the balcony of Salem Custom House as he stood beneath a gilded eagle and a blue slate roof. He and Constance had lived on Chestnut Street, where he wrote tales set in the time and place in which he now found himself. The best of them contained an element of doubt, as if the storyteller could not entirely be sure that demons had not left the forest in which they had been hiding since creation's first instant to harry New Englanders. The more Isaac struggled to purge himself of medieval superstition, the more mired he became in "error."

Isaac Page was born, Minerva-like, from Nathaniel Hawthorne's brain, which ought to have left him no room to harbor thoughts or desires of his own. But could Hawthorne be sure that a rebellious thought would not sometimes cross his creature's mind? Would he not resent his author, as his author sometimes did God, and wish to disenthrall himself? What is the chain that binds a creator to his figment? Are the links adamantine or gossamer? Invoking Magistrate John Hathorne that he might be rid of him, how could Hawthorne hate him who, long ago, had passed into dust and—the final stop in humankind's mournful recessional—words? Nothing was left of his great-great-grandfather to hate, since one cannot abhor a noun, a jostle of adjectives, or even the verbs by which men do wrong.

—∿∿∿—

Isaac thought of the Puritans' first winter, 1630, when the livid bay at Boston's ragged hem had frozen. He pictured himself shivering in a wattle and daub hut, huddling by an inadequate fire, and straining his eyes to read dismal tracts by the light of a tallow candle, a scene such as John Winthrop had described in his journal. In vain did Isaac try to imagine the taste of boiled acorns chased with water neither sweet nor wholesome. Trembling with fevers and in fear of the Devil's own savages, two hundred souls perished before the *Lyon* returned from England with supplies. Isaac admitted to himself that he could not truly picture or imagine the desperate circumstances from which his ancestor had sprung. Lives are bound to be stunted when seeds are sown among tares.

It's folly to think I can judge him honestly! The fault lies in our stars.

Then a voice, which might have been his, whispered, "Remember who you are, Isaac Page, and the guilt you carry in another's name."

What keeps me from boarding that Dutch *fluyt* straining to be away with the tide? Isaac asked himself, sick of his wavering. I could travel to the Spice Islands, in the Banda Sea, delight in the odors of nutmeg, clove, and cinnamon, and dine with the *senapati* of Java on fish and coconuts. I could claim an uninhabited island and declare myself lord of its mosquitoes. I would make it my capital of Naught and pray, as John Winthrop did, "O Lord, crucify the world unto me!"

Isaac was startled by a hand clapped on his shoulder, a hand heavy and raddled as a ham.

"By the glaze in your eye, I guess you are a seafaring man looking for a ship."

"I'm no seafarer and have never ventured onto any deeps, save what a ferryboat could reach," replied Isaac, who noted the milky cast of a cataract covering the other man's eyes.

"Well, friend, you've the look of a man out of his element."

"I am that," replied Isaac. The element is time, he added to himself.

"Smoke?" asked the other, who had opened his pouch.

"Thank you, no, I've a canker."

The man prepared his pipe. Shall I describe him as he busied himself with the totems of his vice? One would call him an old man, although he had lived six less than threescore years. His face was darkly seamed, his hair white, his back bent no matter how he tried to stand erect, and his feet were well gone in the arches. He gave the appearance of being someone who had toiled much and hard in every sort of weather.

"Seth Grimes is my name," he said, having put his kindled pipe between his teeth and offered Isaac a hand to shake. "Shipbuilder here in Salem Town. I came out to see the *Beverly*. I laid her keel. These days, my sons bear the brunt." He studied Isaac's palm as though to read the younger man's destiny in it. "By your calluses, you're a farmer or mechanic."

"A carpenter," said Isaac. "I'm looking for work."

"Can you let a rabbet into a sternpost?"

"I think you mean something other than what I eat in stew; but if it be joinery, one join is very like another. I'm handy with a drawing knife, mallet, augur, and chisel."

"You speak sense, mister. Would you like to learn boats?"

"Aye, if it be for wages. I've had enough of Salem thrift."

"Like you the sound of five shillings and found?"

Isaac agreed and shook hands on it with Grimes, who clapped him on the back again. The two men walked to a dock on the harbor's far side, where the noise of hammering, sawing, and gouging timber—each noise peculiar to its tool—escaped the open casements of a long, narrow shed on which was painted with a flourish:

Grimes & Sons, Shipwrights

—⁓⁓⁓—

Grimes and his three grown sons taught Isaac the refinements of their craft—far stricter than the joinery he had learned at Brook Farm. Errors are intolerable in a shallop or a ketch. His ears delighted in the chuck of a mallet, the skirl of a file, the chuff of a saw, the sweet sound of a brace and bit, the silken whir of a plane or an adze as he shaved the tender wood like a barber following the grain of a man's cheek with a razor. A false note would raise the father's eyebrows and cause his fellow musicians to frown. Seldom did they misplace a note or sour a tune unless it be that the wood was at fault because of a knot or a scab of resin. Isaac enjoyed his work, and the days passed—one very like another.

He had a room above a ropewalk. He ate his dinner at Gedney's tavern, often in the company of the old widower. After a chop or a roasted bird, the two liked to play Put or Nine Men's Morris. They drank ale, and if they scoffed at the "one and done" rule, they took care not to become besotted. "The stocks be a poor breakfast," said Grimes, who was not talkative, except as it concerned a boat taking shape in the yard or anecdotes of his sons. Later, Isaac could recall their having discussed, once only, "the witch business in the village."

"The times are passing strange, Isaac," said Grimes. "I wonder at them and at the stories I hear of goings-on in the village. I try to pay them no mind, but my friend Philip English has had to flee the town, and his wife, Mary, whom I know to be a good soul, is locked up in Arnold's jail for witchery. She's confined with Goody Nurse, as well as that Emerson woman, who buried her newborn twins in the garden, and Grace, the black slave, who birthed her child down a privy hole. Or so they say."

"They do have much to say," said Isaac.

"Aye, and much rubbish besides." He smoked pensively. "It's said that Rebecca Nurse's specter choked Mary Warren, so that she couldn't testify against her, and Philip's specter pricked the girl with a pin. For the life of me, I can't fathom how those simple girls can weave such fancies into stories that the whole province accepts as God's truth!"

"He keeps His truth well hidden," said Isaac glumly.

"It be plain enough for masters Corwin and Hathorne—God rot them!"

"It's difficult to know what God wants of us," said Isaac.

"I tell my sons we should build an ark. You'd be welcome to sail with us. Ah, but my boys only laugh at me! Young men are fools."

"You think He intends to drown His people in New England?"

"I think it won't be long before George Herrick comes to take us all to jail."

III

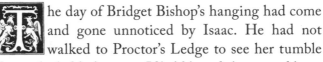

The day of Bridget Bishop's hanging had come and gone unnoticed by Isaac. He had not walked to Proctor's Ledge to see her tumble down the ladder's rungs. If he'd heard shouts and huzzahs carried on the wind to Derby Wharf, he would have mistaken them for the screech and cries of seabirds, which were ample at Salem Harbor. He would have remained blissfully unaware of her execution and extinction had it not been for another of Richard Pierce's broadsides, which Isaac did not read till weeks after the event.

NEWS OF PERSONS PREVIOUSLY EXAMINED IN SALEM VILLAGE

{Published at Boston, on the 1st day of July, in the Year of Our Lord 1692}

2 June. Bridget Bishop, of Salem Town, is convicted of witchcraft.

10 June. Bridget Bishop is hanged at Proctor's Ledge, in Salem Town.

16 June. Roger Toothaker dies in Boston jail.

29–30 June. Rebecca Nurse, Susannah Martin, Sarah Wildes, Sarah Good, & Elizabeth Howe are sentenced to death by magistrates John Hathorne & Jonathan Corwin at the Salem Town House.

Isaac sat with the paper on his lap and stared at Salem Harbor through the open window of Grimes's shed. Gold disks of water sliding in the evening sun entranced him as he pictured the hangman kicking away the gallows ladder and dropping Bridget, bound and hooded, into Heaven, Hell, or oblivion. Only this was sure: She broke her neck at the end of the rope and was put into the ground.

"What be your opinion, Isaac, in the matter of witches?" asked Caleb as he dipped his bread into his ale. The two men were eating their supper. Caleb had not spoken to him before of the madness. The eldest of Grimes's sons, he appeared troubled, as if a warrant had been issued for his arrest and Deputy Herrick was on his way to serve it. "I took her for a scold but not a witch," said Caleb, stabbing the broadside with his thumb at the place where Bridget's death was reported.

Isaac stuffed his mouth with bread, so that he would not have to answer.

To be sensitive in callous times, one must be like an oyster, which needs to hide its tender part inside a shell; so it was with Caleb. At first, he had seemed careless of Isaac and his feelings. "You're not building a privy," he would remark when Isaac had drilled a crooked peg hole. "If Noah had left the girdling to you, the ark would have foundered before reaching Mount Ararat," when he had scanted the timbers set around a hull. "You're not making a shave horse," if Isaac had chosen planks for a false keel without enough heft. However much Isaac resented the other's carping, he realized that it was not only needful but also given without malice. Until that time, the most complicated structure Isaac had built *was* a privy. At the end of the day, Caleb would clap him on the back or tousle his grizzled hair, as if Isaac were a young apprentice, when, in fact, he was a dozen years older than Caleb. Isaac admired his uprightness—all the more so because of his own backsliding. He'd let his purpose dampen, and not even Bridget's death was spark enough to rekindle it.

Caleb had been used to keeping the Sabbath by rowing across the harbor to Marblehead to worship in secret with a Baptist enclave. Lately, he had been keeping to his father's house or his own on Brod Street. He knew better than to be seen to stand apart in a dangerous time, when a word shrieked in spite or fear could blast a man, woman, or child. In Salem Town, the Court of Oyer and Terminer had been convened on May 27 and was grinding the accused with the pestle of the zealots' law. Grim judges were probing consciences with the fervor of a surgeon hunting for an abscess with a knife. After Governor Phips brought the province's charter from London, making Massachusetts a law unto itself, death warrants held in abeyance could be executed. One of them had swept Bridget Bishop to Kingdom Come—God's or Satan's. The sea winds that had once seemed to cleanse the atmosphere of Salem Town blew ill; its stink carried far and wide.

"Think you those girls are wicked?" asked Caleb.

Isaac was afraid to answer him, knowing that a man can seem honest, but it is cunning that makes him appear so. He turned the table and asked Caleb what he thought of the invisible world.

Caleb gnawed a crust. "I think there be hidden shoals, which can tear the bottom of the staunchest boat."

Isaac nodded warily.

"But I don't suppose God puts rocks in the way of ships to drown men." He chewed his crust some more and then concluded: "Nay, I don't believe in spectral evidence. I don't believe people can be judged by proofs of devilry that only some can see, and they be unreliable. By God, who are these children to say yea or nay to who should live or who should have his neck stretched? I say they are wicked and should be flogged!"

Isaac guessed that Caleb's rancor was caused by the flight of his friend Philip English, whose wharf stood empty. His ships had been seized and his goods distrained. "I'm of the same opinion," said Isaac after a pause in which he'd debated with himself how to respond.

Caleb looked relieved. He may have had doubts of his own concerning his apprentice's beliefs and, despite them, had resolved to risk his property, liberty, and life by being round with him. Thus will like-minded persons find each other, no matter how much the world conspires to keep them fearful and apart.

"It's not safe for me here," admitted Caleb. "I've been working against them, you see. I expect any day to hear the sheriff banging on my door."

Isaac was amazed by this intelligence. "Working against them, how?"

"There be men and women who don't much like what has happened in Salem. I won't give you names, though I trust you, but they are not mine to give, because it would be the death of them were they discovered. They be good people—I tell you that much, friend, and we had hoped to put an end to the business. But now it may've gone too far to stop. We fear a pack of vicious girls, who have power to send us to jail or the gallows. Why, even Cotton Mather and John Hathorne dance to their tune! Hathorne has a stone for a heart, and *that* be frozen. It is the nineteenth of July, and Rebecca Nurse, Susannah Martin, Elizabeth Howe, Sarah Good, and Sarah Wildes were, this day, pushed from the gallows ladder."

"More will follow," said Isaac with the confidence of foreknowledge.

The massacre of innocents—"Desolation of Names," in Cotton Mather's words—would not end until September 22, when the last convicted witches twitched at the end of the hangman's rope. Not till October would Governor Phips forbid the use of spectral evidence in court after Increase Mather and Thomas Brattle had condemned it as unreliable. Even so, the holy terror continued into January 1693, when Chief Justice Stoughton ordered the executions of women whose hangings had been delayed by the unborn children in their wombs. Fortunately, his order was countermanded. Salem had finally lost its appetite for murder. The snow was unpacked from the hearts of its people. It was stained like that in a stable yard, to continue the figure.

"I do fear to be in Salem during the humiliation," said Caleb.

"Then you must leave at once!" asserted Isaac.

The General Court had called for a day of humiliation, when "all persons are required to abstain from bodily labor and to resort to the public meetings to seek the Lord."

"The people will pray and fast for deliverance from Satan's power," said Caleb. "In their zeal to worm the body politic of wizards and witches, I may find myself delivered up to prison."

Isaac could have told him that nowhere in the notorious history of Salem did the name of Caleb Grimes appear—not among those cried out, examined, or jailed, those who fled, died in prison or on Proctor's Ledge. An early death could not have been foretold by reading Caleb's palm, hidden by a pewter mug half-emptied of its ale.

"Then you must be off this very afternoon!" exclaimed Isaac, unwilling to dissuade him on the evidence of history, which is not wholly reliable.

"Think you that God will judge me a coward?"

"'And when they persecute you in this city, flee ye into another,'" said Isaac, quoting from the Gospel of Matthew.

Caleb was satisfied of Isaac's loyalty. "I leave tonight." He took Isaac's hand and said, "It's arranged, but my house is being watched."

"What can I do?" asked Isaac, carried forward by a sudden gust of comradeship.

"We're shaped alike, our height and shoulders much the same. After sundown, when I'm wont to leave the yard for the day, you'll put on my cloak and hat and walk to my house, where you'll stay till morning. In the dark, I'll row across to Marblehead. Friends have engaged a ship to carry me thence to New York," where there were no witches, only the crafty Dutch, crusty Germans, Catholic French, Protestant Swedes, Sephardic Jews who had emigrated from Brazil, and the lordly English. "Will you do me this service, Isaac?"

"Gladly!"

And so this Prince Hamlet of a man, who had allowed his purpose to blunt, promised to save Caleb Grimes from the great-great-grandfather whom he had sworn to obstruct or, if need be, pay in kind for the terrible judgments he had wrought.

IV

hen the potboy from the tavern in Eccles Lane arrived with Caleb's beer, as he did every night, Isaac noted the presence of a darkly mantled figure lurking in the thickset trees. By then, Caleb was on the way to Marblehead.

Isaac fell asleep after finishing the beer, which tasted sharply of spruce. In the morning, he broke his fast with brown bread and ale, the custom of the time, locked the house behind him, and walked toward the wharf.

In Essex Street, a man accosted him. "Mister, what business had you at Grimes's?"

"I fed his cat."

"A cat, you say? What kind of cat?"

"A house cat."

"Imp familiars do often assume the shape of a cat."

Isaac's words had been reckless, and he tried to make light of them. "I assure you, it is an ordinary cat with an appetite for nothing larger than mice."

"You seem a comical fellow."

"The Lord bids me to be joyous."

The black-suited man fell silent a moment. "And where is Grimes this morning?"

"I don't know."

"Am I to believe he entrusted his house to you without saying where he was going?"

"A master need not take an apprentice into his confidence."

"Did he say, at least, when he would return?"

"Tomorrow, or the day after," replied Isaac with a vague shrug of his shoulders. "Till then, I'm to watch over his property."

“Are their thieves in Salem Town that he should fear for his goods?”

“Is it not written that ‘. . . the day of the Lord so cometh as a thief in the night’?”

Isaac’s impious gibe angered his inquisitor. “You take the Lord’s name in vain!”

“I do not, sir, unless it be vanity to quote from Scripture. If that be the case, there are a great many vain persons in Salem. The words I spoke are from First Thessalonians.”

“I know it! I admonish you not to trifle with Holy Writ nor with the pleasure of the court, which has writs of its own to hobble impudent fellows!”

Isaac felt the silver piece sewn into his pocket. Taking courage, he remarked flippantly, “Why do you trouble an innocent citizen on his way to work?”

“I suspect there be mischief in you!”

“There be none, I assure you. If my words offended, I beg pardon. It’s a fault for which my friends have often reproved me. I’ll strive to amend it. With your permission, I’ll go about my business, which has only to do with boats and ships and nothing at all with mischief.”

“I’m not done with you yet, fellow!”

“I’ve told you all I know of Master Grimes’s comings and goings.”

“‘He hath made a pit and digged it, and is fallen into the pit he made.’”

“I pray you are mistaken, sir, but in any case, I am well clear of it.”

"Nonetheless, I'll watch again tonight. As the Lord said, "'. . . I set watchmen over you.'"

"Then you must come in and sit to rest your feet awhile. When the boy brings beer, we'll drink a jar together—one and done, of course."

His antagonist relented, but he took down Isaac's particulars in a small red book, which frightened the people of Salem, as though it were the Devil's own, where diabolical contracts were recorded in blood. "What church are you?" he asked, having paused in his writing.

"I'm new to Salem Town and have not yet decided the matter. In that it be a grave one, I think I ought not to consider it in haste. I tell you, sir, if a man be reckless and stumbles, it is often the Devil who picks him up. I would keep the Devil far from me, for the good Lord's sake."

"And your own soul's, Goodman Page."

"Aye, my soul be precious to me."

"Grimes is not of our church," said the spy, insinuating a depraved character.

"He's not spoken on the matter."

"Why should he wish to make a secret of his faith? Were he covenanted, he would gladly boast of his good standing with the Lord."

"There are some who've taken faith so deeply into them and hold it so jealously to their breast, they are loath to speak of it." Isaac smiled. "Master Grimes is a man of few words."

"Faith, if it be genuine, ought to be shouted from the rooftop. It pleases God's ears to hear it."

"Those who are mistaken in the truth of their sanctity will not be saved," replied Isaac.

The spy, who accounted himself God's own, had been sent by the magistrates to sniff out sin. "It may be that Caleb Grimes is a Baptist."

"Is it not allowed?"

"It be frowned upon. It would have gotten his tongue pierced by a red-hot poker when the Bay was still a colony. I would reintroduce the practice."

A few more minutes of sharp palaver followed before Isaac was allowed to go his way, with a warning that, at a time of extraordinary affliction, when the Devil was at his last gasp, the court would punish evildoers harshly.

After his flip encounter with civil authority, Isaac rebuked himself for being a fool. Now you've made yourself remarkable! And by the time the evening shadows had begun to lengthen into night, he had frightened himself. He heard a plangent voice whose source may have been his own mind or the Devil, who whispers sweetly to those at the end of their rope: "Go forth and hang yourself."

At that alarming instant, the memory of Constance, whom Isaac had all but forgotten, swept over him like a breeze in which a half-familiar odor and a half-remembered music were entwined, and something else—the taste of a kiss when kisses were new and love had not yet declined into affection, which is both greater and less than love. Feeling the coin in his pocket, Isaac was again seized by the wish to go home.

"Caleb got away," said Seth Grimes, laying a hand on Isaac's shoulder.

"What's that, you say?" So distracted was Isaac that the old man's words had been like the noise of a fly.

"Caleb got away. In two days, he'll be in New York. Pray God he will be safe there! He's a good son and a godly man. His contempt is for the elders of Salem and the rings the lying girls have put through their patriarchal noses."

"What of Timothy and Alan?" They were the old man's other, younger sons.

"They have wives and children and are not part of the opposition. I'm grateful to you for helping Caleb escape. You're a friend to my son and me, and I ask the Lord's blessing on you."

They shook hands warmly.

"Seth, I would ask a favor of *you*."

"If it be in my power to grant, you shall have it."

"Tomorrow, I'd like to borrow a skiff and row to Marblehead."

"What do you want there?" asked the old man with neither a suspicion nor a challenge.

"I've no wish to be in Salem on the day of humiliation, when the righteous flail themselves into ecstasy."

"You can have the boat that took old Rebecca Nurse home."

The night of her execution, the family disinterred Rebecca's remains from their hasty grave on the lower ledges, near the stream that flowed into the North River. Caleb rowed her washed and shrouded corpse to the estuary and onto the Woolston River, which divided Royal Side from Northfields. He continued up Crane Brook to the village, where the Nurse family kept a piece of ground for the burying of its own.

Isaac stayed a second night at Caleb's house "to mind the cat." The spy did not return to skulk among the poplars or to put his feet up and share a jar. The potboy brought beer, and after Isaac had finished it, he fell asleep. Unlike the previous night, he was troubled by dreams. The black-suited, high-crowned officer of the court was examining him.

"The court sent to Rhode Island and has discovered that none remembers an Isaac Page."

"An itinerant carpenter would not be memorable."

"What say you, fellow? Did you hope to deceive Salem's magistrates in order to work some devilry?"

"I know not how to work devilry."

"Tut, tut."

"I tell you, sir, I am harmless and blameless of deceit!"

"You've been cried out as a witch!"

"Who calls me so?"

"Bridget Bishop."

"She was hanged a month ago, and more!"

"If she say you are a witch, then you are one. Dead witches needs must speak the truth; it is God's punishment on them for their wickedness."

"This is foolishness!"

"You are in contempt of court, man!"

"I see no court, only an unkindness of ravens and a knot of toads!"

The officer had indeed resembled a raven when, thrusting his hands behind his back, the black skirts of his coat had stuck out stiffly. And when he squatted to cosset a passing cat, he looked very like the dank creature that witches stir into boiling pots.

"Hear that!" he croaked. "He invokes toads! Surely, this be proof he is a wizard!"

"I know nothing of it!"

"You are damned and will not taste God's mercy or look upon His face!"

"No one can see into another's breast to discover if he be saved or not."

"God's ministers and magistrates will sniff out your corruption, which is as an evil stench in my nostrils."

"None can know if another has received God's saving grace, which is His free gift to mankind."

"Not to all, Isaac Page! He gives it only to His saints."

Then the scenery of the dream had shifted by invisible hands. What is a dream if not a play, and what is witchery if not that, also, and who, if not Salem's shamming girls, were the most consummate actors in the dreaming Province of Massachusetts Bay?

Now Isaac was in the forest where he had walked with Hannah the night he'd supped at the Buxtons' table. He sensed the presence of a mystery, sinister and dreadful. It hemmed the path amid the closely ranked trees, which disclosed imperfect glimpses of the moonless, starless sky. The enormous pine tree burned—a fiery finger pointing not to enjoin the villagers to look to Heaven but to guide the witches to an unholy conclave, where souls would be signed away. Isaac knew he was not alone in the woods, though he could see none but himself and his own two feet as he made sure he was earthbound. Fronds of bracken rattled, and crushed sweet fern released a dark perfume. Hooves clattered on the path but left no mark as unseen congregants rasped and hissed where no church had ever been gathered nor solitary Christian prayed.

The Devil spoke to Isaac, promising luxurious living and supernatural power if only he would sign his registry. Dark words poured into Isaac's ears, like loathsome matter running in a ditch. He vomited what seemed like the contents of a fen. Then the Devil changed his tune, and Isaac blushed to hear that master of blasphemous revels play, with the nimblest of fingers, a carnal rhapsody on invisible strings. The infernal anthem was not meant to be sung by troubadours or Meistersingers. Not even the covetous wretch Salieri, who wished Mozart dead, could have led those impish musicians and satanic choristers. How very great and fearful was the noise they made as Isaac stumbled over roots and ruts toward the great witch meeting!

He came into a clearing lighted garishly by fire streaming upward from the crackling tree. He watched virgins, goodwives, and crones shed their clothes, their bodies clad in nothing but a coppery light. They behaved shamelessly, dancing widdershins around the inexhaustible pine. Painted on canvas in lurid colors, the scene would please a juiceless rake ogling it in his closet, but it appalled Isaac. It would've done so in any century.

Merry and licentious as the rest was a young woman wearing naught but ribbons in her loosened hair. Lustily, she sang as she danced:

Ye Devil she crys,
I'll tear your Eyes,
When Main seiz'd,
Bum squeez'd,
I Gallop, I Gallop, I Gallop, I Gallop . . .

"Hannah!" cried Isaac, appalled.

She turned to him and, gesturing lewdly, beckoned him to join her.

"Hannah! Save yourself!"

But she would not be saved. She lay down on the beaten earth and writhed.

Again, Isaac heard voices. Unintelligible in that havoc, they were punctuated by screams, shrieks, and lamentations loud. He recognized them as the utterances of history, as though time's sharp wind had stripped the accounts written in all the languages ever spoken on Earth.

Isaac cried out and awoke, to find himself in Caleb's house, all the lights gone out.

V

The following morning, Isaac Page set out across Salem Harbor, which the Naumkeag call *Massabequash* (in a language that will someday be as dead as the people who spoke it). He might have been pulling his oars through molten lead, so heavy did the water seem and so heavily did he sweat. The July heat was unrelieved by the fitful wind ruffling the harbor too genteelly to raise whitecaps. The large bay seemed to tilt as gray disks of brackish water rolled around the crawling skiff, its groaning lapstrake planks a ground bass to Isaac's labored breath. He was hardly more than half a mile from the wharf and already regretting the crossing. Scribes and scribblers are a pitiful lot, having strength to drag their pens about the page and for little else.

You're halfway there, Isaac. You can find a tavern at Marblehead, slake your thirst, and rest before rowing back to Salem.

He caught sight of the *Bellevue,* a sloop built by the Grimeses. Having found a favorable wind unavailable to Isaac's skiff, she was spanking northerly toward Winter Island. He had heard of a public house there, which, like Thom Croft's ordinary, was let alone, if not countenanced, by the Puritans. It looked to be no farther than Marblehead, whose long, dark back he saw. Why not go there instead, Isaac? One outpost is as good as another, so long as you're away from Salem's madness.

A cormorant dropped like a stone into the bay.

When it lifted its head from the water, Isaac watched it swallow a fish until nothing of it was left to see but a lump in the bird's throat. "Good or bad, nothing can happen to me, because I belong elsewhere," he said to the bird. He thought of Lenox and his former occupation. "I was too shut up with books and my own fancies. I should've been like Melville, who went on voyages before putting words to paper. If I could only take this home." His arms opened to embrace the water, the distant island, and Salem as he had come to know it—"as only I can write of it in my own century." Isaac's ambition, which had been cold, rekindled; he thought of the book he would write when he was at his desk inside the red farmhouse. Shameless, he imagined his fame after his book—unprecedented in its scope and moral grandeur—was published.

The clouds were piled softly up unto the brink of eternity. A wind bellied the canvas of the scudding sloop. "A pity I have no sail," he said matter-of-factly. The clouds soared. In the distance, Salem Sound was blue. The water surrounding the boat was pewter, which will not shine no matter how strenuously it is burnished. He dropped oars and, biting into the water with them, made for Winter Island.

The Atlantic opened its tidal gate, and a stiff current pushed against the bow. Seabirds wheeled, their wings flashing a meaningless semaphore. Glancing on the water, the light hurt Isaac's eyes. Again, he regretted his decision as the birds cried mockingly. He shipped oars to consider the matter, but the ocean did not allow for deliberation, and the boat fell back toward Salem Town. Having left it behind, Isaac had entered an uncanny space, which could not have been surveyed by Digges's theodolite or described by mathematics. He had blundered into the geography of a dream, where "he sees his nothingness."

Isaac worked his oars against the current until he came within sight of Cat Cove, which divided Winter Island from Salem Neck. He made for a pier and brought the boat to rest against it. His head reeled, and his eyes stung. Worn by his struggle against the will of water untamed and unconfined, he walked into a grove, lay down beneath the aspens, and quickly fell asleep to the murmur of their leaves.

Words alone can restore a village or a house when nothing of its past remains. Waldo Emerson's "Concord Hymn" rebuilt the ruined North Bridge, where the "shot heard round the world" resounds in perpetuity amid mute stones. How much harder is it to resurrect a man by utterance? A student of human nature must guess at the truth of his subject, trusting either in the persistence of a nub of goodness or in an ineradicable stain on character through the ages. Had Isaac been born other than a New Englander and a scion of a notorious ancestor, his nature might have been optimistic, his outlook cheerful. He was born in Salem, however, and its tainted past was also his. Isaac did not believe in the transubstantiation of bread and wine into the body and blood of Christ.

And so it was that Isaac Page, who had left his home

in latter-day Massachusetts to alter history and save his family from disgrace, found himself in exile on a tiny island a dream away from the author of that disgrace and shameful history—an exile no less involuntary, appearances notwithstanding, than Tiberius's on Capri or that of Defoe's castaway in the Carib.

VI

That evening, Isaac walked the ambit of the little island, beginning on its leeward side at Cat Cove and Smith Pool, rounding Juniper Cove at its north end, then turning down its windward shore, where the South Channel seethed below a headland. His curiosity could not have been more quickly satisfied had he worn the famous ogre's seven-league boots. The student of the classics of Arcadia would delight in Winter Island, where sheep grazed in salt-grass meadows noisy with insects, while butterflies, their delicate sails dyed brightly as Javanese cloth, quietly went about their aerial business. Few from Salem Town visited there, except those who rented pasturage for their beasts or brought their fishing boats to the sheltered winter anchorage of Cat Cove. In spite of the commonplace name, Smith Pool appeared enchanted, as though gloomy suspicions had not yet darkened it. A small fort erected on the southernmost part of the island protected Salem Town from French and Dutch warships and the Canadian privateers, known as "Turkish pirates."

Isaac counted a dozen stone houses with thatched roofs, a saltworks, sheds and racks for drying cod, and a cooperage. The public house had been a stubby Dutch merchantman, which had foundered. Casks were trimmed, sealed, and fastened to the breached hull to float her off the rocky shoal. With much ado, a team of oxen dragged the wreck ashore, where she was put up on blocks, dismasted, and converted into a tavern called De Zeeslang—in English, the Leviathan. The ship's master, Pieter Koorne, decided to remain on the island with his ship (happy not to have gone down in her). Corpulent and genial, he was just such a human type as inhabits Washington Irving's tales. Indeed, he might have served as the model of Irving's portrait of old Manhattan's governor Wouter van Twiller, who had "not a little the appearance of a beer-barrel on skids."

Dressed in Hessian boots and galligaskins, cinched with a waistband to keep his belly in check, and topped by a Spaniard's rakish hat, which he wore indoors and out to keep his brains conditioned, as if they were pickled in Holland gin in the cask of his skull, Koorne had a laugh such as had not been heard in Massachusetts since Miles Standish slew jollity at Merry Mount. Koorne was called by his friends, who included every other person living on the island, "St. Nicholas." At Christmas, he gave nuts, apples, and wooden toys to the handful of children who mended nets or shepherded their parents' flocks. In the way of the Dutch, he was accompanied by Zwarte Piet, or Black Peter, who smutted his face with burnt cork. On all other days of the year, St. Nicholas's pursy helper was called Cornelis Bok, a fleshmonger, formerly of Leiden.

Having made up his mind to stay on the island, Isaac spent his idle hours, which were many, at De Zeeslang. He liked Koorne's gin, which the Dutchman flavored with tart mulberries. The two played Old Sledge, bowls, and shovelboard, smoked long clay pipes, and ate pickled herring, sacred fare to the Hollanders. Koorne always called to mind a passage from Irving's comic novel *Knickerbocker's History of New York*: "Who ever hears of fat men heading a riot, or herding together in turbulent mobs?—no—no; it is your lean, hungry men who are continually worrying society, and setting the whole community by its ears." In the islanders' view, Salem's ministers and magistrates were just such stringy men. They had, in Shakespeare's words, "a lean and hungry look."

A boatswain aboard the *Dolphijn*, which had put in at the cove for repairs after a voyage from the Dutch colony at Recife, lost his tame monkey to Koorne at cards. The monkey had made himself at home in De Zeeslang till a fire started in the cabin where Koorne and it slept. Afterward, the animal roved the island with none to molest it, except the drover Jacob Watts's collie dog, which had a prejudice against monkeys.

The antic creature kept mainly to the burying ground, among gravestones worn thin as Communion wafers. Isaac often wandered there because of the view it afforded of the Atlantic. In his day, the place would be known as Execution Hill, where sixteen-year-old Stephen Clark was hanged for setting fire to a hay house. A Salem drab named Hannah Downes had denounced him. (Like the poor, informers and defamers are always with us.) Six lines of doggerel tearfully declaimed from the gallows' little stage were printed on a black-edged card circulated at the time.

> Be warn'd, ye youth, who see my sad despair:
> Avoid LEWD WOMEN, false as they are fair.
> By my example learn to shun my fate:
> How wretched is the man who's wise too late!
> Ere innocence, and fame and life be lost,
> Here purchase wisdom cheaply, at my cost.

Isaac doubted that a pyromaniac could have touchingly exhorted a crowd of gaping spectators in rhyming couplets. It must be said, however, that people spoke fairer then.

Ten days following his arrival on the island, Isaac was once again staring into the misty distance from the vantage of the graveyard. The air tasted of brine. With his back turned on Salem, he felt its malign attraction lessen. Straining to see a ship on the horizon, he imagined himself traveling far from the meetinghouse and Salem Town House, where magisterial judgments were turning ordinary men, women, and children into diabolical agents and, by the inexorable process of man's law, living beings into carrion. Their damned souls were accounted unfit for the genteel company of the future's resurrected elect, their breath smelling of the sweet fennel they chewed in church to keep their stomachs quiet.

Suddenly, Isaac heard two voices coming from far away and, mingled with them, shrieks and cries. The interrogatory voice belonged—he knew for a certainty—to the man he'd come so very great a distance to confront.

"Goody Nurse. Do not you see these afflicted persons and hear them accuse you?"

"The Lord knows I have not hurt them: I am an innocent person."

The words had been spoken on March 24, 1692. They'd been carried from Salem on a seaward breeze and circulated in the upper air until such time as sympathetic ears could hear them and a compassionate mind comprehend them. Isaac could not work out why they hadn't frayed into silence months before reaching him.

"It is very awful to all to see these agonies, and you, an old professor, thus charged with contracting with the Devil and yet to see you stand with dry eyes when there are so many we—"

"You do not know my heart."

"You would do well if you are guilty to confess and give glory to God."

"I am as clear as the child unborn."

"I pray God clear you if you be innocent, and if you are guilty, discover you. And therefore give me an upright answer: have you any familiarity with these spirits?"

"No, I have none but with God alone."

"How came you sick, for there is an odd discourse of that in the mouths of many—"

"I am sick at my stomach."

"Have you no wounds?"

"I have none but old age."

"You do know whether you are guilty and have familiarity with the Devil, and now when you are here present to see such a thing as these girls testify a black man whispering in your ear, and birds about you, what do you say to it?"

"It is all false. I am clear."

A sea wind lashed the high hill, scattering words of accusation and brave denial like petals stripped from branches in a squall. Isaac recalled Hamlet's colloquy with his father, the murdered king, on the battlements at Elsinore.

> HAMLET: Alas, poor ghost!
> GHOST: Pity me not, but lend thy serious hearing
> To what I shall unfold.
> HAMLET: Speak; I am bound to hear.
> GHOST: So art thou to revenge, when thou shalt hear.

In his morbid fancy, Isaac saw himself amid the grave markers on the Nurses' farm in the early hour before Lauds. The ghost of Rebecca Nurse rose into the clammy air, silencing the nightjars, the frogs croaking grumpily on the riverbank, and very nearly Isaac's consternated heart. Were she to bind me to her in a covenant of blood, this old woman who had been among the gentlest and most sweet-tempered in the village—if Rebecca Nurse were to demand that I take vengeance on her murderers, what would I tell her? asked Isaac of himself.

He was saved from having to answer by Pieter Koorne's monkey, which jumped on top of a grave-board and screeched defiance at a shrieking gull. Isaac was immediately addressed by another voice, belonging neither to Hamlet nor the ghost of his father, Rebecca Nurse nor the magistrate.

"I'd like a word with you, fellow."

Isaac turned, to see the blurred shape of a man walking toward him out of the dazzling sunlight.

"What word would you like?" asked Isaac, shading his eyes with the edge of his hand.

"I'm hunting an accused wizard who fled Salem before he could be judged. His name is Philip English, a merchant and shipowner of the town and, by all accounts, an atheist."

"I don't know him," replied Isaac, who recognized the man standing in front of him as a constable by his black staff of office.

"Why, he be among the best-known men in the parish! He sent his specter to cut Susanna Sheldon's throat and chop her legs off if she would not sign the Devil's book."

"I've not been in Salem. I came from Rhode Island and have never heard the name of him you seek."

The constable took off his hat and mopped his bald head, richly watered by his sweat. Isaac took out his stone bottle of cider and offered it to the constable, who drank from it appreciatively.

"It must be hot work to hunt a man."

"Aye, but God's will must be done. I tell you, goodman, the times are out of joint."

"Because of the witches."

"They besiege us night and day. I tell you, they be more dangerous than savages because you can't see a specter to kill with a musket, lance, or ax. A man would sooner part with his scalp than his immortal soul."

"They mean to do us harm."

"I was at Salem Town House when Mary Warren witnessed against Job Tookey for the spectral murder of six persons. The ghost of one of them, who'd been living in Bermuda, told Mary that she dropped down dead when Tookey stabbed her poppet likeness through the heart. Why, he murdered two of his own children! The poor mites' ghosts were under the magistrates' table, howling to be avenged. The others were buzzing in Mary Warren's ear. At first, we thought a hive of wasps under the eaves had been disturbed. Though I be a burly man and an officer of the law, it caused me great affright."

Isaac did not disdain the man for his credulity; on the contrary, he admired him for the earnestness with which he expressed his belief in entities bent on bringing misery to honest folk. He hunted fugitives not for his two shillings a day, but for the townspeople's sake. When he bid Isaac "Godspeed," Isaac bid him likewise.

Isaac preferred death by an arrow or a knife, a musket ball or a farmer's scythe than by "the rage and malice of Satan." He did not think he had Giles Corey's fortitude (or was it plain cussedness) to ask his judges for "more weight" as stones were being laid atop his chest. Could the old man have foreseen his agony, would he not, also, have run?

To be rid of the sensation that a weight had been set upon his own chest, Isaac filled his lungs with the savory odors of the tidal marsh, the salt bay, and the ocean, eternally grinding like a pestle in the mortar of its ancient bed. Like musk, the mixture never failed to stimulate his appetite. He shook off his fancies and walked to De Zeeslang to eat in the lively presence of the Dutchman.

"Pieter, what think you of sorcery?" asked Isaac as he sat musing over his gin.

"I don't think much on it," replied Koorne. Isaac noticed an uncharacteristic shadow pass across the other's face. "The subject makes me bilious." The Dutchman fished up a slab of roast meat from the salver. "Puritans who sharpen the bones in their arses on hard church benches and privy seats while they strain at stools are mad." He waved his fork at Isaac. "I don't trust a man who has no flesh on him." He put down his fork and took up his glass. "One and done. By God, did you ever hear such foolishness?"

"What do the Hollanders in New York say about the Puritans?"

"That they are all beggars."

"Why 'beggars'?"

"They beg for mercy, for fear of a scorched backside. There is no good in them, because there's not a thimble's worth of sin in them. 'God loveth a cheerful sinner.' Does it not say so in the Bible?" He chewed his meat with gusto. "God loves a fat man!" exclaimed Koorne, clapping his bulging stomach with a pair of beefy hands. "And of all fat men, He loves Dutchmen best."

"You'll never squeeze through the eye of a needle," said Isaac, laughing.

"God loves the Dutch more than the stingy English." Koorne drained his cup of gin, belched, and spooned up a tender piece of herring. "Look at a Puritan's face, and what do you see? Biliousness and choler. The saints look as if they have a bellyache. On the Sabbath, they should worm themselves!" He filled his cup again. "Unless God gave them a colicky face for the same reason He gave a rattle to the envenomed snake."

Koorne's talk of scrawny Christian nonconformists called to Isaac's mind the lard-caked frames of John Buxton and his dame. They, too, were zealous in the matter of meat and drink, and had no more appetite for the spiritual food provided by John Calvin, John Robinson, and John Winthrop than did the convivial Dutchman. But they had not Koorne's openhandedness or joie de vivre.

"I supped with a fat Puritan and his fatter wife."

"Then they are not the sour-pickled Puritans who bow their heads and pray to the music of their belly's winge and rumble."

"No, but they have the covetousness and bile of the skinniest Puritan in Massachusetts."

The Buxtons' table may have groaned under the weight of plenty, but most other boards in the Province of Massachusetts Bay were not so festive.

The winter had been harsh. The sap in the wood piled on the hearths had frozen, as had ink in the inkwells and bread on the Communion plates, which to gnaw made some think of the heart of Jesus—frozen and past caring for the chosen people of the New World. During Isaac's stay in Zion, the cornfields were sere and the rains reluctant. Famine has a fearsome prospect, which can make Aztecs of Christians willing to offer the savories of their neighbors in exchange for a good harvest.

"Eat some herring, you long-faced Bunyan!"

"You'll die like a rat fallen into a barrel of meal!"

"A barrel of beer, you mean!"

Koorne held a spoonful of herring under Isaac's nose.

"God damn you for a thick-skulled, fatheaded Dutchman! Get your fish out of my face!"

Laying down the spoon, Koorne took offense. "This morning I listened to you praise the sachem Massasoit. Now there was a glutton! He'd have died in an agony of constipation during one great feeding if Governor Bradford had not sent for a physic."

Isaac held his head in his hands.

"You look as if you could use a physic yourself," said Koorne, his resentment forgotten.

"My eyes hurt."

"A seed of wild clary put into a sore eye does cleanse it."

Isaac suspected that the true cause of his distress lay beyond the skill of herbalist or leecher to correct. What its cause might be, he guessed, had to do with his transplantation to Old Salem. How many generations of herring separated the alewife that lay pickled on a plate in front of him and the fish he had served to Herman Melville during his last visit to the red farmhouse? What a gulf of time lay between the sprats with which Massasoit had fed the famished Pilgrims and those that Moby Dick would have eaten had it not been a figment of Melville's brain! The water Isaac and Herman had stirred into their whiskeys had been a vein of Arctic ice in 1692. The atoms of air they breathed in the tobacco-fumed sitting room in Lenox had been excited by winds prevailing in the summer of the witches. The strain of so great a variance in time must take its toll. Isaac had become a divided man, who could not ascertain the honesty of the ghost he had come to chastise. He could search the weight of pages in *The English Physitian* and not find a single remedy for doubt.

"'The light of the body is the eye: if therefore thine eye be single, thy whole body shall be full of light. But if thine eye be evil, thy whole body shall be full of darkness. If therefore the light that is in thee be darkness, how great is that darkness!'"

"You surprise me, Pieter!"

"Even a thick-skulled Dutchman who likes his pipe and tipple may, now and again, read the Scriptures, especially at sea, where time is slow and danger quick to rear. Fear is an excellent tinder for religious fervor."

As much as any New Englander of 1692, Isaac feared the Wabanaki, their French allies, and the Canadian wild men, the *coureurs de bois,* presently at war with the English fifty miles north of Salem. Seventeen years earlier, the Wampanoag, Nipmuc, and Narragansett, led by Metacomet, had scorched more than half of the English settlements and murdered some eight hundred souls among the Christian population. Isaac's fear—the more it grew in him—made him less inclined to interfere in the spiritual authority and civil government of 1692 Salem. His scalp was not his own, as it had been in 1851 Lenox. A savage might claim it.

"Care for a bowl of suet pudding?" the Dutchman asked.

"Thank you, no."

Isaac had been born in the nineteenth century, had attended Bowdoin College, ascended in a balloon, sent a message by telegraph from Boston to New York, and traveled by steam train to San Francisco, a city unimaginable in its vitality and bustle, at the opposite end of the continent, whose immensity, marvels, and wealth none in the colonies could have foreseen. His mind had been shaped by a knowledge of his nation's history, which, in 1692, could hardly be said to have begun. Isaac's thoughts were modern, John Hathorne's medieval. Doubt kept Isaac on the boil; dogma kept his ancestor sullen and assured. The age was blind to other points of view. Celebrated, even adored, in the nineteenth century, Emerson would have been shunned, examined, exiled, or hanged in the seventeenth.

Who am I to censure someone who lacks the advantage of a fortunate birth in a time when science is erasing the shadows of obscurity and lighting the streets of great cities? Isaac asked himself. Old Salem's streets at night are dark indeed! Still darker is the forest. Is it unimaginable that a black hog, which is a witch's familiar, would be loose in it? Is it inconceivable that women would dance in the night woods and, by the heat of lust engendered in their loins, summon the Black Man?

Even so, what justification could there be for enchaining and imprisoning a four-year-old girl or hanging a septuagenarian midwife and a contentious scold who liked to wear a red bodice and had let her pigs stray into the Ship Tavern's yard?

And yet John Barton, a court-appointed surgeon, did discover a witch's teat on Bridget Bishop, in the hidden place between her "pudendum and Anus." Moreover, John Bly swore that his son had found poppets stuffed with black swine bristles in her cellar wall, which Bridget had hired them to remove. Goody Lacey had cried, "Oh, mother! We have forsaken Jesus Christ and the devil hath got hold of us!" And little Dorcas Good had left her tooth marks on Annie Putnam for all to see at Ingersoll's ordinary. Are facts like these not sufficient to prove that demons are busy in New England?

Are you still unconvinced, Isaac Page? Do you need more proof of witchcraft?

The Herrick girl from Beverly, who had cried out against the Reverend Hale's goodwife, recanted after the apparition of Mary Easty told her that it was the Devil in disguise and not Sarah Hale who had been tormenting her. The girl's retraction proved that Satan could take the form of innocent persons when he went abroad. (John Hale signed death warrants for seventy-two of them.) Didn't Samuel Wardwell, self-proclaimed fortune-teller of Andover, Margaret Jacobs, and, for a time, Mary Warren herself, whose testimony had undone so many, repent of their accusations?

No one denied the existence of Satan. In 1706, the grown-up Annie Putnam, the most vociferous of the young accusers, admitted that she had been deceived by "a great delusion of Satan." All that desolation had been the Devil's fault and not her own.

"The dreadful business couldn't have been a delusion! God would never have allowed the ministers and the magistrates to be in such grave error!" Isaac had spoken aloud.

Koorne looked up from his pudding. "What's that you say?"

"I was arguing with myself."

"You'll find no argument in me!" The Dutchman returned to his dessert, and Isaac to his thoughts, which his mind had been turning on its lathe into more and more desperate fancies.

I'm a modern man born to an age of science. But if

I were to peer down the barrel of van Leeuwenhoek's microscope and see, amid the infusoria and animalcules, Satan's face leering up at me—what then?

VII

ne afternoon as Isaac was walking the island's circuit, keeping the water in view because of the pleasure it gave him, he happened on a young man squatting beside a square-rigged boat, some fourteen or sixteen feet in length from its stem to a broad stern affixed with a rudder. He looked as Alexander may have the moment before he drew his sword and cut the Gordian knot. In other words, reader, the stranger gave every appearance of being perplexed and provoked.

"What be your trouble, friend?" Isaac had taken him to be a white man, but as he drew near, he saw that he was an Indian dressed like an English laborer.

"The skeg!" He pointed to a triangular piece of wood near the aft end of the keel.

"Sea worms have made a meal of it," said Isaac. "I can make a new one. My tools are at Pieter Koorne's, where I board."

"I know him," said the Indian. "I've brought him soft-shell crabs." He picked up a sack by the neck. The coarse cloth bulged and leaked water. "He has an appetite for them."

"He has an appetite for most things and a belly large enough to accommodate them," said Isaac. All in all, he liked the Dutchman and had meant the remark kindly.

"I could name you some well-nourished Salem folk who love their victuals overmuch, though gluttony is a sin with them."

"Their consciences have no teeth if the sin is toothsome!" retorted Isaac scornfully.

"You're not one of the high-minded sort, I think."

"I'd sooner stand with the condemned than with their self-righteous accusers." Once again, Isaac had spoken rashly to a stranger.

The Indian looked over Isaac's shoulder, as if he feared to see the sheriff ready to seize the apostate and show him the amenities of the jailhouse. (Wags claimed that Hell would be an improvement on Arnold's jail in summertime and worth the sins of admission to escape a New England winter. God's eternal absence could be more easily endured than the misery of biting flies or sleet borne by a nor'easter.)

"What's your name?" asked Isaac.

"Joseph Quapish, of the Naumkeag people."

"Are you a Praying Indian?"

Joseph spat in contempt either for Christian Indians or for the New Englanders who had forced the survivors of King Philip's War to choose a life of enslavement in Bermuda or one of conversion in a Massachusetts prayer town. Most preferred to sing psalms in common measure than to cut sugarcane in an infernal climate and die of fever. The Naumkeag people had already been cut down by plague in 1617 and smallpox in 1633—gifts of European adventurers. The survivors had been poised on the brink of extinction even before John Winthrop's fleet landed at Boston and discovered "the Lord's waste" waiting for Christians to claim, divide, sell, rent, and squabble over.

"I don't pray to your God, though I have to pretend to be a Christian now that Christ is no longer a lamb. I spend as much time away from Aquinnah and its congregation of righteous red men as I can." Joseph laughed scornfully. "An Indian dressed in a buckled hat, broadcloth coat, and britches worn out at the knees from kneeling is a pathetic sight. It pains me to see my father so."

"Do you miss him?" asked Isaac, remembering suddenly his own faraway family.

"I spend the winter at Aquinnah, the prayer town where my parents repent of the sin of having been born savage and eat the body of Christ. Six days, my father plies the salt maker's trade, and on the Sabbath, he puts on a tall hat, walks up and down the street, and pretends he doesn't hear the English boys laughing at him."

"You speak well."

"For an Indian, you mean." Isaac made no reply. "I was taught by Mistress Deliverance Bagley, who took it upon herself to civilize the Praying Indians of Aquinnah. She'd been one of Anne Hutchinson's flock."

"Your boat needs caulking," observed Isaac, tired of the eternal wrangle over piety.

"You seem to know your business."

"I was apprenticed to Caleb Grimes."

"I know him; he's a good man."

"Aye."

Joseph's boat was named *Pequot,* meaning "destroyers of men." Most of the Pequot had been themselves destroyed by the English and their Narragansett and Mohegan allies during the Mystic Massacre, of 1637, when their village was set alight. The fire was so hot that the Pequots' bowstrings burned like candle wicks. (The Indian word would descend through the generations that followed the carnage to become *Pequod*, a corruption of the original word that Melville gave to Captain Ahab's whaling ship.)

"Shall we get my tools?"

The two men walked in silence, as people do for whom conversation can be burdensome.

"Hallo, you dirty Indian!" shouted Koorne on seeing Joseph.

"Hallo, you great tub of lard!"

Koorne got up noisily from the settle. He went to greet his friend, with the rolling gait of a fat man or a seafaring one. Sniffing Joseph as Isaac had seen him do a plate of oysters, he said, "You smell ripe."

"And you stink of muskrat!"

"You make me hungry!"

"I've a present for you," said Joseph, handing Koorne the damp sack.

He peered inside and smacked his lips. "Ah, there's nothing so delectable as soft crabs fried in brown butter!" He poured three cups of Hollands and toasted Joseph: "*Gezondheid!*"

Isaac left the tavern and returned, shortly, with his tools and timber from the woodshed. Joseph was toasting the Dutchman's health in what Isaac supposed was Naumkeag. A comedy ensued as the two men praised each other fulsomely in their respective languages.

"Come to supper!" called Koorne as Isaac and Joseph were leaving.

"I can get a better price for my crabs in Salem Town, but I don't like dealing with the elders," explained Joseph as they walked back to Smith Pool, where the sailboat was beached. "If I had my way, I wouldn't go near the place. These are mad times, Isaac, and the English fear 'savages' as much as they do their white witches."

"Does John Hathorne buy them for his table?"

"He does. But I'm told he picks at them, as if the shells were stuffed with the tender flesh of Jesus."

"What do you think of the magistrate?" asked Isaac cunningly.

"He is a man eating himself alive."

Isaac did not know what to make of the observation.

Noting Isaac's puzzlement, Joseph explained, "Hathorne is a true Puritan, and Puritans are hungry for the next world. They gnaw on their own hearts, hoping to please God. The pious ones have no flesh on their bones, and the hypocrites think to prove their good standing with the Lord by the flesh they carry."

By Smith Pool, Isaac faired a board to the shape of

the *Pequot*'s ruined skeg. He also strengthened a bracing timber by the mast. He sent Joseph to gather moss to caulk her seams, having no oakum to hand.

"An abandoned cooperage at Juniper Point has plenty of pitch we can use to coat her seams," said Isaac. "The moss will keep her dry while we sail around the island."

"Are you going, too?"

"I've nothing else to do," replied Isaac, who had once again been swept up in an outbound tide leading to forgetfulness. He put the caulking iron and mallet in his satchel.

"It'll be dark soon," said Joseph. "We can leave in the morning."

"Will we try the Dutchman's crabs in brown butter?"

Joseph nodded, and they walked to De Zeeslang as the last of the long day's eastern light drained from the Atlantic.

VIII

At Juniper Point, Isaac and Joseph boiled pine resin in an iron kettle. The abandonment of the cooperage had incited speculation among the islanders. A faction of gossips, who wore leather doublets and breeches (not skirts and bodices), believed that Enoch Rhodes, owner of the works, had been murdered by Naumkeag Indians; a second faction argued that he had been arrested by the Puritans and taken to Boston jail. Those with no opinion had lost their tongues to the chief magistrate Death.

Joseph painted the seams with pitch. Finding needle and thread, Isaac mended the sail by the clew. The *Pequot* was once more seaworthy. They searched the cooperage and the house for anything left behind that might be useful to them. In the kitchen, Joseph found a letter inside an ivory casket.

> Whosoever shall find this letter, know ye that I have Wickedly & Feloniously practiced Detestable Arts called Witchcraft & Sorcery, within the Township of Salem, upon & against Magistrates Corwin & Hathorne. Several times, in the Day & Night, I Hurt, Tortured, Afflicted, Pined, Consumed, & Wasted them. Whosoever seeks me will not find me, no matter where they search, for I have gone to the Devil. Know ye, also, that I have set a Curse upon this House & the Generations of Men who may desire to inhabit it. They shall be torn Limb from Limb, their Bowels roasted & fed to the swine, & their Eyeballs nailed to the lintel until ravens pick them clean. For this Dire Curse, Satan is my guarantor.
>
> Enoch Louis Rhodes, Age 52
> Juniper Pt.
> 14th of May, in the Year of
> (I will not say "Our Lord") 1692

"You've been to John Hathorne's house," said Isaac, clearly disturbed by the letter.

"I have," responded Joseph, seemingly unmoved by Rhodes's confession and curse.

"Did he seem hurt, tortured, afflicted, pined, consumed, and wasted?"

"I told you, he looked like a man eating himself alive." He fell silent a moment and then went on to say, "He's consumed by faith and despair. Unless it be by worms such as those that ate my skeg."

Faith and despair are in feverish opposition within a human heart, which only death can reconcile. The struggle for supremacy can eat a person alive—even a man like John Hathorne. Perhaps the contest waged within his gaunt ancestor was Isaac's inheritance, which had made him melancholy.

"Do you believe in sorcery?" asked Isaac. He had spoken with an odd intensity, as if he thought that Joseph, being of a savage nature, might be closer to the truth of such dark matters.

"I believe there is evil in the world and there be those who wish it on another. They might as well be called 'witches' as anything else."

Just then a third man entered the room. "Who are you men?" he demanded. "What is your business here?" Large and well knit, he was not to be denied a civil answer.

"We heard the place was deserted," replied Isaac. "We needed pitch to caulk the boat."

"You won't find it in the kitchen!"

Isaac glanced at a ragged curtain hanging at a dirty window overlooking an overgrown garden where a dozen pear and apple trees stooped, their leaves sickened and bark scabbed; at the kitchen's plastered wall, grimed by the soot of a hearth where not so much as cold ash gave evidence of former warmth; and at the barren table, where conviviality seemed never to have been.

The man ripped the letter from Joseph's hands. "You'd no right to open it!"

"It's addressed to 'Whosoever shall find this letter.' We found it," said Joseph evenly. "We opened it."

The man appeared ready to strike him.

Isaac spoke quickly. "We're sorry for our trespass. We heard that no one lived here."

"Heard from whom? The loafers at the Dutchman's alehouse, I'd hazard to say."

Isaac affirmed the man's guess with a nod of his head.

"A shiftless rabble! You and this Indian are likely no better. I suppose you came to find doubloons buried underneath the floor? More than once I've wanted to burn the fat Dutchman's place to the ground and see him roasted in his own lard."

Isaac noticed a blur of movement—a flirt of light like the underside of a gull's wing as it lifts toward the sun. Joseph had leaped on the man, and before Isaac knew it, he held a knife at his throat.

"Have a care, you bloody Indian! You'll cut me!"

"Joseph!" I admonished him.

"The 'fat Dutchman' is my friend!"

"Your pot companion!" sneered the other. "Now take your knife away, Indian!"

"Keep still, or my hand could slip," said Joseph softly.

Fascinated, Isaac watched the scene unfold. He'd had no experience of gutting a fish or dressing a stag whose blood was still hot, much less of cutting a man's throat, and none at all of men who flung themselves furiously at each other. He might have been an ancient Roman sitting drunk with bloodlust in the Colosseum while two gladiators fought to the death. Violence has a strange power to enthrall and becalm. Some men love it as they do the pipe, the dram, or to lie beneath a lady's skirts.

Joseph put away his knife and indicated, with a nod and a syllable, which might have been savage, that the other man should sit. They regarded each other for a time made audible by the breath each drew, according to his mind's upheaval. Joseph looked at Isaac as if to say, I've said enough; now it's for you to speak.

Unsure of the tone he ought to take, Isaac began in conciliation and ended in defiance. "We've apologized and hope you'll make no more of it. We did not come to loot, only for resin. We looked inside the house, as anyone would who is capable of curiosity. We borrowed a needle and some thread—the tools and wood are mine—and would have shortly been on our way if you had not abused us!"

The man looked calmly at Isaac. "I could forgive your trespass and the theft of a little thread—"

"We did not steal it!"

"The thread was not yours to take. I would not have begrudged you it and the needle or the resin.

My brother has no more use for them. I'm perplexed, however, by your prying into his cupboards and drawers. What did you hope to find in that casket? Queen Isabella's jewels?"

The man's rebuff had been honest and correct.

"You say this is your brother's house?" asked Joseph after the silence had grown loud enough to hear a fly's last agony as it surrendered its tiny life to the sticky jam left on a spoon.

"Aye, it belongs to Enoch Rhodes—he who wrote this!" he replied fiercely, clutching the letter, as if he intended to hand up a true bill and indictment against God Himself.

"What became of him?"

"I took him to where magistrates and constables cannot find him." He shook the letter, as though to curse Heaven with its contents. "Did you read it?"

"We did," replied Joseph quietly. Rhodes gazed at the Indian's weather-beaten, somehow injured face, and his own expression softened.

"Then you know my brother is mad. For a man or a woman to be mad in Massachusetts is to be a witch. The magistrates and ministers make no distinction. Whether Enoch's wits were turned by Satan or some distemper of the brain, it matters not at all to them. I don't want to see him tied feet to neck till the blood runs out his nose, only to be hanged."

"How came he so?" asked Isaac.

"Who can say what drives one person mad, another to put his hand to an evil purpose, yet another to make a career as hangman? Juniper Point is not far from Salem Town, and if madness be contagious like the pox, Enoch was liable to the catching of it. He was a sensitive, fanciful boy. Later, he studied theology at Harvard and, in the summer, helped Father make barrels and casks. Enoch used to say that he could see into a human heart. Who can see such a thing and not go mad? He should not have gone into theology—it bedeviled him, and his mind fell to pieces. He heard so much talk about witches that he came to believe himself one. It would've been better for him had he thought himself afflicted and behagged, but Providence is sometimes perverse. In his distempered mind, Enoch became a wizard who sent his specter to the magistrates, especially Corwin and Hathorne, who are the worst of them. My brother became a sorcerer to destroy them because, as he said, 'Evil cannot be defeated by goodness.'"

"I should like to meet your brother," said Isaac.

Rhodes turned to Joseph, who was staring out the window. "And you, do you want to meet him also?"

Joseph nodded, his eyes fixed on the sickly trees outside.

The man considered a moment and then said, "I'll take you if you will lie down in the hold."

"You don't trust us," said Joseph.

"You're right not to," said Isaac. "To trust is to put yourself in another's hands, which may close around your throat or open and drop you into your grave." He cupped his palms and opened them. Rhodes glanced at the floor, as though Isaac had let something fall. "We are all sinners in the hands of an angry God."

"Will you lie belowdecks like two slaves during the Middle Passage?" asked Rhodes, scowling.

"Aye," replied Isaac.

"And you, Indian?"

Grunting, Joseph acquiesced.

"What name has she?" asked Isaac.

"*Desire*, though I dare not paint the word on her stern, since human joy is outlawed in the province."

Much later, when Isaac was again himself, he read in Winthrop's journal that the Salem ship that had carried a cargo of Indians defeated in the Pequot War to sell in Bermuda returned with "salt, cotton, tobacco and negroes" in her hold. The ship was named *Desire.*

IX

saac and Joseph stretched out beneath the shallop's planked deck, where fish would gasp their last breath on the way to the gutting board and drying rack. Isaac could feel the sea beat against the hull as the boat tacked. Rhodes was at pains to conceal his course to what turned out to be Tinker's Island. Named for the abundance of tinker mackerel running close to shore, the island lay two leagues southeast of Juniper Point. Lulled by the water's lapping against the hull, Isaac fell to dreaming.

He was in his rowboat, *Pond Lily,* on the Concord River, not far from Egg Rock, where Henry Thoreau and Waldo Emerson sat with their backs to the water. Waldo was declaiming, "The good, by affinity, seek the good; the vile, by affinity, the vile. Thus of their own volition, souls proceed into Heaven, into Hell."

Seemingly beside the point, Thoreau said, "I dislike lawful assemblies more than I do hecklers and troublemakers; the first makes empty and vainglorious speeches, which the second rightly interrupts."

"That smacks of anarchy!" chided Emerson.

"The first smack on the backside sets the infant squalling in protest and revolt," retorted Thoreau with his customary bite. "The best human beings don't let up until the undertaker sews their mouths shut."

The two men philosophized awhile, until they were surprised by the abrupt appearance of Isaac stepping ashore.

"Why, Isaac!" exclaimed Emerson. "We heard you were dead."

"I was in Salem, working for the revenue service."

"A plum appointment!" said Emerson with his customary enthusiasm.

"Isaac, you were nothing but a highfalutin tax collector!" said Thoreau contemptuously.

"How do you find the afterlife?" asked Emerson.

"I tell you, I'm not dead! I'm in the Province of Massachusetts Bay!"

"That is where all the trouble began," said Emerson, swiveling his head like an owl.

"Do you think that it was some evil in my nature

that took me to Salem and not, as I had supposed, a pair of my ancestor's spectacles?"

"We are all carried onward by Fate," said Emerson. "This fact does not relieve us of the obligation to choose how we are to live our lives. There is little we can do for one another."

"Did you see your great-great-grandfather?" asked Thoreau slyly as he coiled the beard growing at his throat around his finger.

"I—"

The shallop knocked against a mooring, and Isaac awoke.

"I hope you were not incommoded," said Rhodes, whose Christian name was Matthew. He had coved *Desire* on the small island's windward side and thrown open the hatch. To leeward, Marblehead would have been visible in the wavering distance. Matthew watched his two passengers squint in the sudden glare. Lending each a hand, he tugged them from the hold. He asked Joseph whether he had an inkling of where they were.

"It might be Misery Island for the stink in my nostrils and the stiffness in my bones."

"It might be," replied Matthew craftily. "Whatever it be called, there is none here but my brother and us. He gathered the things he had taken from the house—clothing, a pair of shoes, a few books, an iron skillet, and a large pot. "The island belonged to my father. Now it belongs to me, who also hopes to lie here, unless the steeple hats put me in their burying ground and confiscate my property—or impress me as a sailor when they decide to make war on Rome."

The three men settled into a dory lashed to the mooring. Joseph slipped the line, and he and Isaac rowed ashore. Matthew sat in the bow, holding the pot on his lap. He resembled the Budai, vulgarly known as the "Laughing Buddha." Isaac had admired a small bronze of the monk at Thoreau's cabin, a gift from Emerson. Tinker's Island was desolate, except for a seal lying on its belly atop a granite outcropping exposed by the retreating tide, and an ugly seabird squat against the water-blackened sand. The sound the boat made as it beached reminded Isaac of the day he had met Hannah Smyth, when she poured dried corn into a trough, amid the pecking chickens.

"How do you live?" asked Joseph as they walked deeper into the pinewoods. He had put the question simply, and Matthew took no offense.

"I catch mackerel, cod, and striped bass, dry, salt, and exchange them for rice, molasses, sugar, whale oil, brandy, cloth, fruit, and Dutch tobacco with Virginia traders whose merchant ships stop here on the way to Portsmouth. I have a kitchen garden, and all the wood, salt, and fresh water we need. I've said good riddance to the world and would gladly strike the spark to send it to blazes."

They walked some minutes in silence before Matthew took up the thread of recollection.

"I was a schoolmaster at Wenham and, summers, caught blackfish to sell for their oil till I had my fill of the tablets of the law as handed down from God to Calvin, Cromwell, Winthrop, Mather, and John Hathorne! What a sour, misery-loving wolfish pack of Christians they be!"

Isaac recalled a fragment of his dream belowdecks—a gnomic exchange between Thoreau and Emerson:

"History has judged them."

"What is history if not the spectral evidence of the past?"

"Waldo, you think too much."

"A man cannot think too much, although too often he thinks too little."

"Too much of it can make a Hamlet of a man!" Henry had cracked his knuckles. "What would happen to my bean rows if they were left to the dithering prince of Denmark to weed and hoe?"

X

our house is well hidden," said Joseph.

"Father traded in liquor and had no use for the Crown's 'hog reeve.'"

"Massachusetts men will throw tea into Boston Harbor rather than pay the king's tax on it," remarked Isaac imprudently.

"You mistake your tenses—unless you're the Devil's man and can foretell the future."

"You don't strike me as a pedant, Master Rhodes," said Isaac, in the hope of changing the subject.

"Grammar is a bulwark against confusion in men's

minds and in their government," said Matthew, who finished his assertion in a sigh. "I *am* a pedant, if no longer a master of boys. Now I give instruction to the gulls, which mock me."

Nothing could be heard of the ocean seething at the island's edge or of the shorebirds silenced by human trespass and bickering. The three men entered a clearing, where a timber-framed house stood. The bays were wattled and daubed in the manner of the first rude houses built in New England. The place was gloomy, damp, and mossy. His eyes having pained him since leaving the hold of the shallop, Isaac strained to see a felicity of aspect in either the house or grounds that might recommend them as picturesque. (The storyteller's affliction persists even in a desert or a polar waste.)

The gray sky brightened abruptly. Having knelt to tie his boots, Joseph was struck by the sun's glance. His face and hands shone in a beam of light, which Jehovah might have flung earthward to mark some new prodigy of creation. Isaac cried out his astonishment at seeing Joseph so transfigured.

Joseph looked up from his boots to regard Isaac's face. "What be the matter?"

"You're shining, man!"

Matthew gave a bark of laughter. "It's fish scales that bedazzle you, Master Page!"

Joseph glanced at his palms and saw that they were shining. Absently, he cleaned them on the grass, which, in turn, sparkled as though sown with brilliants. Once again, dark clouds shuttered the sun, the ray of light withdrew, and the grass gave up its radiance.

"It was a pretty sight, and I don't blame you for thinking an angel had come among us," said Matthew, fingering a wen on his neck.

"Widow Bagley says that the Holy Spirit is inside every man, woman, and child," said Joseph, amused. "She'll be glad to know it shone in one of the least promising of her charges."

"'How art thou fallen from Heaven, O Lucifer, son of the morning!'" shouted the mad brother Rhodes, who appeared as unexpectedly as the light had done on the dull grass.

"Enoch, where have you been?"

"Cleaning my harquebus." He spoke to Joseph, who was still kneeling, his hands on a bootlace. "If He be inside each of us, how, then, can we damn anyone to His eternal absence? It would be to banish God from His own creation—a logical impossibility."

Isaac thought the case too clever by far to have been put by a madman. Recalling Dill's imposture, he grew wary. He had encountered much in New England that was not as it seemed.

With a smile as radiant as a lunatic's, Enoch went to Joseph and, with a regal movement of his hand, bid him arise. "I saw you through the window," he said, jerking his head toward the house. "I couldn't decide whether you were a fish pulled from the Sea of Galilee by Simon Peter or a dead carp washed up from the Nile after God had set His curse on the Egyptians." He paused and then went on with devilry in his voice: "Unless you be my lord Lucifer, the shining one."

Matthew introduced him grudgingly: "My brother, Enoch Rhodes."

"Even a dead fish will shine in the sun; it's a property of its scales, you see, and not its flesh, much less its state of grace. Thus do men put on the majesty of the law—even God's—though they be putrid and corrupt." Enoch's voice had a rough beauty. Isaac had not heard its like since Abraham Lincoln's stump speech for Zachary Taylor, in 1848. "I see that *you* have no scales." Enoch studied Isaac as intently as a boy does a dead bird lying on the grass.

"I do not," said time's castaway as he dredged up from his mind's abyss Polonius's words concerning Hamlet's fancies: "Though this be madness, yet there is method in't."

"Then you are an abomination!" thundered Enoch. "For God said, 'And all that have not fins and scales in the seas, and in the rivers, of all that move in the waters, and of any living thing which is in the waters, they shall be an abomination unto you.'"

"Joseph lay where the mackerel rub against the stem and scrape the scales from their backs," said Matthew, exasperated by his brother. "Isaac did not. Joseph, let's walk to the inlet, where you can wash your face while I see if there are any eels in the ox head. Abomination they may be, but I do dearly love the flesh of an eel!"

"It is a creeping thing, Matthew, and defiles the man who eats it."

"And you are an ass, Enoch!" snarled his brother. "You may not eat of an ass, for so it is written!"

Matthew and Joseph walked toward the inlet. Enoch led Isaac into the house.

—∿∿∿∿∿—

"I read your confession," said Isaac, sitting in the chair offered by his host, who was not, Isaac decided, insane.

He laughed. "It was a merry prank I hoped to play on them who would seize my house and goods. I dare say, none in Salem cares to live in a house accursed by its infamous owner, for whom Lucifer himself stands as guarantor."

"The casket, I think, is a rare thing. How came you by it?"

"An uncle gave it to me. When a young man, he'd been in the East India Company. The curse I got from Midiates, who got it from a curse tablet inscribed in ancient Greek. I knew the ivory box would attract the avaricious. The curse inside would prevent the superstitious from stealing it."

"Enoch, why do you pretend to be mad?" He had once asked Dill a similar question.

"We are all mad who live in these times. I was one of God's ministers. I had a small church in Beverly and preached on the Sabbath until the autocrats of holiness charged me with heresy."

"What heresy?"

"You're right to ask, since there be many, and mine

is as detestable as the rest in the eyes of the Puritan ministers. Like them, I preached that Christ had made a covenant with the Father: He let Himself be betrayed, scourged, and nailed to a cross to atone for the disobedience in Eden. Unlike them, I taught that He died for everyone and not only for the few elected to salvation before they were born. As the Hollander Jacobus Arminius had done, I rejected the theology of man's entire depravity and unconditional election. Even if we sinned in Adam, God gives us all sufficient grace for faith. Like Anne Hutchinson, I believe we can enjoy direct revelations from God, apart from Holy Scripture and without the ministers' intercession. My heterodoxy makes me a danger to them and an affront to the Almighty, who might send His all-devouring wrath against His chosen people in Massachusetts to punish them for my errors."

Enoch took a sharpened quill from his desk, as though he intended to write—what? His confession? A jeremiad? Theses that he would nail to the meetinghouse door? But it was only to rid a fingernail of a speck of dirt. "Men suffer most when heresy and treason are accounted one and the same."

In the colony's first decade, Anne Hutchinson and Roger Williams had taught that one could earn life everlasting by acknowledging God's sovereignty, the authority of the Scriptures, and Christ's redemption of our kind's sinful nature. She preached that man, in utter helplessness, was led toward salvation by the Holy Spirit, which God placed within each person by the grace of His son's death and Resurrection. In her opinion, the Puritans had fallen into error by placing the Covenant of Works above that of Grace. She avowed that an outward show of godliness was no guarantee of good standing with God for even a covenanted church member.

"Anne Hutchinson and Roger Williams shook their fingers and bit their thumbs at Winthrop and the ministers of the Bay," said Enoch. "If not stopped, they would cause what Massachusetts feared worse than savages—a schism. Divisiveness ends in bloodshed when men's faith is rabid. God is no good reason to go to war against one's neighbors. Men, not He, are responsible for the evil that befalls them."

The colony's churches were insufficiently Calvinist for Roger Williams, who wished to purify the Puritans of their lingering attachment to England and its idolatrous church. Had John Winthrop and the General Court not banished him from the Bay Colony, he would have held its congregations to an impossible standard of holiness. The many who flaunted their sanctity were, for Williams, deluded or hypocritical. (In his zealotry, he declared that Quakers should be scourged for having "set up a false Christ.") He came to realize how preposterous his standards were when he could find no one in Plymouth Colony—the place of his church in exile—saintly enough to share in the body and blood of Christ, save his wife, and her only grudgingly. In time—that bitter solvent—he would embrace "the dung heap," as

Winthrop put it, and tolerate other faiths, no matter how repugnant they seemed to him.

Faith, like liquor, taken at full strength can addle the brain and bring whole nations to grief.

"I believe that children are not born desolated and depraved!" said Enoch fervently. "It's a sweet thing to contemplate, Isaac—too sweet for the sour faces of the ministers and magistrates of Salem, who call this misstep or that misdeed a 'sin,' when God Himself has not forbidden it in Scriptures. They would hang us for our thoughts!"

Abruptly, he rose from his chair and went to a sideboard. "I've been a thoughtless host. Will you take strong water or beer?"

"Some beer, thank you."

Enoch poured two tankards of beer from a handsome Rhenish jug.

"In Beverly, I preached a toothless covenant made between God and His creatures, which does not require them to gnaw their own vitals. We needn't crucify ourselves or one another for His love. In fine, I taught that no one is predestined for Heaven or for Hell; the afterlife will be as our acceptance or refusal of Christ's gift of redemption shapes it. Isaac, there be no visible saints or signs of God's saving grace legible to any living soul! We can't see the truth about ourselves, much less others. We are poor sinners, and the best of us—the godliest among us—are troubled by fear and uncertainty."

Seldom had Isaac heard the matter so nicely argued.

"And they call this 'heresy'!" he said, his voice shaken by indignation.

"It's the string of a commonplace discord too frequently harped upon since the beginning of our vexatious relations with the Almighty," said Enoch, wiping foam from his bearded lips.

"A hymn for martyrs."

"I haven't the courage of Saint Catherine, Anne Hutchinson, or Roger Williams. I was glad to let my brother hide me. Why, the magistrates will hang George Burroughs, formerly the minister of Salem Village, because he can lift a matchlock by a finger inserted in the barrel and a barrel of molasses with only his two good arms—feats of strength, it is said, that are impossible without the Devil's assistance for a small man like him! It seems that only weak and puny men are without sin."

"And if you are brought before the magistrates?"

"Who can say whether or not I'll renounce my convictions and henceforth polish a bench with my backside in Salem Meetinghouse?"

When had Isaac and Constance last sat together in the familiar pew, beneath the hymn board, listening to the minister raise subjects no more controversial than the next church social or the state of the church's drains? Isaac wondered at how remote that Sunday morning was from the house on Tinker's Island—*was* and, at the same time, *will be*! He smiled to think what tense schoolmaster Matthew Rhodes would propose for such an absurd chronology.

"I'm fortunate to have no wife to care for," said Enoch. A deep sigh belied his words.

Constance, said Isaac to himself, and then he repeated her name aloud with a tenderness that begged the other man to ask, "Who is Constance?"

"My goodwife."

"Ah! Is she safe?"

"She is far from *this*." His glance took in the simple furnishings, the brass and pewter plates and cups standing in a rack nailed to the plastered wall, a fowling piece, a tin cartouche box, a linen chest, a press, a churn, a scale, a wheel—the movable property of a householder who was better off than the general but not nearly so well-off as a Salem merchant or magistrate. Isaac's gaze had taken in the Rhodes brothers' few things, but the word *this* comprehended all of New England in the second year of the final decade of the seventeenth century. "She is safe at home."

"God grant she remain so," said Enoch.

Once again, Isaac nearly yielded to the desire to have done with his fruitless sojourn in an alien civilization, which he could entirely despise if only his mind's wavering would end. He longed to palm the silver coin until he could feel it sear his flesh with the recollected heat of its minting and recall him to Lenox and Constance. He yearned to take her in his arms. Never more would he punish her with his melancholy. Henceforth he would write sunny tales of piazzas in Rome and not spend another brooding thought on John Hathorne or his execrable times.

Isaac noticed an hourglass on Enoch's sideboard, standing next to the bottle of strong water, which, in a later age, he would call brandy. There is, he told himself, a moment so brief that it is measured by the time it takes for one grain of sand to pass through the hourglass's neck. Although impossible to detect it, there must be an instant when the number of grains below and above the neck are equal, when the past and future have reached an equilibrium and time is in abeyance. At that instant—too brief to be called one, too improbable even to be called a rarity—the doorway—for so it can be imagined—stands open. What if I'm here on Tinker's Island by virtue of time's open doorway and not that of Hathorne's spectacles? A grain of sand having fallen into the glass's bottom half and the equilibrium at an end, what if the doorway closed, never to be opened in my lifetime? Squeeze the Liberty dollar as hard as I can, I can't ever go home. What then?

"You look tired and worn," said Enoch kindly, and Isaac thought that there could not be two more dissimilar brothers in New England than Enoch and Matthew Rhodes. He considered telling Enoch his own extraordinary tale and, by it, pull the thorn stuck in the tender flesh of his brain, his heart, or that undiscovered organ where guilt and sin are lodged. He stopped short of admitting to a journey as perilous as Hannibal's crossing the Alps, Cain's flight from Eden to the Land of Nod, or, to speak presumptuously, Christ's dire passage from the Mount of Olives to Calvary. Isaac knew that he was alone in the New

World of 1692 and sensed that he ought not relax his vigilance. It's a short walk to the gallows, he told himself, and for the first time in his exile, he felt at risk of the executioner's expertly knotted rope.

"Does your brother truly believe you're mad?" he asked his host.

"It gives him satisfaction to hear that I send my spirit out to torment the magistrates. Though no spirit of mine flies across the sound to kick Hathorne and Corwin in their pompous arses, I pray they will feel the scorch of my ire. Ill will can do as much harm as specters, when it be hot. Mine is piping. I tell you, Isaac, that there be many mad folks in Salem, whose brains are boiling in resentment."

Having his own cowardice in mind, Isaac said, "You do more than I."

"I've done nothing, except to leave a paper curse for tyrants to find. I should have nailed my theses and my challenge to the meetinghouse door! The intolerance of God's people in Massachusetts is a wonder to me, since they themselves were persecuted in the Old World."

"I've heard it said that John Hathorne is not necessarily an evil man, though he does evil things," said Isaac, canvassing still another person in the matter of his ancestor.

"Evil things are done by evil men. Or do you think, as *I* have heard said, that a kind of plague has turned men's wits against themselves and their neighbors? You might as well blame it on the flour with which they make their bread. To say that Goodwife Tomlin split her husband's skull with a felling ax because he complained his roast meat was raw or that the Reverend Cripps should be forgiven for beating his slave because his worry over other men's souls had made him irritable—these be feeble defenses, Isaac Page!"

"Some say the hostiles have made every man fear his neighbor," said Isaac doggedly, trying to justify the evil that men do—to salve his pricking conscience, which had been lately insisting that he carry out his purpose and return to the family he had all but forgotten.

"There will be those who blame the Indians until the day comes when there are no more Indians. Then they will turn against their negro slaves. Aye, New England *is* nervous about the 'savages.' In January, they burned York, Maine, until nothing but charred timber and scorched stones were left. Fifty Englishers were murdered, and another hundred taken into bondage. At Salmon Falls, the Indians roasted Christians on spits. In Cotton Mather's gaudy words, the attack was a 'diabolical satisfaction.' The Europeans have had enough satisfaction of their own, since our first trespass in the New World. The province also dreads the French, the Dutch, Parliament, the Act of Toleration, and King William, who may decide that Massachusetts is impudent for behaving in a manner 'repugnant to the laws of England,' which, in many ways, are more just than those of the city upon a hill. I detest the smug saint who beats his Bible and his wife with equal fervor."

Isaac had seen the same fierce glint in Enoch's eyes in those of evangelists in the 1830s, during the Second

Great Awakening in New England, as well as in Methodist camp meetings in the "burned-out districts" of New York after the fires of revivalism had swept through them.

"I don't doubt your sanity," said Isaac as he filled an earthenware cup with strong water poured from a squat green bottle. "But I do the wisdom of such an outspoken airing of belief to a stranger."

"Are you one of Hathorne's or Corwin's men? Are you a deputy, an officer of the court, or a witch hunter?"

To each, Isaac answered, "Nay."

"Then why must I be wise? New England is filled to the hawse pipe with such wisdom 'as makes cowards of us all.'"

"You know the play?"

"*Hamlet*? It's the book and gospel for those who prefer doubt to the overweening vanity of conviction."

"It teaches us to hesitate."

"I'd rather hesitate to imprison a child, hang a man or a woman, confiscate the person's property, and deny the survivors an inheritance. In this age of unshakable belief, hesitation is strength and not weakness. Who is Hamlet if not a man who cannot accept spectral evidence?"

Isaac grew quiet as he ran his finger around the rim of his cup.

"What brings you here, Isaac Page?"

Enoch's question broke the spell cast by Isaac's revolving finger. By "here," did Enoch mean Tinker's Island, or the New World of 1692?

"Curiosity," he replied evasively.

"About the letter in the ivory casket and its author."

"And what your brother had to say about you."

"Matthew means well, though he can be prickly."

Isaac helped himself to more brandy as Enoch continued: "During the 1640s, when the king's neck ought to have itched in anticipation of the ax, which, at the end of the decade, fell at the people's pleasure, the English Puritans held a majority in Parliament. No longer hunted and oppressed, the nonconformists ceased their exodus to New England: The Great Migration ended. With no new planters to buy their clapboards, cattle, corn, and fish, economic necessity obliged the colonists to sell Massachusetts cod to the Roman Catholics of Spain, whom they detested in principle. Dearth, it seems, can compel even saints to do business with the Devil."

"Your point being?"

Enoch shrugged. "The thought was in the air, and I plucked it."

Isaac put down his cup. He rubbed his eyes and moaned.

"What's the matter, Isaac?"

"My eyes—I can't see clearly."

"The fault of ardent spirits—or of a new thought," said Enoch slyly. "If the cause be ocular and not oracular, you'd be wise to visit the spectacle maker in Boston. I have a feeling that you're not wise, as men go."

"I have spectacles," said Isaac, remembering the pair he carried in his pocket. "But they aren't mine."

"Whose are they?"

"John Hathorne's." The cause of this remarkable imprudence could be set down to the pain in Isaac's eyes, which distracted him, or to the brandy, which was nauseating him.

"How came you by them?" asked Enoch, amazed.

"Fate," replied Isaac, and he would say no more.

Enoch opened his mouth—Isaac supposed that he meant to question him further—but he apparently decided to go no further into the matter. Enoch may have rejected the idea of witches, specters, and apparitions, but he accepted that of fate, which rules us even now, reader, in our own day.

"Let's see what abominations Matthew has caught for our supper," he said, rubbing his hands in anticipation.

The two left the house and walked toward the inlet. The ocean noise grew louder as the dense woods standing between them and the shore thinned. When they stood face-to-face with the Atlantic, waves came clashing on the shingle. Enoch and Isaac watched Matthew haul the remains of an ox head from the water and onto the gravel beach. Rags of pale gray flesh waved obscenely in the churning water, and—to Isaac's horror—black rivulets of eels poured from the mouth, neck, and eye sockets of the beast's ruined head. It might have belonged to Moloch, the Canaanites' god of child sacrifice. Isaac dredged up from the murky depths of his revolted mind a passage from *Paradise Lost.*

. . . *Moloch*, horrid king, besmear'd with blood
Of human sacrifice, and parents' tears;
Though, for the noise of drums and timbrels loud,
Their children's cries unheard that pass'd thro' fire
To his grim idol.

The eels squirmed madly, each naked body tracing the letter *s* against white and yellow pebbles, which hissed as though to give voice to beasts. Deftly, Matthew gathered them into a barrel partly filled with seaweed and saltwater. Joseph stood impassively, Enoch gazed on the scene benevolently, and Isaac retched. So violent was his upheaval, it could have raised the bloated corpses of those who had sailed from England in high hopes, only to drown, or dug from a dismal fen the ancient key that had locked the gates to paradise. He vomited, as if he would be rid of the last particle of humanity and henceforth be a stone. Isaac wondered at how plainly he could see the grisly, monstrous form of Moloch, whole and entire, while the other men remarked only on the eels.

"We shall dine royally!" crowed Matthew as he banged the barrel lid shut with the heel of his hand. To make amends for having insulted Pieter Koorne, he told Joseph, "When I take you and Isaac back to Jupiter Cove tomorrow, I'll give you a sack of eels to treat the Dutchman."

With a nod of his head, Joseph tersely acknowledged Matthew's appeasement.

"Father was taught to bait eels with the severed head of an ox by a man who'd lived in Friesland," said Enoch.

"A putrid carcass cannot fail to excite eels, which, for a time, are happy dwelling in corruption."

Isaac remembered the immaculate swans on Wilkins Pond and shuddered to picture them passing sedately above a controversy of serpents.

Matthew ran two stout hickory poles through two pairs of iron rings fastened below the barrel head and, taking hold of the end of a pole, as if it were a handle, he bid the others do the same. With a grunt, they lifted the heavy cask and carried it between them, like a sedan chair in which some Byzantine eunuch sat.

On a knoll above the inlet, Enoch stopped, and they put down the barrel. "Father wanted to be buried by the sea. We honored his wish and laid him to rest here." He knelt and poured the sandy ground onto his palm and watched it drain between his fingers. "Sadly, a prodigious storm unearthed the coffin and flushed it out to sea." Enoch stood and dusted his hands on his breeches. "May it please God to have sent him drifting as far as the Fortunate Islands."

Matthew said nothing, and the four men carried the barrel the rest of the way in silence. Isaac pictured the bones of old man Rhodes, damned by an inscrutable deity to sail, in an endless Middle Passage, inside his coffin ship—drawing no nearer to paradise than a honeybee shut up in a bottle does a field of wildflowers.

That night, Isaac dreamed that two men wearing cloaks carried him to a hill above the inlet and made him fast to iron rings hammered into a granite rock. Moloch walked from the ocean, eels streaming from his mouth, eye sockets, and nose. With his claws, he dug the eyes from Isaac's face and gave each to a disciple kneeling at his feet, who ate it. Between their teeth, the eyes crunched like stale Communion bread. Isaac shrieked.

Of a sudden, John Hathorne appeared. He released Isaac from the granite stocks and, putting an arm around his shoulder, comforted him. "What have they done to you, dear Isaac?"

"My eyes! They have taken my eyes, and I can't see!"

"You've only to put on my spectacles to see what you have glimpsed till now."

Isaac groped inside his doublet. "I cannot see to find them!"

Hathorne put his hand inside Isaac's doublet and brought forth a leather case. Removing the spectacles, he put them on Isaac. The magistrate's hands were shining, as if he had wiped them on the scales of Leviathan, of whom it is written in the Book of Job: "His scales are his pride, shut up together as with a close seal" and, also, "He maketh a path to shine after him," like a slick of blood.

"I see clearly!" cried Isaac, entranced as he had been earlier when he watched the eels whip themselves into a frenzy on the strand, the instant before he vomited.

"Tell me what you see," said Hathorne kindly, so that Isaac wept grateful tears.

"Moloch."

"What does he want?"

"For me to go to Salem and denounce the Rhodes brothers."

Hathorne patted Isaac's head affectionately, as if he were a child. "That is what you must do, then."

Isaac awoke. Shut up inside the dark chamber, the terror of his dream persisted. He felt as he had done on certain nights as a boy when he would awake with a dreadful jolt—half in, half out of a nightmare. Uncertain and afraid, he would hide beneath the bedclothes. There he would close his eyes and listen to the clock in the parlor tick amid the heavy silence. In the Rhodeses' second bedchamber, which he shared with Joseph, who'd slept through Moloch's and Hathorne's visitations, Isaac strained to hear something of the familiar world—a clock, a night bird, a rusty cicada, a sleepless fly. He'd like to hear a dog barking in the distance. When he was a boy sent to bed for the night, he loved to hear the barking of the ostler's bitch chained inside the stable. Now on a strange bed, in an unfamiliar darkness, Isaac began to shiver. *Not a dog!* he said to himself. *The Devil and his legion make familiars of dogs. My nerves couldn't stand to hear a dog in the night!*

His hearing became preternaturally acute, as is said to happen to compensate the blind for loss of sight. He heard a borer worm in the hornbeam tree outside the window, a beetle scraping its armor against the lath inside the plastered wall, a louse crawling through Joseph's hair. Isaac shivered a second time and would have prayed for morning to make haste, but his voice—even that which droned ceaselessly within his own mind—stammered.

How sharp the Devil's hearing must be that he can eavesdrop on secrets whispered by adulterers, on sins confessed fervently into the ears of priests, on the sighs of the forlorn, and the groans of those ready to sell themselves for meat when the body is famished or to bargain away their souls for love when the heart is starved!

Isaac awoke beneath a shadow lying across the bedclothes, cast by the hornbeam through the window. Joseph had dressed and gone downstairs. By the smell of ham frying in the skillet, Isaac guessed he was already at his meat. He put on his clothes, tied his hair sailor-fashion, and looked out the window. He could see the distant inlet shining above the tops of the black pines, though, on that windless morning, no sound of foaming wave or hissing sprawl reached his ears. He listened for the worm in the hornbeam, the beetle in the wall, but heard nothing. Instead, he was delighted by the song of a bird and the drone of an industrious wasp building a paper house beneath the eaves. He gazed at the thickly sown conifers and, in the clearing between the saltbox house and the woods, at a shed where Matthew Rhodes stored fishing gear, a brew house, and a half-buried stone outbuilding where he smoked his hams. The world was not in focus, and Isaac fretted that he might never see it clearly again, until he remembered what his ancestor had told him in his dream: "You've only to put on my spectacles to see what you have glimpsed till now."

They were on the dresser. He took them from their cracked leather case, unfolded their wire arms, and put them on. Never till that moment had Isaac known such clarity! His eyes roved the bedchamber and saw horsehair wound into a plaster wall, two warrior ants in mortal combat, a scratch on a heavy oak dresser, concealed by an embroidered cloth. Even more uncanny, Isaac saw, as a seer would have done, the *cause* of the scratch. In his mind's eye, he watched a woman, drab and plain, take a horseshoe nail from her apron pocket and—with pent-up fury and the bitterness of disappointment—scar the dresser top. Isaac knew for certain what a mentalist might pretend to know, that she was marking the face, its effigy, of him who one day would die in this house and, after being defiled by nature's equally solemn rage, go to sea in his coffin. Like the vengeful asp, a shadow flickered its tongue from beneath the bedstead. As it slipped into the room, Isaac saw the dead man's ghost and knew it was hunting for the wife who had poisoned him.

Aghast, Isaac tore the spectacles from his face, and the view clouded, as if by cataracts. What does it mean? he asked himself, trembling. Having no answer to give, he returned the glasses to their case, saying aloud, "Never did I know such clarity, save when I stood on the shingle and watched the eels slide from the ragged head!" He went downstairs to appease a hunger that lay outside the remedy of breakfast.

Enoch was buttering toasted bread when the pilgrim sat down to breakfast. He poured Isaac a cup of ale.

"Would you care for a hash of potatoes and ham?"

"Yes, thank you, Enoch."

"Did you sleep well?"

"I was troubled by a nightmare."

"Perhaps the eel didn't agree with you."

Isaac had not touched the eel. As he sat by the fire with a plate on his knees, the flensed and quartered flesh did, indeed, seem an abomination.

Eating his hash, Isaac felt the weight of the other man's gaze. "What, Enoch?" he asked peevishly.

"I'm sorry you're leaving us. There be much more I'd like to say to you."

Isaac laid down his knife and spoon and asked brusquely, "Such as?"

"Nothing more alarming than theology, Isaac, I promise you."

Isaac frowned. Of all things in that New World, theology was the most to be feared.

"You're right to make a face. Theology has many branches. Underneath some of them, mandrakes grow from the seed of hanged men. Women, too, are dropped from branches, but I can't guess what root or weed might be bred in the shadows of their skirts."

His appetite deserting him, Isaac set aside his plate.

"Isaac, I do beg your pardon. Religion and politics are unfit subjects at breakfast, when the stomach is impressionable." He laughed, and once again Isaac couldn't decide whether the other's mirth was innocent or perverse.

"My brother wants to be away with the tide. But hear me first, Isaac: Go wide of Salem. It's a noxious place! Whether the poison be distilled from the blasted hearts of our race or from the mephitic waters of Lake Avernus, whose vapor would choke birds to death that flew across its face, I cannot say. But mark this, friend: The Devil is only another point of view, contrary to the general. Stay well clear of Salem! One can't always hold his breath long enough to escape a stench. Forgive the lecture. The habits of a preacher—who, in happy days, was a student of the classics—are hard to break."

Avernus, entrance to the underworld. Yes, thought Isaac. So had Salem seemed when I walked out of the forest and into anno Domini 1692.

As they headed for the beach, Enoch asked, "What if Christ had not arisen from the dead after His three days' harrowing of Hell? What if Satan had triumphed and assumed His form and radiance? What would that make of our religion?"

Isaac gave no answer other than to kick a stone from his path. The two walked the rest of the way in silence.

The tide was high and full of noise. Seawater captured by an iron salt pan trembled in the early-morning light. Matthew and Joseph had brought the shallop close to shore. In two hours or so, Isaac would be on Winter Island. Enoch offered him his hand, which he churlishly refused. "Return to your own place!" he urged. "To breathe the foul air of Salem and to see as *they* do will drive you mad!"

What did he mean by "your own place"? asked Isaac, but only of himself.

He waded from the shingle to the boat. Joseph pulled him, dripping, over the gunwales.

"Stay clear of Salem folk!" shouted Enoch above the drumbeat of the luffing sail. "You may already have tarried too long to . . ." The rest of the caveat was lost to a freshening breeze, which stretched the canvas taut.

Watching Enoch dwindle to a dot onshore, Isaac was stricken by a pain behind his eyes, worse than before. He shut them, and after a moment's darkness veined by threads of light, he opened them on Salem Sound as the boat beat northeasterly from the island's windward side. Impulsively, he put on the spectacles, and the ache and uncertainty fell away, as though scales had, indeed, been covering his eyes. "But if thine eye be evil, thy whole body shall be full of darkness."

Through John Hathorne's spectacles, Isaac gazed on the distant shore of Tinker's Island. To his amazement, a giant was striding knee-deep in the water, as if in pursuit of him. The great beast stepped onto a sandbar and shook its brazen fist at Heaven, and by Heaven's trembling light, Isaac saw Moloch. The two other men saw nothing. Matthew was watching the sail, and Joseph was looking out to sea.

Though there be fury on the waves,
Beneath them there is none.
The awful spirits of the deep
Hold their communion there . . .

Looking at the girdling horizon, Isaac saw Scylla, Cetus, Poseidon, and Hydra—fabulous sea monsters, which had once decorated the ends of the world's oceans on ancient maps. Beasts, he now knew, were of the world as it truly was. Isaac laughed at his previous ignorance, and the remnants of his former consciousness dissolved as his mind fused with the universal. Moloch was raging in a stentorian voice, which mimicked the roaring surge, while mewing gulls flew up before him, as if Moby Dick were hurtling into their midst, lashing the water white with its flukes.

"The Devil is only another point of view!" What heresy! Enoch had honed his mind on the Devil's stone! Isaac comprehended, as he had not before, how dangerous was the theology of the Antinomians, which imagined the Holy Spirit dwelling within each human breast. What if it be not God's radiant person but Satan's shadow that sits in the plush chambers of the heart and whispers blandishments into men's ears? Without God's Word breathed onto the pages of His Book, we would certainly be deceived. Without the church's ministers and teachers, we would lose our way, like children walking amid the high corn. "Stay clear of Salem folk!" Ha! Isaac would denounce Enoch to the magistrates, and his brother, Matthew, also, for having hidden the apostate. He swore that two

Rhodes brothers would be added to the desolation of names before the week was out. In his thoughts, Isaac glorified the Lord's men, saying, "These have power to shut Heaven, that it rain not in the days of their prophecy: and have power over waters to turn them to blood, and to smite the earth with all plagues, as often as they desire."

Isaac's thoughts then turned to Merry Mount and the madness of Thomas Morton, who had styled himself Comus, cupbearer of Bacchus, and a Lord of Misrule, who had, as it were, opened a school for atheism and debauchery in New England. In Concord, Isaac had heard him lauded by Thoreau, when the Transcendentalist had made himself giddy with dancing and spruce beer. He believed that Morton had been unjustly persecuted by Bradford and the Pilgrims for his liberality and for being "a light in that dark world of dour Englishmen." Had Thoreau been nearby, Isaac would have dragged him before the magistrates and declared him Satan's tool.

From a dyer in Salem Village whose father had been a governor's assistant in Plymouth, Isaac had learned the truth about Thomas Morton: He had sold fowling pieces, muskets, pistols, powder, and shot to the Indians and instructed them in their use. He'd sold them molds with which to manufacture their own shot. Morton had done all this to purchase the means to nourish the drunkenness, gluttony, and licentiousness of his cohort. For this reason, Miles Standish and his men arrested him and took him to Plymouth, so that he could be sent to England and have his treason published. By his great cunning, Morton escaped punishment. Sinners, heretics, atheists, and practitioners of the black arts, regardless of their artfulness, will not escape me now that the scales have fallen from my eyes! avowed Isaac, besotted with self-righteousness.

Arriving at Juniper Point, Matthew dropped sail and docked at the abandoned cooperage. He embraced Joseph fraternally and nodded to Isaac—coldly, he thought.

Isaac glared. You'll regret your aloofness, as will many another secret sinner in our midst. Henceforth, I'll use my spectacles to unmask them. I'll burn them, as boys do ants beneath a magnifying glass!

"It shall be yours to penetrate, in every bosom, the deep mystery of sin, the fountain of all wicked arts, and which inexhaustibly supplies more evil impulses than human power—than my power at its utmost—can make manifest in deeds. . . ." How prophetic those words had been, which Isaac had given the dark figure in his tale "Young Goodman Brown" to speak!

I'll go to Salem Town and tell my great-great-grandfather that the Devil *is* abroad in the world, and I have seen him! declared Isaac, as if he were already standing before the magistrate.

"Remember to give the Dutchman his eels!" called Matthew, tossing the squirming sack onto the dock. The sail bellied, and the boat stood to for the southeast.

Isaac had cast out the beam from his eye.

XI

'm sailing to Aquinnah to visit my father. Why not go with me? You can talk religion with the widow Bagley."

"I've business in Salem," replied Isaac tartly.

"You'll be safer among the Praying Indians."

"I have business in Salem! I'll be obliged to you if you'll take me to Cat Cove."

His churlishness offended Joseph, who grunted his assent.

On the way to the cove, the two men kept a wary eye on each other—Isaac's behind the spectacles, which granted him a godlike omniscience. He looked into Joseph's heart and saw that it was savage. A stoical countenance hid the wildness and vice of a race of "wicked imps . . . like the Devil, their commander," as Captain Underhill had described the Pequots. By exterminating them, New England had done what was needed to save its people from "exquisite torments and most inhumane barbarities." Or should they have waited till the savages roasted their babes and ate them? demanded Isaac silently and furiously of Joseph. The heathen nations are joined with Satan in making war on the saints of God's earthly kingdom.

Joseph had turned his face to the water; his beardless lips were set in a grimace. Isaac recalled from memory's well words of John Winthrop vindicating the Puritans' settlement of New England: "For the natives, they are near all dead of the smallpox, so the Lord hath cleared our title to what we possess."

At Cat Cove, Joseph brought the boat close to shore. Isaac clambered over the gunwale. His feet slipped on slime-covered stones as he sought a foothold in the waist-deep water. An aphorism of Winthrop's rose to the surface of his agitated mind.

> When a man is to wade through a deepe water, there is required tallnesse, as well as Courage, and if he findes it past his depth, and God open a gapp another waye, he may take it.

Isaac would take the way that God had opened for him, which led to Salem Town and his great-great-grandfather, whom Isaac had defamed.

"My things!" he snarled. Hatred, as flammable as oil, had seeped into his soul.

Joseph took Isaac's satchel and pack and slung them onto the beach. He would have hit him in the face with the sack of eels had Isaac not jumped away in time. It lay moiling at his feet, endued with alien life.

"Go home and pray," shouted Isaac, "though you will never see the Lord's face—neither you nor your ridiculous steeple-hatted father!"

Joseph cursed him in his native tongue. Having put about sharply, the *Pequot* headed toward the South Channel and open sea.

Isaac stood, sopping, amid the saw grass. Drops of water glinted on the glass panes of his spectacles. A solitary gull laughed in mockery at God and His botched creation, which the devils in Salem were pledged to destroy. The warm, earthy smell of harvested salt hay, once so pleasing to Isaac, made him retch. Enraged, he cursed Joseph and rejoiced as the heavens smote him with a beam of light and set his boat ablaze.

Isaac had been too long in Salem. A better nature can be forgotten, and the rabble's cause taken up as one's own. He had put on another's spectacles, whose lenses were biased.

Isaac's stomach griped at the stink of a Spanish cigar. The Dutchman was eating and drinking lustily, his fat face flushed and sweating as it beamed good-naturedly on his laden table, like a lord surveying his domain. Isaac found his conviviality irksome, and his appetite repugnant. He couldn't wait to put this gorging, swilling Falstaff out of sight and rest his clear gaze on scrawny Christians who would one day dine in paradise while swine like John Buxton and Pieter Koorne cleaned the Devil's hooves.

"I've missed you, Master Page!" shouted Koorne affably. "Sit you down while I carve a haunch of venison for us. Will you have beer or gin, or both?"

"Nothing!" shouted Isaac fiercely.

"*Sacremente!* What ails you, friend? Do your eyes still hurt?"

"I'm not your friend, Dutchman! And I want no more of your hospitality, which be the Devil's own! As for my eyes, they're sick at the sight of your guzzling. Give me my bill; let me pay it and be gone!"

"*Als't u beleeft,*" replied the Dutchman tersely. "As you please."

Insulted, Koorne wiped his greasy mouth on a cloth he kept tucked in his sleeve for the purpose and went to his ledger. He scribbled Isaac's debt—his plump hands shaking with rage—and slapped the bill on the table, as if to say, I, too, can be incensed, although I'd rather not be. Anger is bad for the digestion, bad for the heart, and bad for business.

Without another word, Isaac paid the sum. He was about to leave, when he noticed a broadside on a table. He stuffed it into his pocket and left the tavern. If he could have seen his face in a looking glass at that moment, he would have noted its resemblance to those of many in Salem—saturnine and choleric. The likeness would have pleased him. He would inform the magistrates, he told himself, that the Dutchman's familiar was loose on the island in the shape of a monkey.

In gravelly Dutch, Koorne growled words that were surely a curse on Isaac Page.

Recalling Matthew Rhodes's gift for the landlord, which Isaac had left in the yard, he fetched the dripping sack, undid its neck, and shook out a turmoil of eels onto the sand-strewn floor. They made a black knot on the planks. Squirming, they unlaced themselves and slithered—with a hissing noise—toward Koorne, as though they meant to suckle at his breast.

RECENT HANGINGS AT PROCTOR'S LEDGE. HANNAH SMYTH, ACCUSED OF WITCHCRAFT & LECHERY.

{Published at Boston, on the 31st day of July, in the Year of Our Lord 1692}

19 July. Rebecca Nurse, Sarah Good, Elizabeth Howe, Susannah Martin, & Sarah Wildes are hanged at Proctor's Ledge in Salem Town.

22 July. Martha Emerson, daughter of Roger Toothaker, is accused by Mary Warren & Mary Lacy Jr.

23 July. Mary Toothaker is examined by Magistrates Hathorne & Corwin.

29 July. Hannah Smyth is accused by Sarah Bibber of witchcraft, whoredom, & licentious carriage.

Isaac rejoiced in the news of Hannah's arrest. She had seduced him. She'd danced naked in the forest, the lascivious light of the inextinguishable jack pine licking her belly and thighs. She would have seen him damned. He would march on the Salem Town House like Joshua and accuse her of lewdness. He would fall upon Hathorne's neck and weep. To be reconciled with his ancestor, Isaac realized at last, was his reason for going to Salem; that, and to hound the witches from their holes and tree them up Proctor's Ledge. "Thus I was humbled, then thus I was called."

When do we learn shame, and when forget it? In April, Isaac would have known how to answer. April had come and gone in another life, however; in this life, at this time, he feels none—a denial that is strange, since shame is a weapon that frightened people use against themselves. The flagellant lashes his own back, even though the strap is handed him by another. Never mind his having sold muskets to the Indians, Thomas Morton needed to be destroyed because he was resistant to shame. Shameless, he would have laughed to be shown the whip, the manacle, or the cross and told to embrace it. He would have made God's chosen people in the New World the laughingstock of the Old.

XII

saac rowed across the broad harbor to Salem Town and made fast to the pier from which he had departed. He shuddered to think that he had helped Caleb escape God's wrath, and intended to denounce Seth Grimes as a confederate of his son's treason. Isaac felt his new purpose like a goad and would have mortified his flesh in Essex Street if he'd had a strop or a birch branch. He told himself that he would keep the fire of His just retribution burning beyond the September 22 executions of Martha Corey, Margaret Scott, Mary Easty, Alice Parker, Mary Parker, Ann

Pudeator, Wilmott Reed, and Samuel Wardwell. As recorded in the history of the province, they were the last persons hanged in Salem for witchery.

Along with his zeal to do the Lord's work came the ambition to make himself visible in the world. Worldly success and godliness were not inconsistent attributes of a man or woman in Puritan Massachusetts; they were signs of God's saving grace. In gratitude for my collaboration, John Hathorne might build me a house, mused Isaac as he pictured himself and his great-great-grandfather at table, discussing grave matters of state over a cup of sack and a plate of oysters.

He hurried to the Salem Town House, where the grand jury was in session. As he drew near, a hymn arose, a slow and mournful strain, such as the pious love, but joined to words that expressed all that our nature can conceive of sin and darkly hinted at far more. Its source, Isaac knew, was Hell. Rampant on the roof, a creature bred of fire and brimstone and nourished with the flesh and blood of infant sacrifices stood. Its leering eyes were rubies, and its great lapping tongue rasped like flint against the chimney stones, as if to strike fire into the frenzied hearts of the righteous, who, at that moment, were enjoining sinners to confess their wickedness and to accuse others of having signed the Devil's book. In Earth's bowels, Hell's choristers lifted their voices in ecstatic discord. Many people inside the hall would later say that the hymn was passing sweet to the ear. They were the hypocrites.

Isaac threw open the door and strode inside to add his solemn voice to the excoriation of the witches, who stood in attitudes of dejection or defiance, according to their faith and stamina. In the dock, a woman cringed. She seemed familiar to Isaac, and in an instant, he recognized her as the witch and wanton Hannah Smyth.

"You would do well to confess and give glory to God!" warned Hathorne, a vein on his damp forehead bulging.

"Isaac!" she cried as he went to her. "For mercy's sake, say I am no witch!"

Forgotten was Christ's admonition that, long ago in Lenox, Isaac had planned to hurl at the magistrates: "For with what judgment ye judge, ye shall be judged: and with what measure ye mete, it shall be measured to you again." Instead, he shouted, "I know her for a whore!'"

His words caused a sensation.

"I am not!" she shrieked, as if she already felt the hangman's rough hand on her shoulder. "I swear I am a good Christian woman."

"And what of the Devil? Are you his creature?" asked Corwin.

"I have no knowledge of the Devil!"

"Speak the truth, harlot!" enjoined Hathorne. "You must speak it now, as you shortly will before God."

Sitting blackly above him on a dais was the object of Isaac's long and, until that moment, fruitless quest to confront the source of his ancestral shame. He looked upon the man with pride and admiration. Isaac had on his spectacles and, perforce, must see the world as John Hathorne saw, and despised, it. It was his dread, magisterial duty to annihilate the corrupt tree and its evil fruit. Is it not written in the Gospel of Matthew: "Every tree that brings not forth good fruit is hewn down, and cast into the fire"?

"The Lord knows I am no harlot, and that man—he, also, knows it!" cried Hannah, weeping and gnashing her teeth.

Isaac wondered if there mightn't be the briefest of moments before the noose tightened around a neck—a knot in time between "about to be hanged" and "hanged"—when the sensation of the rope against the skin was indistinguishable from that caused by the gentle hands of a lover as he gazed into the face of his beloved. Isaac shook his head, amazed that, even now, his mind could entertain such fancies.

"Identify yourself, sir, and say how you know this woman!" commanded Hathorne.

"My name is Isaac Page." He pointed a damning finger at Hannah, who was near to fainting under the strain. "She seduced me and made me lie with her in the field like a beast. Later, I saw her in a Morris dance. She circled widdershins around a flaming pine tree in the woods at Andover. She did entreat me to dance with her. Fondling herself, she tempted me with her nakedness. Affrighted, I fled the forest." Isaac's eyes glinted in sympathy with his inner eye, which was entranced by the lurid spectacle, as though it had indeed happened as he described it.

"Naked, you say? And in a Morris dance?"

"Aye, she behaved lewdly. I hurried from the Lord's waste, and till this moment, I've not seen or spoken to her for my sweet soul's sake."

"Mark his words—*naked* and *lewdly*!" rejoiced Hathorne, eyes bulging like the vein on his brow. His thin lips were parted. His teeth, which were small and pointed, showed in gums that were oddly pink and seemed themselves indecent. "These be high and dreadful offenses!"

The assembly made noises of exultation, which is next door to fury. Hathorne glared, and the leering faces disappeared beneath masks signifying abhorrence.

"Saw you any witch marks on her person when you lay with her?"

The gawkers leaned forward expectantly.

"I saw none." He would not go so far as to say he'd had sight of her pudendum and anus.

"No witch's teat to give suck to Satan's imps?"

"I did not!" replied Isaac, blushing, although the others packed into the hall—magistrates, ministers, and watchers—were not the least embarrassed.

Hathorne was manifestly disappointed. "How often did you fornicate with the accused?"

"Once only." Glancing at her face, which he had thought comely, Isaac was repelled by the scars left by smallpox.

"Why once and no more?"

"I saw that she was not honest."

"How so?"

"I thought her face turned wolfish."

"Wolfish, when?" asked Magistrate Corwin.

"The moment we had knowledge of each other," replied Isaac, his face coloring.

"There's a generous bounty set on wolves," said Hathorne, his eyes alight with malice.

Almost as one, the spectators sniffed, as though to get the rank scent of the animal.

"Are you certain you saw no witch's mark?" asked Hathorne, adopting the insinuating voice so useful to those in authority who wish to conceal their stony hearts.

"I saw none," replied Isaac, who suddenly wondered if he had not seen tooth marks on Hannah's breast. "I saw her naked."

"And dancing widdershins. Did she, perchance, send her succubus to you in your sleep?"

"I don't entertain women—neither visible in the flesh nor invisible—in my chamber at night!" replied Isaac. He was immediately alive to the impertinence of his answer and smiled at Hathorne foolishly. Guffaws in the courtroom only served to increase the magistrate's ire.

"I warn you not to make light of these proceedings, or you'll come to know—and soon—what passes through a man's mind the moment before he drops!"

Isaac's blood ran cold, and he threw some meat into

the arena to make the magistrates and the others slaver. "She sent her specter out to kiss my eyes."

"Mark that!" said Hathorne gleefully. "She tried to bewitch this man's sight, so that he could not see truth!"

The onlookers gabbled like turkeys in a yard.

"What say you, mistress trollop?"

"It's a lie! I swear upon my soul, I never sent my spirit out to this man or any other. And on my oath, I never danced naked or clothed in the woods, save as children do, innocent of foulness."

"Swearing and oath taking are easily done by one of Satan's brood. Hannah Smyth, I'm of the opinion that you are the Devil's creature. What say you, Magistrate Corwin?"

"I'm not sure, John." Jonathan Corwin appeared uncomfortable sitting at the high table between Hathorne and a third magistrate, Bartholomew Gedney. Gedney's brother owned the Ship Tavern, in whose vegetable garden Bridget Bishop's pig had routed.

Isaac considered if Corwin might not have had carnal knowledge of Hannah, the depths of whose wickedness he was only beginning to fathom. Studying her, he saw a monkey's face underneath a starched cap, while on her shoulder a spectral bird with a woman's head sat. He shivered in fear.

"How? Not sure!" exclaimed Hathorne indignantly. "How can you doubt she is a witch, man? She has shown her backside to the Devil!"

"I am blameless!"

"I've heard enough of witches!" Corwin's voice was pitched between exasperation and exhaustion.

"Careful you don't end up in the same sty as this harpy!" Hathorne turned to the crowd and, in John Winthrop's words, warned, "'The eyes of all people are upon us; so that if we shall deal falsely with our God in this work we have undertaken and so cause him to withdraw his present help from us, we shall be made a story and a by-word through the world.'"

He turned to Isaac. "Whence came you?"

"From proselytizing the savages on the western frontier," he replied with a ready lie.

"We have a great suspicion of strangers," said Hathorne. "They can bring with them the pest or, worse, outlandish ideas repugnant to the one true faith."

"I bring only the desire to destroy the Devil and his servants."

Hathorne appeared satisfied. "How long have you been among us?"

Isaac would have replied if the door had not been thrown open. Deputy Herrick led a man wearing chains into the hall, who shouted at Isaac, "You're a liar, Isaac Page!"

"Silence, or I will have your ankles tied to your neck!" ordered Hathorne, having gotten to his feet. Trussed up until blood issued from their noses, the most refractory of witches would speak truth and confess. "Who is this person who dares to disturb us in our grave business?"

"He's called Dilly," replied Herrick. "His Christian name is William Dill."

"Whether or not he be a true Christian remains to be proved," said Hathorne airily. "What reason had you to arrest him?"

"Why, by your own warrant!" exclaimed Herrick.

"I've issued a prodigious number of them!" Vexed by the man's impertinence, Hathorne would have a sharp word to say to the deputy after the day's bearbaiting.

"Geoffrey Hance, of the village, denounced him for having made his chickens sick."

"Hance, who was denounced Monday by Martha Tyler—I remember now. We're up to our withers in witches this week!" nickered Hathorne.

"If I be a witch, that man is the Devil himself!" shouted Dill, shaking a finger at Isaac.

A sound like swine routing in rotten vegetables greeted Dill's charge. Fascinated, Isaac watched as the onlookers, expectant of a new revelation that would disturb the commonwealth and excite the gossips, changed into veritable beasts before his bespectacled eyes.

"Explain yourself, man!" said Hathorne. His voice replete with menace, he had no need to raise it to silence the court.

"I've proof that he came neither from the western frontier nor from Rhode Island, as he told many in the village, but from a century and more hence."

Isaac felt the blood drain from his face and recalled—from far away—a stanza of a song by the Bay Colony minister, physician, and poet Michael Wigglesworth that he had read beside Fairhaven Bay while Thoreau tramped the woods in search of their negro friend, the fugitive slave Samuel Long.

He that was strong at first
    Immediately grew weak;
And let the stock of Grace run out,
    Like vessels that do leak.
Hence we are all made weak,
    And neither have Free-will
To chuse, nor Power to do what's good,
    But only what is ill.

"Show me your proof!" demanded Hathorne, who had stepped down from the dais.

"He's a fool, Your Honor, and his words are foolish," explained the deputy sheriff.

"He lives in a beast house and eats at Widow Stowe's pig trough!" sneered the Reverend Parris, who, for a niggling sum, recorded trial testimony.

"He is simple, John," said Corwin. "They call him 'Dilly the daft' hereabout."

Hathorne ignored his colleagues. "Do you feel yourself being drawn toward salvation by God's irresistible grace, William Dill?"

"I do!"

"And you love God and will not be forsworn?"

"I am a truthful man and know not how to lie."

"Will you kiss God's Word, which is to say His lips, which uttered it?"

"I will!"

Hathorne gave Dill a Bible to kiss. He could not

have done so more eagerly had he been Adonis bussing Venus as the poet Shakespeare rhapsodized: "Pure lips, sweet seals in my soft lips imprinted, / What bargains may I make still to be sealing?"

"You say you have some evidence against this person." The magistrate turned his barbed gaze on Isaac.

"Yea," replied Dill. "And it be hidden *on his person,* sir, for he would not go without it."

"Search him!"

A pair of soldiers put down their halberds and, having subdued Isaac, searched his boots, stockings, hat, and clothes. They found the Liberty dollar sewn into his pocket. One of them put it in Hathorne's outstretched hand.

"What is it? A coin? What does a coin prove, William Dill?"

"You've only to look at it closely to have your answer."

"What does it mean?" asked the perplexed magistrate, having examined it.

"It's a counterfeit," said Isaac weakly.

"And what else might you have counterfeited?"

"He told lies about me!" cried Hannah, hoping to save herself from the gallows.

"Hold your tongue!" admonished Hathorne. "Thou hast a whore's forehead."

"I had the coin made for sport," said Isaac, feeling the floor on which he stood grow hot like Hell's own stove. "To amuse my friends."

"Methinks it was not made in Boston. On Satan's forge, perhaps."

"He brought it with him, sir, from the days that have yet to come," said Dill proudly, as someone would do who was keeping a marvelous secret, forgetting that, to reveal it, could send him to his death.

"This Dill is not honest! He makes a pretense of weak-mindedness," said Isaac. "Now that you hear him speak, you needs must know him to be a fraud and dissembler."

"God has made him sensible, so that he can cry you out."

"What is written on the coin, John?" asked Corwin.

"That it was minted in the year 1851, in a place called the United States of America."

The crowd gasped, as though the stench of brimstone had been in the air.

"The coin is his talisman," said Dill. "With it, he did fly from uncreated time."

"Fly, you say? Did you hear, Magistrate Corwin? The man flies!"

"He is no man!" said Dill, who would have rubbed his hands together in triumph had they not been manacled.

"He reads immoral books!" said Isaac, exasperated.

"William Dill read books!" scoffed the Reverend Parris. "I tell you he is a natural fool."

"God has cast the demons from my mind, which kept me long in ignorance. Hallelujah!"

"Hallelujah!" shouted the crowd, to this most entertaining of spectacles.

"Dill is in the Devil's pocket!" shouted Isaac.

"I have you in *mine!*" retorted Hathorne, shaking a finger in admonishment at him.

"You have the Devil by the tail!" cried Parris gleefully.

"I doubt you, Isaac Page; I suspect your honesty! I believe you are the Devil himself or his envoy and are in New England, directing your foul witches to afflict the people. Deputy Herrick, be quick and lay hands on this fiend before he wreaks havoc!"

The deputy hesitated while Isaac shouted, "Satan is on the rooftop! I saw him as I came nigh to the Town House!"

"*He* is Satan!" cried eleven-year-old Abigail Williams, one of the original afflicted girls, who had brought the people to their knees and made them quake in terror of the rope.

"Why, child, does he hurt you?" asked Hathorne.

"I see his great leather wings, his red eyes, and—do you not see?—a tail that whips back and forth like an eel!"

"I see it!" shouted another of the girls, then another, and still another in a fearful chorus.

"I see it!" agreed John Indian, Tituba's husband, who had been among the first to say he was tormented by impish familiars.

"I see it, also!" cried Cotton Mather, who had been dubious of specters and of spectral evidence and would conclude, after the witch frenzy had cooled, that the Devil had hoodwinked the ministers and magistrates "into a blind man's buffet, and we [were] even ready to be sinfully, yea, hotly, and madly, mauling one another in the dark."

"See where it stretches its immense wings!" exclaimed Gedney. "Satan, get ye hence!"

"Satan, be gone!" intoned John Indian and the afflicted girls in unison.

A few who had been leaning forward on the Town House benches to see this dreadful play unfold crossed themselves like papists, as if they feared that only the Roman Church could do battle with the Prince of Evil.

"Lucifer has shown himself!" declared Hathorne.

"The stink of corruption is almost past enduring!" shouted Parris.

"I see Chaos come, and Ancient Night!"

"I hear the gibbering of fiends!"

"He will drag us down to Hell!" groaned Mather, raising his Bible against the beast.

"Quick, Deputy, throw the double chains on him, or none will be safe from this day hence in New England!" commanded Hathorne.

Aghast, Isaac cried, "I'm not the Devil or his man. I am—"

"Is this not the Devil's coin?" asked the magistrate, holding the silver dollar between his finger and thumb for all to see. Few remained to take note of it. Most had rushed pell-mell into the street, where several persons of notable vision and probity swore that a scarlet beast was, indeed, prancing on the rooftop. "I have you now, demon!"

"I would speak to you in private!" begged Isaac.

"Nay, I am no fool to give solitary audience to a fiend!"

"I am no fiend!"

"How came you by this token of the future? Perhaps you'd have us believe that you are a prophet."

"I'm neither a prophet nor a wizard; moreover, you will be amazed by what I have to tell you."

"I think you are the Prince of Liars."

"A word, please!"

"It's a trap, John!" warned Corwin.

"Do not parley with him!" urged Gedney.

"I am one of Almighty God's earthly representatives," said Hathorne coolly. "He will see that no harm comes to me as I go about His work."

"I can recite the Lord's Prayer!" declared Isaac, who knew that a witch or a wizard could not.

"I will not permit such a supreme blasphemy!"

"Put as many chains on me as you like; I'll offer no resistance."

"Herrick, why are you dithering? Chain him up!"

The deputy loaded Isaac with four lengths of heavy chain, so that he could scarcely stand upright under the weight of them.

Satisfied, Hathorne said, "Though you be Lucifer himself, I fear you not. I'll hear what you have to say. Clear the room!" he bellowed.

To the noise of benches scraping against the floor, and in some instances toppling, the room was cleared of all but Hathorne and Isaac, who heard halberds clanging on the stairs as the soldiers hurried to the street.

—~~~~~~—

"MAY I SIT?" ASKED ISAAC. "These chains are ponderous."

"They were forged according to *The Hammer of Witches,* written by the Dominican inquisitor Heinrich Kramer. In it, he set forth the methods by which witches can be known and destroyed." Hathorne smiled. The aspect of that smile evoked both the words *rapture* and *raptor.* But Isaac was too preoccupied to think like a storyteller. "It be rare sport to hammer a witch."

"I can no longer bear the weight of iron you've piled on me!"

"Sit, then." Hathorne studied Isaac's face. "Even as I forged their links, reading God's Word while they annealed, I did not believe they would be proof against Satan. How is it you do not burst them?"

"Because I'm not he!" Isaac had spoken vehemently, so that the spectacles flew from his head and their panes were dashed against the floor.

At that instant, the lenses in the spectacles John Hathorne was wearing cracked, as well. He took them off and gazed on them, astounded. "This be the Devil's work!" He held the broken object, as though *it* were a talisman with which to conjure all the potentates of Hell. "Unclean spirit!"

"These I wear once belonged to you!" shouted Isaac, retrieving them despite the burden of his chains. "By them, I was able to come to Salem *this year* from *that stamped on the silver coin.* The spectacles that you're holding now came down to me through five generations.

Yours and mine are one and the same. If one breaks, the other needs must also!"

No longer seeing through his ancestor's biased lenses, Isaac gazed on a world lacking the playhouse machinery by which Hell was hauled up through a trapdoor and Heaven lowered from the flies. Isaac knew himself again as a man belonging to the rational world, where Passion plays survive as quaint reminders of humankind's darker age. He knew, as well, that he could die on Proctor's Ledge, which, in the nineteenth century, would be called "Gallows Hill."

"You're a subtle beast!" sneered Hathorne. "Little did I know when I arose from my bed this morning that, at two o'clock in the afternoon, I'd have one of the powers of Hell shackled before me, perhaps the Black Man himself."

"There are things that can be explained without resorting to the occult," countered Isaac, thinking absurdly of the locomotive in the Housatonic Valley, which, in Lenox, had affirmed for him the greatness of the age of science.

"Recite the 'Our Father'!" ordered Hathorne, since none was there besides himself to hear the blasphemy.

Isaac had been straining to hear the steam locomotive's chuffing through the open sashes.

"By your silence, Isaac Page, I assume you cannot say the 'Our Father.'"

Shaking off his reverie, Isaac recited it without faltering.

"I think the Devil could say the prayer."

"I damn him!" shouted Isaac. "The Devil would not damn himself!"

After a brief silence, his interrogator asked, "Who are you, then, if not he or one of his servants?"

"My real name is Nathaniel Hawthorne, your great-great-grandson, born in Salem in 1804."

The magistrate's face blanched. His expression changed from astonishment to disbelief, from mistrust to anger. "You must be a lunatic and, as such, belong to the Evil One!"

"I'm the son of Nathaniel Hathorne, who was master of the *Nabby* when he died in Suriname in 1808 of yellow fever. His father was Daniel Hathorne, who fought bravely in the American War of Independence against Great Britain and died in 1796. *His* father was your son Joseph, who would live peaceably, a sea captain and a farmer, until his death in 1762. *You* will die in 1717, a disgraced man known in my time as the only unrepentant judge in the prosecution of the witches. *You* will be held accountable for the arrest of two hundred innocent souls and the execution of twenty. Your father, Major William Hathorne, arrived with John Winthrop on the *Arbella* and is chiefly remembered, when he is at all, for having had the Quaker woman Ann Coleman whipped through the streets of Salem. That is the paternal lineage of the Hathornes in America." In his mind, he finished the condemnation: It was to rid the family name of tarnish or, failing that, to wreak vengeance on you that I came to this godforsaken place and time. It was to hide my shame of you that I changed the name to Hawthorne.

His wits recovered, Isaac knew that he had waited too long to achieve anything useful in Salem. It may well have been vanity to believe that he could have done. "Hence we are all made weak, / And neither have Free-will / To chuse, nor Power to do what's good . . ." He wanted only to return to his wife and children, to Lenox and his books. Never again would he meddle in what was past. The present would be enough. He would try to repudiate his grim inheritance, and if he could not, he'd live with it. Is not sin the great theme of his tales? Who can say if he could have written them without it. Powerless as he might be to ameliorate the ills and evils of the world, he would write as though he were able.

"You speak like a sorcerer of the future, yet you insist you are not demonic," said John Hathorne, grinding the tabletop with a thumb whose nail, Isaac saw, was black.

"Is God, who sees the end of time, a sorcerer?" shouted Isaac, out of patience with this man, an ordinary fanatic—Isaac saw plainly—whose face betrayed ambition, spite, fear, and a childish belief in a simple world where outcomes were decided by grave combats, such as two boys will wage in a schoolyard with sticks and stones. Isaac could almost pity him were he not the cause of so much suffering, so many deaths, and his distant scion's own unhappiness.

"You pile blasphemy on blasphemy, so that I must condemn you!"

"I am innocent to a witch. I know not what a witch is."

"You say the words of Bridget Bishop, as if they were your own. I cannot think but that you whispered them in her ear. You are wily! I shall call for more chains to prevent you from gathering another parliament of specters in the Reverend Parris's field."

"No more weight, I beg you! I can scarcely breathe for it."

"What dissembling is this? Satan beseeching me to lessen his pain."

"Were I Satan, I would not humiliate myself—nay, not even in my cunning. Were I he, I'd blast these chains apart with a glance! I'd change you into the ass that you most surely are!"

"Then you're a common trickster," said Hathorne sadly. "And your coin is but a pretense with which to gull the ignorant. By Heaven, I wish I had the Devil cornered! I'd nail him to the church door; I'd flay him like an eel; I'd tear off his wings, as boys do flies'! You're nothing but a halfpenny witch, dressed in a cheap Birching Lane suit. I've dealt with a hundred and more like you these past months. But I will have you notwithstanding!"

"Do I hurt you? Have I sent my spirit through the air to give you colic? I am innocent to a witch! We are all of us—accused, imprisoned, or dead by your arraignment—innocent!"

"I will have your life, fellow!" said Hathorne, whose piercing gaze might well have seen his descendant's guiltlessness and found it infuriating. "I'll nip the head in the hatching!"

Isaac knelt and wrung his hands pitiably. "I swear I am what I say I am!"

"Tut, man! You are spineless, like a girl. If you truly are my grandson twice removed, I'm ashamed to acknowledge the relation. Is it so hard for you to die? Do you covet your life this much that you would mewl at the prospect of losing it?"

"Great-Great-Grandfather, please!"

"You're in God's hands, not mine."

"It's your rope that will bruise my neck!"

"I've listened to your tale, and I judge your wits to be afflicted. Say by whom, and I will make room for you in John Arnold's jail."

"And you will not send me to the gallows?"

Having judged the man groveling before him harmless, though not innocent, Hathorne assumed the irony with which he habitually cloaked his cruelty. "Nay, sir, I would not hang my *heir*! Now get up off your knees!"

Isaac stood with difficulty because of the chains and his will's weakness.

"I shall name you a name," agreed Isaac.

"Say it."

"William Dill."

"We have it already from Geoffrey Hance!"

"I will corroborate it."

"Oh, very well." Hathorne was weary of the interview, which had gone on too long and produced nothing of importance.

"And you say I will not hang?"

"I say it!" intoned Hathorne, speaking in the voice he used to examine and condemn. "In return for clemency, I would know the purpose of this coin."

"It's a pretense, as you said—a thing to gull the gullible." By dismissing it as nothing more sinister than a childish prank, he hoped to turn the magistrate's interest from the coin, which Isaac must have or be becalmed in a leaden sea where hope was sunk and joy rationed—one and done.

"I think not. Methinks it has a significance, and I needs must know it, if only for the sake of curiosity." In Hathorne's voice, Isaac perceived the cunning that had undone so many.

Isaac acquiesced. "It is marked."

"How marked?"

"With a scratch."

"What meaning is there in a scratch?"

"Look hard," said Isaac. "Harder!"

"I see no scratch." Hathorne rubbed his myopic eyes. "I need my spectacles, which your black art made worthless."

"I used no arts," said Isaac suavely.

"The scratch!" said Hathorne, employing the peremptory tone with which he bullied and harassed.

"It's been carefully hidden in the design," said Isaac slyly.

"By whom?" Hathorne turned the coin from front to back and back to front again.

"By *his* art, the Devil put it there," said Isaac softly. "Old Scratch. It is his signature."

"Show me it!" commanded the magistrate, his eyes alight with both zeal and greed.

Isaac held out his hand.

Hathorne gave him the silver piece and watched as he pressed the coin against his palm until it burned.

WINTER 1851
LENOX, MASSACHUSETTS

hat do you think of my story, Sophia?"

"It will disappoint those who praised *The Scarlet Letter* and may put off any who would otherwise read *The Blithedale Romance.* No, Nathaniel, I don't care for it."

"For once, I want to write a book without giving a thought to the booksellers!"

"And in return, they won't give you a thought or it space on their shelves. Your fixation on your great-great-grandfather is unwholesome. You're not living in the Salem of 1692!"

"In those papers your pen has been scratching, I *was.*"

"As far as I can see, you've accomplished nothing of what you'd hoped to do. Bridget Bishop was hanged *twice*—once in fact and now in fiction. I don't suppose she'd thank you. We can't exchange our ancestors for some others more suitable. Your melancholy distracts you and offends me."

"A knowledge of human nature is the corrosive that eats away at a cheerful temperament. All men and women are equal in guilt and besmirched by sin. That—"

"Husband, I am not guilty, and I haven't sinned!"

"—is a New Englander's bleak view, and in that I am one, the desire to forgive is always opposed by a compulsion to censure."

"You make too much of yourself, Nathaniel!"

"I felt compelled to produce a moral tale."

"Mr. Ticknor will dislike it. Besides, I can't see a moral in it, except that we are helpless and, without free will, cannot choose but ill."

"I think that may be the case, Sophia."

"Then you have written a bad book!"

"Be that as it may, I've only extemporized one."

"I'd throw these pages into the stove, but I can't stand it when you sulk!"

"Manuscripts were once written with ink made from gallnuts. Think of the bitterness of their pages!"

"Your gloom is ostentatious, Nathaniel! Don't I cheer you? Haven't I set aside my own art for yours? Do you remember what Lydian Emerson said when we were last at Bush? 'Save me from magnificent souls. I like a small common sized one.'"

"Then I'll leave my story for the Tooth Rat to gnaw."

"You'll give it up?"

"I'll give it up. In any case, I've work to do on *Blithedale* before I give it to Ticknor."

"I'm glad of it."

"Your eyes, dear, they no longer pain you?"

"They are better—and I'll be obliged to you, husband, if you allow me my complaints without bestowing them on your characters."

"I do beg your pardon."

"There are days when I wish the ink in *your* inkwell would freeze."

"Sophia, I'm ashamed for not having encouraged your ambition. You surrendered your art for me without protest, as you did your maidenhood. I remember your joy at seeing your *Isola San Giovanni* hanging in the Athenaeum and Waldo Emerson's delight in the medallion portrait you painted of his brother Charles. My 'Gentle Boy' will always look to me as you drew him. I allowed you to waste your gift, and I'm sorry for it. You're right: I make too much of myself."

"That reminds me, Nathaniel: The lenses in your great-great-grandfather's spectacles *are* cracked. I noticed it when I was dusting the curio cabinet this morning."

"They could not bear to look again on Old Salem. They're happier in the cabinet, where they can see your pretty face. What's that you've drawn? Is it me wearing a steeple hat, asking for your forgiveness? Or John Alden stammering before his Priscilla?"

"Pshaw! You're an incorrigible fantasist, Nathaniel!"

"Whose throat is dry."

"I'll make us tea, shall I?"

"Yes, please, my dear."

Who remembers Bridget Bishop now that 160 years have passed? Who knows or cares what hardships and agonies she bore and whether or not she did so bravely? In any case, did she not bring them on herself? She would not hold her tongue, and *she would wear the red bodice*! I think that it was not the slanders of John Indian and the village girls, nor the frontier raids by the Wabanaki and the French, nor drought and fear of famine that turned the province upside down, but the Puritans' covenant with God, which promised His chosen people that confession followed by punishment would atone for sin and bring an end to their affliction. We are not the chosen ones, and there will be no end to affliction. Each of us has his own complicated business to oversee, which may succeed for a time but must inevitably fail, as stars fall according to laws other than Divine. Let men and women look to their own welfare, for governments are blind!

On the subject of God's existence, I have nothing original to say.

"India or China, Nathaniel?"

"China, I think."

"I'll cut you a slice of currant cake."

"I'm not hungry."

"There's little nourishment in words, husband, even those you might come to eat."

If there is witchery, it is in the stories that we tell,

their power to enthrall, transform, uplift, and corrupt. A scarlet letter or a great white whale—what are they if not figures in a tableau behind which lie truths that can crack the foundation of the world and let the angels or the devils out into broadest day!

L'Envoi

Dear Sophia,

When people or places disappear, they leave a shadow behind them where stories can take root, grow, and sometimes become perennial. There the dead can quicken, and a town long before changed beyond recognition can be restored. A hand can reach up through the ages from its grave and touch another's beating heart—quickening or stilling it. Wanted or not, stories thrust themselves upon me. They are devilish hard work for small recompense. Yet I tell them as though—leaky or not—they were the vessels of Grace.

Your Nathaniel

In that *whiter Island*, where
Things are evermore sincere;
Candor here, and lustre there
          Delighting:

There no monstrous fancies shall
Out of hell an horrour call,
To create (or cause at all)
          Affrighting.

—Robert Herrick,
from "The White Island;
or Place of the Blest"

Afterword

Doubt is the tooth of the covenant we inherit;
it can bite and gnaw where conscience has its quick.

Many books have been written about the Salem witch trials. *Tooth of the Covenant* is not intended to be one of them, although the madness of 1692 is stitched in scarlet threads into the fabric of this novel. Nor did I set out to correct our misconceptions about the Puritans, who were likely no purer in their time than we are in ours, although they may have been more guilt-ridden. Nor is this novel a revenger's tragedy, although allusions to Hamlet and his problem are ample. (Like Isaac Page, Hawthorne's proxy in the tale, the Danish prince wrestled with the problem of spectral evidence.) In *Tooth,* I wanted to show a mind slipping its moorings, gradually losing its way amid an unfathomable reality, and ending in delusion—in the case of this novel and of the Salem of 1692, a commonly held one.

What the novel *does* concern is the power of storytelling to raise the dead and, by its persuasive and transgressive art, to confront a persistent ghost. To imagine the burden of the ancestral guilt carried by Nathaniel

Hawthorne was reason enough to want to write this book. To suggest that his melancholy, taciturnity, and habit of producing somber narratives regarding sin and remorse are due to familial shame is nothing new. How he might have used his craft to silence his great-great-grandfather Hathorne (the most vigorous prosecutor of Salem's accused) is a novelty that combines literary biography and the metaphysics of fiction writing. The novel shows the ultimate failure of the storyteller's quixotic quest to alter history or a human heart—another's or one's own. Isaac Page's failure to remake the world is our kind's tragic patrimony. It is also a salutary reminder that no one ought to presume to impose a point of view.

> A better nature can be forgotten, and the rabble's cause taken up as one's own. He had put on another's spectacles, whose lenses were biased.

Aside from the fascination of considering Hawthorne's unattractive qualities as the result of a predisposition to guilt, if not sin, is the disturbing idea that few individuals immersed within a culture (those fitted with the "spectacles" of a particular way of seeing) can judge it clearly and fairly. When Isaac puts on the spectacles, he assumes John Hathorne's point of view; moreover, being a man of ordinary character, he cannot resist the strength of the communal delusion. I stated the dangerous dilemma in the novel this way:

> In 1851, Isaac was open to ideas as long as they were sensible. In exile, however, his intellectual toleration would lead him to an uneasy recognition of Satan and his cohort. That was no more astonishing than clear water's turning dark by the process of infusion—a minor marvel witnessed in a pot of tea.

The best of nineteenth-century literature was not small in scope, nor did it consider moral, social, or political ideas outside the jurisdiction of fiction. My ambition has been to confer on readers a larger view of the American present by writing essential stories of a nation being violently made, unmade, and remade. To reach toward the sublime, I have found it necessary to lean away from myself.

Acknowledgments

In writing this tale *for* Nathaniel Hawthorne (a singular presumption), I strove to simplify the complex Puritan mind without falsifying the spirit of the times or the possible motives of the central figures whom I have chosen to represent them. I could not have minimized the theology and history that I include in the book. Seventeenth-century Puritans cannot be understood outside of their faith and history; their mind is alien to ours in many respects. I peppered my story with invention and exercised a storyteller's prerogative to shape events. (Time is shapeless, after all, a fact that makes the composer's art possible.) In some instances, I have consolidated characters, sketched actions, and taken liberties with actual places. For example, I exaggerated the distance between Salem and Winter Island to suggest Isaac's temporary isolation from the mainland and its fevers. There was a public house there, licensed by Salem Town, which used the island as a wintering place for its fishing fleet and as a pasturage. The inhabitants were few. (Salem Neck and Winter Island would not be conjoined until much later.)

History is a complication beyond my powers to unknot. In the case of a character in a story buried underneath history's avalanche, however, the creator need not inquire much further into his circumstances than the rock that struck him. I leave remote causes to students of time's accrual, whether they be historians, archaeologists, or theologians. They are better equipped than a novelist, at least *this* novelist, to penetrate what Perry Miller called, in his book by that name, the New England mind.

I acknowledge a debt to the following persons for having corrected some of my initial misunderstandings of Puritanism: E. Brooks Holifield, Ph.D., Emory University, author of *Theology in America: Christian Thought from the Age of the Puritans to the Civil War*; William Huntting Howell, Ph.D., Boston University, author of *Against Self Reliance: The Arts of Dependence in the Early United States*; and Emerson W. Baker, Ph.D., Salem State University, author of *A Storm of Witchcraft: The Salem Trials and the American Experience.* (For any errors that remain, the fault is mine.)

The language used in this novel is steeped in seventeenth-century prose. Like Arthur Miller's in *The Crucible* and Hawthorne's in *The Scarlet Letter* and his colonial New England tales, my antiquing gives the necessary illusion of an appropriated time without attempting to reproduce its peculiar usages or orthography, except as they may appear in excerpts. *Yeas* and *nays* there are, but *thee* and *thou* have been purged from the story's vocabulary as unnecessarily obtrusive.

Passages in the novel beginning with the following words were taken from records kept of John Hathorne's examination of Bridget Bishop and Rebecca Nurse, respectively: "I am no witch" and "It is very awful to all to see these agonies." I have borrowed lines from other Salem witch trial testimonies, as well. (The originals have been altered on occasion, though not their sense, to be consistent with the novel's diction.) I have also quoted several passages by Hawthorne from his tales set in the Massachusetts Bay Colony. (His zealous readers will discover them for themselves.)

I read or consulted: *American Poetry: The Seventeenth and Eighteenth Centuries*, edited by David S. Shields; *A Break with Charity: A Story About the Salem Witch Trials*, by Ann Rinaldi; *The Crucible*, by Arthur Miller; *Emerson Among the Eccentrics: A Group Portrait*, by Carlos Baker; *Homage to Mistress Bradstreet*, by John Berryman; *The New England Mind: From Colony to Province*, by Perry Miller; *Of Plymouth Plantation: 1620–1647*, by William Bradford; *The Puritan Dilemma: The Story of John Winthrop*, by Edward S. Morgan; Salem Witch Trials Documentary Archive and Transcription Project site (salem.lib.virginia.edu); *Six Women of Salem*, by Marilynne K. Roach; *The Times of Their Lives: Life, Love, and Death in Plymouth Colony*, by James and Patricia Scott Deetz; *Visible Saints: The History of a Puritan Idea*, by Edmund S. Morgan; "The Witchcraft Trials in Salem: A Commentary," by Douglas O. Linder (www.famous-trials.com); and *The Wordy Shipmates*, by Sarah Vowell.

Philip Roth's rebuke to the Puritans in *The Dying Animal* and his admiration for the "riotous prodigality" of Thomas Morton and the "mad Bacchanalians" at Merry Mount is passionate; so, too, is William Carlos Williams's essay on the maypole in his book *In the American Grain*. Holding a contrary opinion of Morton, Plymouth Colony governor William Bradford in *Of Plymouth Plantation: 1620–1647* condemned him as one of the "gain-thirsty murderers," a profiteer who would sell "the blood of their brethren . . . for gain."

Occasionally, the reader will encounter a phrase or clause set off by quotation marks that may seem to have no referent in the text. These I found in the secondary sources named above, especially in *The New England Mind*; *Six Women of Salem*; *The Story of John Winthrop*; and *Of Plymouth Plantation*. They are best thought of as expressions of the culture that Isaac struggles to comprehend. Needless to say, my gratitude to the scholars who brought them to our attention is boundless. Borrowings from the Bible are numerous and taken from the King James Version, which likely would have been in Nathaniel Hawthorne's possession, and not the Geneva version, which the Puritans would have read. References to *Hamlet* are also abundant. (The sentence "An old white horse galloped away in the meadow" belongs to T. S. Eliot; I can think of few more beautiful ones in the English language.)

To tutor my sensibility, I listened to anthems and fuguing tunes by our country's first composer, William Billings, of Boston, a tanner by trade. No amount of acclimatization could allow me to feel and re-create the terror of the time of which I write, not only that imposed by churchmen and magistrates but—perhaps more dreadful—that inspired by the wilderness, which was so readily peopled by devils in the popular imagination. This *wildness* may be considered a major character in the novel.

This acknowledgment is the ninth I have written since Erika Goldman and Jerome Lowenstein, M.D., copublishers of Bellevue Literary Press, first made room for me on its publication list. By now, I thought to have been able to express my gratitude without resorting to the usual formulae, but I find that I cannot. To say it plainly, my thanks to you, Erika and Jerry, and to your able colleagues Molly Mikolowski, Laura Hart, Joe Gannon, and Carol Edwards.

Bellevue Literary Press is devoted to publishing literary fiction and nonfiction at the intersection of the arts and sciences because we believe that science and the humanities are natural companions for understanding the human experience. We feature exceptional literature that explores the nature of perception and the underpinnings of the social contract. With each book we publish, our goal is to foster a rich, interdisciplinary dialogue that will forge new tools for thinking and engaging with the world.

To support our press and its mission, and for our full catalogue of published titles, please visit us at blpress.org.

Bellevue Literary Press
New York